I0817623

LIES
OF A
TOYMAKER

LIES OF A TOYMAKER

a novel

KELLY ANN JACOBSON

THREE ROOMS PRESS
New York, NY

Lies of a Toymaker
A Novel by Kelly Ann Jacobson

ISBN 978-1-953103-51-2 (trade paperback)
ISBN 978-1-953103-52-9 (Epub)
Library of Congress Control Number: 2024951362

TRP-114

Pub Date: April 8, 2025

First Edition

BISAC category code
YAF017010 YOUNG ADULT FICTION / Fairy Tales & Folklore / Adaptations
YAF031000 YOUNG ADULT FICTION / LGBTQ+ / General
YAF002030 YOUNG ADULT FICTION / Animals / Mythical Creatures
YAF030000 YOUNG ADULT FICTION / Legends, Myths, Fables / General

COVER AND INTERIOR DESIGN:
KG Design International: www.katgeorges.com

DISTRIBUTED IN THE U.S. AND INTERNATIONALLY BY:
Ingram/Publishers Group West: www.pgw.com

Three Rooms Press
New York, NY
www.threeroomspress.com
info@threeroomspress.com

For Zoe and Lyla

LIES
OF A
TOYMAKER

PROLOGUE

EXCERPT FROM

THE ARCHIVES OF RUMORS, MYSTERIES, AND MYTHS "THE GREAT WHITE LIGHT"

PERHAPS, ARGUABLY, THE GREATEST OF ALL the myths the fairies still tell is that of "the great white light." Known, now, to be the distant star where the Starsprites eventually made their home, the origins of the light are still told to this day as a bedtime story for young Fae. Though there are many versions, the one most well-known goes like this:

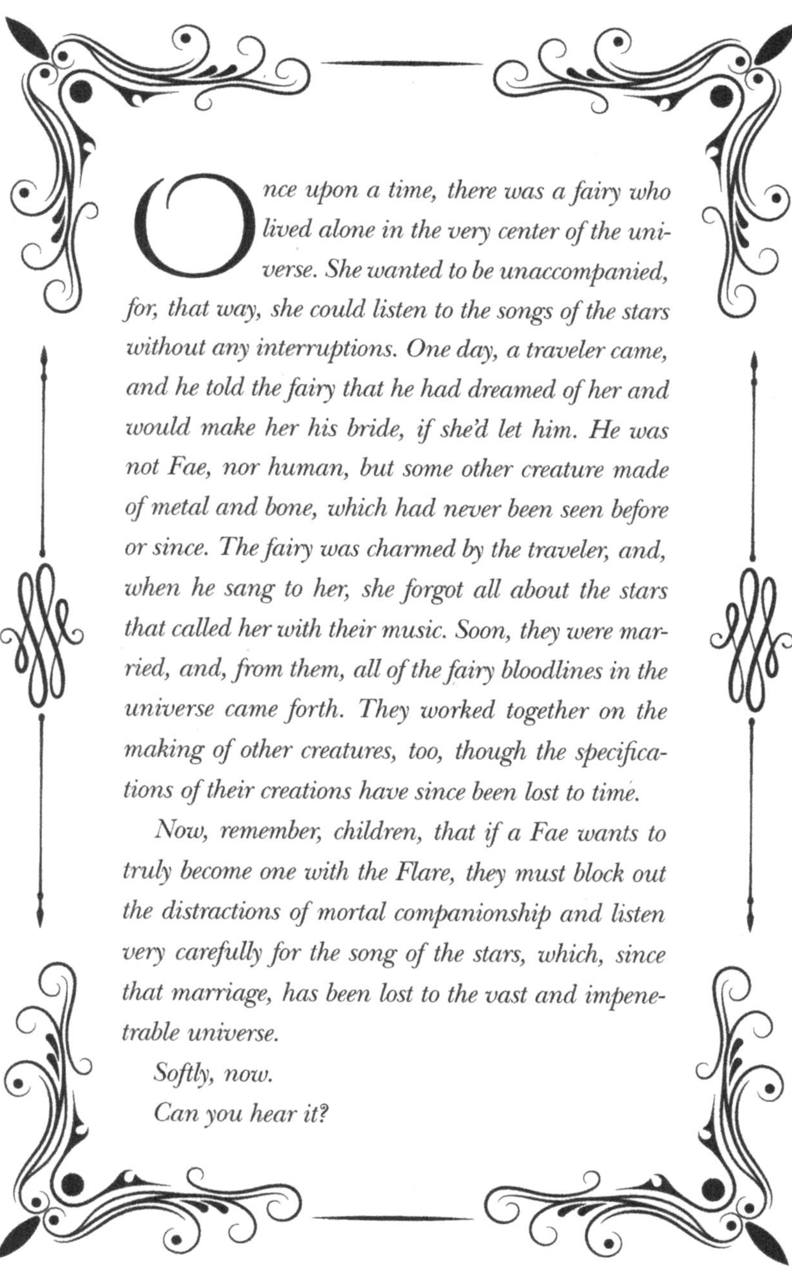

Once upon a time, there was a fairy who lived alone in the very center of the universe. She wanted to be unaccompanied, for, that way, she could listen to the songs of the stars without any interruptions. One day, a traveler came, and he told the fairy that he had dreamed of her and would make her his bride, if she'd let him. He was not Fae, nor human, but some other creature made of metal and bone, which had never been seen before or since. The fairy was charmed by the traveler, and, when he sang to her, she forgot all about the stars that called her with their music. Soon, they were married, and, from them, all of the fairy bloodlines in the universe came forth. They worked together on the making of other creatures, too, though the specifications of their creations have since been lost to time.

Now, remember, children, that if a Fae wants to truly become one with the Flare, they must block out the distractions of mortal companionship and listen very carefully for the song of the stars, which, since that marriage, has been lost to the vast and impenetrable universe.

Softly, now.

Can you hear it?

PART ONE

CHAPTER ONE

PAIGE

By the time the exit for Wintroster appears, Paige has been driving for twelve hours. Her eyes burn, and she rubs them with fingers that smell like cinnamon gum—a nice change from the stiffing sharpness of hemp oil and paint remover. She has bits of sour straw lingering in her molars, which she washes down with the last sips of a diet coke, and her hair is a dry tangle of yarn-y locks. *We couldn't just have gone to Sarasota?* she grumbles in her head to the sleeping form in the passenger's seat, but the internal compass in her mother's lockbox head has pointed toward Virginia.

Now, the great Petta dozes under a saddle blanket, with only her gray waves visible like the foamy top of a fearsome and inevitable tide, and, in the undercurrent, her legs, twig jeans tucked into Victorian leather boots. *What's playing in your head right now?* Paige asks the bear slumbering beside her. *It's been eighteen years, and now you just spring this on me?*

Not that Paige will ever ask these questions, for to bring up her birth state is to send Petta into a frenzy of furious brush strokes on a pig puppet or a yo-yo or a train set or a miniature dollhouse. No, Paige cannot handle another one of her mother's "artistic moods," as Petta called them, not after the last one . . . But Paige can wonder, as she turns around the tight bend of the start of the city, why they would ever come far enough north to see the wind dance russet red leaves from the tall branches of the unfamiliar oaks, which grow here not like spiders extending their knobby legs, but like great raised fans.

"Mom," Paige says softly. Though her mother's head dips off the corner of the blanket she has bunched like a pillow and propped against the door, she finds the comfortable edge again and snores.

Paige's gaze drifts to the pedestrians on the sidewalk, whose regard she has been avoiding: a woman with a white shopping bag full to the brim with pink-wrapped paper. A child holding the hand of a mother weighed down on one side by a diaper bag. A man in a black cap and cook's uniform bobbing to music in his headphones.

"Mom, we're here."

Still no movement.

Paige glances back. Now the people of Wintroster have stopped walking to stare at the wooden caravan behind their truck. *Look*, they mouth. *What is that?*

To Paige, the trailer is just a painted sign in the side mirror: *Petta's Traveling Toys.* She can't see the rickety balcony at the back door, nor the chimes there that tinkle hello to the people who watch them pass. She can't see the toys tied up like fish caught and hung on the line—the newest pig puppet and the wind-blown doll and the nutcracker that slacks its jaw at the bystanders. But she imagines them, now, the way they looked when Petta tied up her final string, clapped her hands together, and announced that it was time to set off on their next big adventure.

"Mom!"

The truck hits a dip, and the tools and loose pieces of wood secured in their trunks clatter. Paige's cheeks warm, but she keeps her eyes ahead at the street signs, which indicate they have almost reached the side street where they have secured a permit to park.

Don't look. Don't look. Don't look.

". . . Hmm?" Petta's low croak finally murmurs.

"We're here."

Petta throws off the saddle blanket like she is drawing away a curtain. She is still wearing her apron over a loose white shirt that is rolled back to her elbows and tucked into her high-waisted jeans. *My completely unavailable look*, as she calls it, though the older men of the town are never persuaded. "We're here?"

Paige glances at the sleepy face and notes that Petta looks surprisingly well-rested. *Must be nice.* The dark circles that have lived under her eyes for months have faded; her mouth has turned up in an optimistic smile. How strange, that she can be so rejuvenated by their relocation, like a cramped plant that has just received a newer pot, while Paige feels like she has aged ten years since she heard the news.

"You have paint on your cheek," Paige says, and turns her eyes to the road.

Her mother wipes at the crusty orange streak, and when crumbs come away, she rubs between her fingers until they fall to the car floor.

"There's wipes in the glove compartment."

"I'm fine." Petta gives the growing crowd a little wave.

The truck meets more bumps as they get closer to the cobblestone entrance ahead. Paige read that the old town calls tourists from all over the world to stop and have lunch on the attractive strip. Through the archway, she can see the black gates of the restaurants' seating areas, where metal chairs wait in neat bunches for the midday rush. Glass display cases shimmer in the sun. A library with its statuesque entrance is on the right—or perhaps it's a government building. *Pretty.*

But they won't be parking in the nice part of town. Rather, at the last traffic light, Paige turns right, and then left, and then slows the caravan to a stop in their assigned location near a bagel shop that claims to be the best in all of Virginia.

Paige unbuckles her seatbelt and stretches as far as her long legs can slip between the pedals. "You have the business license?"

"Yes." Petta removes her own seatbelt and pops open the glove compartment. Her hands are dry at the knuckles and painted under the nails, as though the years of her life have settled below the wrists instead of across her face, like a normal mother's would. "Somewhere."

Paige pulls the sleeves of her Florida State hoodie over her hands and puts them on the steering wheel, where she then rests her burning eyes on the makeshift garnet pillow. "And the parking permit from the city?"

"I'm sure I do." The papers in the glove compartment rustle.

If she keeps her eyes closed, Paige can almost imagine the heat of the sun through the windshield is the result of a humid Florida morning. But she needs to check on the caravan, so she reluctantly lifts her head, gives her mother a pointed look that Petta misses as she pages through the stack of documents on her lap, and opens the car door.

A cool breeze sends a chill through the thick fabric of the hoodie, and Paige shivers.

"A nice change, isn't it?" Petta calls out, and Paige slams the door in response.

She grabs the ends of her sweatshirt and pulls them in to make warmer nooks for her already freezing fingers. At least they aren't going to another conference—or, that's what Petta calls the gatherings of strange toymakers that she organizes whenever she arrives in a new town. *What's the point of making friends you're going to leave?*, Paige always wonders. And it's not like Petta has anything to learn from those other makers, anyway—she's the best there is. *That's what makes shadowing her so frustrating.*

The caravan seems to be intact, though one of the wheels is a little flat. Paige makes a mental note to visit the air pump the next day, as well as clean the back window, which is so dusty she can barely see through it. The doll and pig are alive and well, though they seem to have lost the nutcracker somewhere along the route.

Safe travels, friend, Paige says to her mother's creation, the way she always blesses the toys that leave her hands.

At the caravan's far counter, Paige unlocks the window and raises the wooden slats up so that they disappear along the ceiling of the interior. She hangs her sign, "Open for business," and wipes away some pollen from the long wooden ledge. Then she circles back the way she came, to the back deck, and brushes her fingers through the doll's knotted hair. *Glad you're still with us,* she thinks.

Inside, the caravan is strongly scented by the oils and paints that have not been vented in almost two days. The pillows have fallen from the bunk beds on her left, so Paige rights them and fluffs them twice for good measure. She squares the corners of the comforters, then uses her mother's bunk as a stepstool so that she can set her stuffed animal, Monkey Joe, back in the center of the top bunk.

On the wall behind her bed is a map of all the United States, with twenty-one of the lower divisions colored in increasingly neat crayon. Some of the states have two colors, like the blue-green of Alabama or the purple-blue of Georgia, and then at the bottom that deep dip of Florida, a fiery red-orange-yellow. How Paige used to love to get out the dusty bag from her mother's supplies and select her waxy utensil; how she used to scribble against the hard back of the caravan wall with pride. *Most kids don't ever leave the town where they're born*, Petta used to say, and Paige imagined those children as roots stuck tight in a frozen ground, while she drifted lightly through a dandelion breeze.

Now she knows a dandelion is a weed.

Paige turns away and hops down from her mother's bunk. At the kitchenette just past the beds on the left, she lifts the heavy water jug from the bin screwed to the counter and pours water into the black kettle, then sets the sloshing receptacle on the burner. The dial sticks, but then it turns all the way to the highest setting and begins to warm. She removes two mugs from the small cabinet above the counter and sets a green tea bag in one and a packet of instant coffee in the other. *Hurry up*, she instructs the water as she rubs her eyes again. *I've still got ten hours to go.*

The water is slow, and Paige is strangely anxious, so she moves past the kitchenette to the front of the caravan, where she removes the wooden folding chairs splattered with paint from their hooks on the wall and sets them by the long wooden desk. Here are Petta's tools, secured with hooks and extra cords so that a rogue axe or seamstress's scissors do not leave dents across the floor. There are three tool bins, too, with brushes and drill bits and screws. Her mother has not mentioned a new design, so Paige guesses she will just be painting this afternoon. Another nutcracker, Paige suspects, which means red, green, black, and gold—along with a set of brushes that have dried along the drive. The bristles are soft and pointed, and Paige runs them along her palm before aligning them to the paints and a plastic palette.

Now that her mother's work has been settled, Paige turns to the opening in the other wall, where the antique cash register locked to the interior of the wooden ledge waits. She taps on the worn white buttons in hello, and then she dings open the cash drawer and counts her stash: two hundred dollars, with three hundred more in the safe out of view from the prying eyes of customers. Of course, they should have a newer register, but Petta refuses the harsh modernity of a digital face. *You'd rather get robbed?*, Paige asks, but she knows the answer is yes.

The bills are crisp and sharp in her hands, and Paige reminds herself to be careful when pulling them from their slots. *My domain,* she thinks, fanning the bills and inhaling their woodsy, linen smell. She only relinquishes this spot on days when she has fallen very ill, or when she is needed to paint the delicate features of a face too small for even her mother's reading glasses to see well. After any time away, she always returns to the register to find the bills mixed up and the coins in the wrong spaces.

Speaking of which, where is she? Paige wonders, glancing back at the open door.

Then she hears the call:

"Toys! Wooden toys! Handmade toys! Bespoke creations! Toys sold here!" Petta's voice is high and enthusiastic, as though they hold the very wonders of the world in this sixteen-foot-long space.

I'm getting too old for this, Paige thinks, and then she slips her chin into her hoodie and lifts it up over her blushing cheeks.

CHAPTER TWO

LILY

As Lily Jones walks through the early morning chill of 6:00 A.M. Wintroster, she calls out greetings to the other first shift employees already deeply engrossed in their work. There is Tom collecting the last of the previous day's detritus from the city receptacles and then snapping a new bag open in the air beside him—*More magician than man*, she announces. There is Margot at the bakery window, lining crescent moon croissants in fetal rows and wiping spilled cream from the trays with the edge of her apron, who waves a sympathetic cinnamon roll as Lily briskly passes. There is Joseph, the self-proclaimed bagel master, smoking a cigarette at his own outdoor table, the exhale mingling with the fog in anxious systems carrying the storms to come.

Lot of customers already? Lily asks the bagel master, and he shakes his head no, so that the top hat he wears threatens to abandon the chaotic mind of its wearer and roll away down the empty street.

Not that there are ever many customers for Joseph—he only takes visitors one at a time, and they have to call the number on the window to select which of his three options—cream cheese, lox and cream cheese, or egg and cheese—they've chosen. *If you'd only let me help you adjust your business model . . .* Lily always says, but Joseph just shakes his head and points to the announcement on the window: *Orders by phone call only. You must call! One customer at a time, please! Best bagels in Virginia.* Then he tells her that he might be renting from her father, but if she knows what is good for her, she'll follow the rules like everyone else.

Now, he hands her a brown bag, and she keeps her mouth shut and presses a five-dollar bill into his boney hand. There are goose pimples up his exposed arms, and his shoulders shiver once under the thin protection of his white undershirt.

"Thanks," she says.

"Storm's coming," Joseph replies. He stubs out his cigarette in the ashtray on the table and then removes a bagel with cream cheese from his pocket. Lily tries not to stare as he takes a big bite and then swallows hard.

"Seems like it. All this fog—"

"Not that kind of storm."

Joseph scrapes the metal chair back and then goes inside. Lily thinks about sitting in his place to eat her bagel, but she is already late, and besides, Joseph's shop gives her the creeps. Instead, she eats as she walks, chewing in time to the tap of her boot heels on the sidewalk. *1, 2, 3, 5, 7, 11, 13, 17, 19, 23 . . .*

She loves prime numbers—always has, ever since she first read about them in the first math book she borrowed from the library back when she needed her mother to sit with her and read the pages. Divided only by themselves—not beholden to anyone else to define them. Yes, that idea had appealed to her, and, from there, she had followed the path of algebraic thinking to geometry and then precalculus.

Maybe she should have kept her passions to herself, she thinks now. Maybe that would have lowered everyone's expectations.

Her father's buildings pass in her periphery vision, and she wonders if he will stop by later to play chess with the man who owns the carpet store, or if he will visit the florist to buy a bouquet for her mother to display proudly on the dining room table between the steaming dishes she will spend the day making.

You're just a normal girl going to work, Lily thinks, and she tries to clear her mind of him—but instead, there he is, dredging up from her memory with a bishop between his fingers, slowly twirling the ivory piece against the wiry bristles of his chin. She tries, again, to wipe the slate of her memory clean, but now he is sitting back against the green back of the leather chair, running his fingers over his bald brown head, telling the man that Lily was first chair in the school orchestra for the third year in a row.

What will he say about her today, if he dings the bell on the door and takes up the chess set? Will he brag to the carpet salesman about the million ways Lily is the most superb child that has ever graced the planet? Will he tell the man she is taking a "gap year" between college and some grand career—probably law or medicine—and explain that it's easy to go back, like unpausing a movie? Will he claim that she wants to take over his empire one day? Will he worry out loud that she will never marry, or even go on a date, and does the carpet man happen to know any eligible men between the ages of twenty-five and thirty who would provide Lily with the life she clearly deserves?

I don't want a man of any age, Lily thinks—but she'll never be able to tell her father that. *Now stop living in your head, and remember that you're just a normal girl—*

Lily halts, and the half-eaten bagel drops from her hand. There, in front of her, is something new: a caravan, wooden, with windows and dirty white curtains, and a folding chair set at the back, as though the owner has just stepped away for a moment and left the chair and the steaming cup of tea on the ground at its feet. But the caravan is not the problem—rather, it is the name on the side, Petta's Traveling Toys, that stops Lily in her tracks.

A coincidence, surely.

But could it be? A toymaker named Petta? Lily has never heard of a single other person with that name, not even in her college or on the credit cards of the customers she calls by their last name to create a sense of professionalism.

I wonder if I should call Ms. Vitaly?

Lily might have removed her phone from her leather backpack, or at least spent more time debating whether the owner would appreciate being woken this early in the morning based solely on a familiar name, but then Lily remembers the fallen bagel, and poor Tom, who would have to clean it up if she left it splattered on the cement, and her watch, which slips out from the sleeve of her signature blazer to reveal the gray numbers of the hour: 6:35 A.M.—five minutes *after* she is supposed to unlock the doors for the craftspeople who come every morning to replenish their stock.

I'll worry about you later, she tells the steaming mug, and the caravan, and the parked truck that has towed the wobbly wheels from whence it came. *For now, I need to get to work.*

CHAPTER THREE
PAIGE

Paige takes a long time making her coffee. First, she lifts the bag and feels its flexible toughness. Then, she rips the corner, listening to its scratchy creak. The slow dumping is like sand moving through an hourglass, until the dark granules are a pool at the bottom of the mug she wishes she could dive into. The water is the careful pour of liquid and steam. Slowly, she stirs the floating pellets, until, one by one, they dissolve into a thin liquid she can drink without sweetener or milk. How strange, that five years ago she would have dumped five gas station sugar packets into a cup this size, while now, she can sip at the rich black coffee with the desperation of a woman much older than eighteen.

"Paige?"

"Coming," she calls out the window toward the front of the truck.

Now she begins the process of the tea. But this time, she feels her mother's impatience like a clock ticking in her ear. Rip goes the bag, in dips the tea. Sugar, of course. Swirl, swirl, swirl. She lifts the mugs, which burn at her palms, and lets out a deep sigh. *I'm not ready*, she thinks, and then she turns around and walks out the back door.

Her mother is not visible from the back or the counter side of the caravan, but when Paige rounds the front, she can see her at the right of the truck, chatting with a small crowd of bystanders.

"Here she is!" her mother announces, waving a doll-labored hand theatrically in Paige's direction. "The brains behind this whole operation. Can you believe she's only eighteen? Tell her your requests, and she'll be happy to write you up a preorder slip you can bring back tomorrow for your custom-painted creation."

You have to take preorders because you haven't done any work yet, Paige chastises. How many times has she told Petta, "*Paint first, sell after*"? But her mother needs those slips like a dog at her heels, chasing her over the wooden surfaces of the toys and leaving perfectly painted patterns in their wake.

Paige removes the preorder slips from the pocket of her hoodie, along with blue pens she clicks open before handing them over to the new customers. Most look like mothers or grandmothers, and they coo over the dolls in Petta's hands before writing their own requests: *A little redhead with a white lace dress, just like my little Angelina,* or *A baby Brad with blond curls and a blue woolen suit,* or some such nonsense that will make Paige roll her eyes later as she translates them into simple checkmark tickets her mother will impale on a receipt holder's metal spoke.

Small. Girl. White. Red. White. Green.

Large. Boy. Brown. Brown. Blue.

But they will see their sweet cherubs in these blank faces, and they will marvel at the talents of the great painter Petta. Paige feels suddenly so tired of all of it, but she takes another sip of her coffee and then returns to the register so that she can collect, through the window, the papers with little hearts drawn in the margins and names like Grammy Lane.

And the money, of course. She can't forget that.

***

By nightfall, Petta has eighteen dolls preordered and none of them painted. Now, she instructs Paige to close the window and lock it—*As though I'd be the one to forget*—before getting dinner at the sandwich shop down the road.

"So . . . Are you thinking about, maybe, starting to paint?" Paige tries not to make her tone too instructive, but she doesn't quite reach the breezy disinterest she's aimed for.

"Soon," Petta says, taking a corked bottle of wine from the lower cabinets and pulling the top.

"Mom, we only have—"

"Food first," Petta instructs. She tips the bottle, and the red liquid lines the glass and rises.

Paige pulls a twenty from the register and tucks it into her pocket. She and Petta go to the back balcony, where Petta sets her fold-out chair so that she can watch the people moving through town toward dinner or home and drink her wine. Paige imagines the hurried passersby sinking into their time-worn sofas and watching TV, something she'd kill for if she could only convince Petta to buy one. At least she has a phone now, though she can only stream with free Wi-Fi like the coffee shop from which they are currently stealing a connection.

The sandwich shop is just around the corner. The line is short, and soon Paige has a vegetarian sub for Petta and a turkey and cheese for herself. "I'll be back," she tells the cashier, and what she means is that she will be back every night for the foreseeable future. She'd rather go sit in one of those metal chairs on the strip—but, of course, to do that would cost a lot more money.

Maybe I can just walk over really quickly . . . Paige thinks, looking down at the plastic sandwich bag on her arm. Maybe Petta will notice, but more likely she will finish her glass and then slip back into the studio side to engross herself in her work.

Squaring her shoulders, Paige sets herself in the other direction. After two turns, she is standing on the cobblestone street, plunged into the excitement of a bustling tourist attraction. People push around her, their eyes set ahead at their destinations. Voices call out from the tables, and strangers cut in front of her to cross over the crowd to their friends. In the shops at her sides, jewelry gleams under lamps and antique silver bowls sit on Chippendale furniture.

Then she sees it.

The storefront is a majestic red with gold writing like the metal stamps of an old-fashioned printing press: Toy Palace. Fake red columns are painted with golden tassels, as though someone has pulled the curtains back to reveal the grand displays of the front windows. These are not the wooden toys of her mother's work, but rather living toys, like a pen of animatronic dogs that frantically kick their legs and bat at the gate holding them in place and kittens that nudge their heads at their luscious stuffed beds. Around them, trains on long tracks zip figure-eights and larger circles, and their faint *choo-choos* echo through the glass.

As though pulled by an invisible string, Paige steps through the automatic doors and then into the brightly lit room. Grand shelves house more toys than Paige has ever seen in one place, from tea sets to craft kits to stuffed animals in hammocks tied at every corner. Each section is labeled with a gold-printed sign, so that the long rows of them can be seen from her place at the front of the aisle.

"Grand, isn't it?"

Paige startles. The shopkeeper beside her is a girl about her age, though that is where the similarities end. Her brown hair is neatly curled and sprayed with so much hairspray Paige can smell it. Her makeup is perfect, from the golden eyeshadow above her brown eyes to the uncreased brown foundation across her face to the shiny gloss on her lips. Her t-shirt is the same deep red as the storefront, with the same golden letters, TOY PALACE, across the chest. Her name tag says Lily, and there is a teddy bear stamped in black next to the y.

I really wish I'd changed, Paige thinks, and then she finds her own reflection in a pink plastic vanity top sitting on one of the shelves. Her dishwater blond hair is more mane than made up, and her face is tired and flat. There is a coffee stain on her sweatshirt. And, worse, her bloodshot eyes make her look like some kind of demon, or maybe a vampire.

"Have you visited us before?"

"Uh, um . . . " Paige looks away from the mirror. "Never."

"Then welcome!" The girl, Lily, gives Paige a perfect white smile. "Allow me to give you a brief tour of the store!"

Without getting confirmation, Lily turns on her heels and begins to announce with large waves of her hands the layout of Toy Palace, which was apparently founded by two Italian immigrants, Arnaldo and Rosa, who started the store as a traditional wooden toy shop. It was not until their son, Calvino, inherited the business, that Toy Palace in its current iteration was modernized. "Quite the scandal," Lily says gleefully. "But no one could doubt him once his profits tripled. He offered the business to his daughters, and one of them, Camilla, has kept the store in the Vitaly name until this day. In fact, it was Camilla who came up with—"

"Vitaly?" Paige accidentally walks into a block tower, which falls over and almost trips her in the process. "Oh, sorry, god, that's embarrassing. It's just that—"

"—the idea of turning Toy Palace into an entire experience. Up there," Lily points to an escalator leading to some glass windows, "is the Toy Palace Cocoa Bar. And back there," her hand lowers, "is the Stuffed Animal Nursery, where children can birth their own creations by stuffing them with our state-of-the-art fluff."

"Can I just go back to—?"

"And who could forget the Doll Salon to our right," her hand indicates an actual salon window, behind which real hairdressers' seats wait for new customers with their own mirrors and brushes, "where trained professional stylists can get your doll looking her best in less time than it takes to find a new toy from our many alphabetically organized shelves. And that way is the Maker's Room, where our toys are made with top secret methods that make them so lifelike—"

But something else has caught Paige's attention. On the wall beside the salon is a line of portraits, clearly dating back to the original founders in their fine cotton muslin and fitted wool suit. The final portrait is of two sisters, both brown-haired beauties, one with flowing hair and the other with a neat and thickly sprayed bun. The one with the long hair wears a familiar silver chain with a key at the end, and the other a line of perfect white pearls above a gold chain with a ruby stone that seems to glow—though that is impossible. Both sisters wear cotton shirts, but the pearled beauty with the bun has hers neatly set under a high-collared suit jacket.

"She still looks just the same," Lily says when she follows Paige's gaze.

"No, she's grayed," Paige says, but then she realizes Lily meant the other sister, Camilla.

"What did you say?"

But Paige can't reply. The smell of new plastic mixed with fluff dust must be triggering her asthma, for she's having trouble catching her breath, and the room seems to be getting smaller. The lights are too bright, and the sounds are so loud she can barely hear Lily over the cacophony of them.

"Are you okay?"

"I need to sit down," Paige says, and she drops herself into a beanbag chair next to an end cap of Curious George books and identical stuffed monkeys hanging by their hands.

"Let me get Camilla. Stay here, okay?"

Though Paige tries to tell her not to—*Please, not right now*—Lily has already disappeared. Paige pulls herself up by the plastic shelf of the endcap, but the whole thing collapses under her weight, and she almost tips over again. Men with the yellow hat teeter and fall onto the beanbag chair. The sandwich bag falls from her arm, but she grabs the handles and hoists them up onto her shoulder. Quickly, she bolts for the door, while concerned customers ask her if she's all right and children dive out of the way of her frantic stomping.

Eighteen years.

Paige thrusts herself through the opening doors and into the cooler night air. The crowd parts for her, and she runs, not realizing, until she reaches the end, that she has gone the wrong way. She leaves the strip, and though she thinks she can simply go the long route by taking the next left turn, the side street hits a dead end. Paige presses her back against the wall and fans her hoodie out to let air into the sweaty space beneath her arms, then uses a napkin from the bag to dab at her forehead. Her sandwich is smooshed, though luckily Petta's is still relatively intact.

Eighteen years.

The sudden drive up route 95.

Eighteen years.

The quaint little town in Virginia.

Eighteen years.

Then home.

CHAPTER FOUR

PETTA

On the morning of her eighteenth birthday, Petta is called to Grandma Rosa's apartment to be given a gift. On the phone, Rosa's voice drifts, like a bird being carried on winds that land animals can only imagine. "I have something for you," she says softly. "Tell no one."

"Right now?" Petta is in the middle of sketching a new design, but she pauses at the shoe of the marionette. "I have work in an hour."

"You'll be on time."

Petta says she'll come right away, and then she hangs up and locks eyes with the beautiful wooden doll stretched across most of the pad of paper.

"You'll have to wait," she tells the toy. "And let's be honest, Dad was never going to let me make you, anyway."

She folds the sketchpad closed and tucks the drawings into the drawer of her desk. She knows that the plans in her book are things of the past, and her father is aimed only at the future—but she can dream, can't she?

You're almost eighteen years old, he had told her the day before as he packed for the trip to California that would hopefully secure them a fourth distributor. He has seen the sketches tacked up on her bulletin boards, and the sight has brought a thin-lined frown to his mouth that hasn't budged all night. *It's time you think practically about your future.*

Not today, she thinks now, wishing she'd spoken up for herself before. *Today, I'm still a dreamer.*

Petta goes to her closet. What would Rosa like best? A dress? Rosa would say that such beautiful fabrics don't belong at the worker's bench. Jeans? This is not an afternoon in the garden. She settles on a pair of brown plaid pants, an off-the-shoulder red sweater, and a pair of brown lace-up boots with only a bit of paint on the soles. Good enough for Rosa; good enough to work in for the whole day afterward. She rakes her fingers through her long brown hair, rough on the knots that love to form in the frizzy kinks, and then wipes her sleeve across the pencil marks smudged on her cheeks.

Buon compleanno, she tells her reflection, but something isn't sitting right in her stomach. She wishes she could just sit here all day and draw, could pretend she isn't going to have to do anything but make art for the rest of her life. No meetings. No spreadsheets. No registers.

And she would turn back and take up the pad, maybe even call out sick for the fifth time this month, but she has Rosa to visit and a party to attend that night. So, with a heavy sigh and a final look back at her pencil case, she forces herself out of her bedroom door.

***

IN THE KITCHEN, HER MOTHER, GIANNA, is making a grand chocolate cake. The first three layers are cooling on the racks, and when Petta bends down, she inhales cocoa powder and butter. At the mixer, Gianna pours in confectioner's sugar, then milk, then vanilla extract. She wears her favorite apron, a purple floral design Petta got her for Mother's Day this year, and a loose black dress beneath. Her hair is a perfect wave of loosely curled gray-brown hair, and she wears her diamond earrings. So stylish, even when they're the only ones who will see her—but Petta's father would expect no less.

"Smells good, Mamma," Petta says. She gives her mother a hug from behind, inhaling the way Gianna's hair smells like her creations. They are the same, in that way—though Petta's scents are graphite and oil paints and turpentine.

"*Buon compleanno, piccola.*"

"Not that little anymore." Petta puts her finger in the icing bowl, and her mother slaps it away. "In just a few hours, I'll officially be eighteen."

"*Mio dio*!" Her mother pretends to faint. "Impossible."

"I'm going over to Grandma Rosa's," Petta says.

"And you're working today," her mother reminds her, as though there is ever a day when Petta *isn't* working. "Register, *piccola*. You know your father doesn't want you at the warehouse anymore."

"I like it there." Petta thinks of the lines of workbenches, and the walls of tools and wires and glue. These are just the creators, of course—once a new design is made, the plans will be shipped off to the factory for mass production.

"I know." Her mother waves her spatula in Petta's direction like it's a finger, and Petta knows she's about to imitate her father. "But it's time to think of your future, remember?"

"How could I forget," Petta grumbles.

She takes a blueberry muffin for the road, kisses her mother's cheek, and walks to the door to find her purse. Her black backpack is still there on the hook from when school let out for spring break, and inside, too, the acceptance letter she never bothered to show anyone. What was the point? She should clean the backpack, though—there was a whole meal of crumbs along the bottom when she felt the inside of it last, and probably a few incomplete homework assignments, too. Not like her sister's backpack, which Camilla used to pay to have labeled in neat white stitching and had nothing in it but binders organized with too many dividers and the plain yellow highlighters and black pens Camilla used to take notes in class. This is why Petta's teachers always expect great things from her—and why they're always thoroughly disappointed. *There were no secrets in her backpack,* Petta thinks as she turns away from the hooks. *Nothing but plain-as-the-nose-on-your-face ambition.*

The day is a perfect spring morning, warm but not too hot, sun sweet on her cheeks, neighbors saying hello from their porches or through the rolled-down windows of their cars. Everyone knows her father, and thus everyone knows her, even though they just bought the house less than a year ago. Petta preferred their old house, with its peeling paint and the wrap-around porch where she'd draw the blooming trees, but Calvino had to have the modern farmhouse with vaulted ceilings and an open floor plan that meant that everyone knew what everyone else was doing, all the time. In their old house, Petta could hide away in the drawing room and sip tea from one of her mother's vintage cups or read a book by the window in the sunroom, and no one would look over from the living room side and say, *You're drawing again?*

Now, she just hides in her room instead.

A few blocks later, she is downtown.

Her grandmother lives on the second story of a deli owned by another Italian, Lorenzo, who Petta thinks has a crush on Rosa but who her grandmother calls *The Sandwich Man*. When Petta presses, Rosa just says, *When you've had prime rib, my love, you certainly won't settle for a hamburger.* But Petta likes Lorenzo, who now is sitting by the window in his shop reading the newspaper to his grandson, who is preparing the display, so even though she's in a hurry, she pops her head in the door and shouts, "Anything I need to know about?"

"Ah, Petta, the world is falling apart." Lorenzo shakes his head, so that the thin gray hair on top of his head shakes back and forth in the wind of his disappointment. "Terrible, terrible."

"Well, on the bright side, it's my birthday?"

Lorenzo and his grandson shout a hearty *Buon compleanno* and insist that she stop back in after her visit for a sandwich, on the house. Everything is always on the house for relatives of Rosa's, but Petta says thank you and promises to return on her way out the door. Then she leaves the shop and enters the alley beside it, where a set of rickety metal steps take her to Rosa's entrance.

She needs to be in a home, Gianna always says, but Rosa won't be moved. She claims that if she leaves this place, the life will drain out of her—that the space is what keeps her so alert. *But is she really that alert?* Gianna complains to Calvino. *Last week, she told me that her stuffed koala was speaking to her.*

Petta admits, as she climbs the narrow steps, that Rosa is missing a few of her marbles. She talks to the toys on her shelves. She insists that she was once a beautiful doll. She talks about a fairy, and how he once invited her and her parents to tea. Then again, sometimes she is completely aware of herself, and she and Petta play cards and drink cold beers and talk about a completely different life, back in Italy, that Rosa also remembers. It's like her grandmother is two halves of an apple, cut and then pressed back together to hide the seams.

It would help if her son would visit more. It would help if Camilla could muster more interest in the old days instead of claiming that Rosa is, in her words, *The human epitome of a dusty old book*. Petta likes old books, anyway. They're far more interesting, and you never know what messages you'll find inside the pages.

She knocks on the door, and, upon hearing no answer, turns the knob. The door is unlocked, as she expected it would be. She walks inside and smells the dusty staleness of the toys that line the shelves, and the same carpets that her father once crawled on as a boy, before her eyes actually adjust to the semi-darkness.

"Grandma Rosa?" she asks.

"Here, *cuoricina*." Rosa is tucked under a quilt, so that she is barely visible in her rocking chair. Petta crosses the room and sits on the couch cushion closest to her grandmother, though she can still only see Rosa's coal eyes and the top of her gray head. "Were you followed?"

"Followed?" Petta laughs, but deep down, she's disappointed. Her grandmother is clearly having an off day, and Petta doubts she'll even get whatever Rosa promised to give her. "No, no one is here except me."

"Good." Rosa throws off the quilt, and Petta is surprised to find that her grandmother is not in her pink nightgown and yellow-white slippers, but a neat purple suit with a white blouse underneath. She has squeezed her thick ankles into stockings, and on her feet she wears neat black loafers Petta has never even seen. "Then we must move quickly, *cuoricina.* Time moves differently here."

CHAPTER FIVE
PAIGE

FOOTSTEPS IN THE ALLEY.

Heavy, like the wooden feet of a marionette slapping at a stage's wooden floor.

Paige looks up and finds the makers, two pairs of combat boots, with one pair pointed at Paige and the other pointed a bit inward, like the curved arms of a doll. Above the boots on the left are black skinny jeans; on the right are ripped fishnets, above which a leather mini-skirt snugly hugs a waist. They are girls, Paige discovers in surprise as she reaches the fitted black hoodies, just a few years older than her. The one on the left has straight black hair braided into two pigtails, and the one on the right has a blue fringe cut.

"You okay?" asks the girl with the braids.

Paige shrugs. "Not really."

"Someone hurt you?" asks the girl with the blue fringe, and then she plays with her lip piercing with her tongue. "You can tell us."

"No."

They hoist her up. They smell different, like incense and smoke and hair grease, and Paige wonders if she is in danger. She tries to remember what she has in her pockets: a few dollars, her phone, and a credit card she can cancel in a hurry from Petta's phone if she needs to.

"What's your name?" the girl with pigtails asks.

"Paige. You?"

"Jia." Jia claps Paige on the shoulder a few times and then lets go. Up close, Paige can see that Jia also has a tongue piercing, this one a blue jewel instead of a ball. "How come we've never seen you around?"

"I'm new."

"Lucky you." The girl with the fringe pulls her bangs out of her eyes. "I'm Amber."

Paige feels suddenly shy. These are the kinds of girls she would never normally talk to, though she would watch them from a distance.

Jia lifts up the sandwich bags and smells. "Sandwich King?"

"Yeah."

"Can we . . . ?"

Paige should say no, but instead, she nods. Jia unwraps the first sandwich to check the contents, and then she wraps it back up in tin foil so that she can toss it to Amber. Paige expects the sandwich to fall, but Amber catches it in one hand, throws it in the air again so that it spins three times, spins around while the sandwich is still in midair, and then unwraps it in the time it takes Paige to blink.

"How did you . . . "

"My favorite." Amber shoves the whole end of the turkey and cheese into her mouth, then adds through her chewing: "Thanks."

"I prefer ham, but this'll do," Jia says. In three bites, the vegetarian sandwich is just a pile of fallen onions and green peppers.

"You guys some kind of magicians or something?"

"Or something." Amber reaches into her pocket and pulls out Paige's phone.

"How did you . . . ?"

"Call it a secret talent." Jia reaches into the back pocket of her pants and reveals Paige's brown leather wallet. "Don't worry, we were always going to give them back."

"Sure." Paige takes her wallet and phone and hugs them to her body. "So, you're thieves?"

"Easy now," Amber says, and both girls give Paige hard frowns. Then they catch each other's gaze and laugh, until they're barreled over. "If you want to put it bluntly, then yes."

"But we prefer survivors," Jia corrects.

"Survivors," Amber agrees.

Paige laughs, but the sound is unnatural. She wonders how she can leave the alley without these two girls finding out where she lives—there is the register to think about, after all—and yet she finds that she is enjoying herself, too. When was the last time she hung out with girls her own age?

"So, what are you doing tonight?" Jia asks as she balls up the tin foil and chucks it at Amber.

"Me? Nothing." Paige looks at the discarded ball on the ground. "I mean, I guess I need to buy some more sandwiches."

"Why don't you come out with us?" Amber kicks the tin foil ball to Jia's feet. "We're going to hit up this new spot across town."

Paige thinks for a few seconds and then says, "I can't."

"You don't sound certain." Jia kicks the ball back, but Amber misses it, and the ball hits the back alley wall and bounces.

"I know. But I really do need to get back . . . "

"Let me give you my number." Jia lifts a phone from under her arm, and Paige realizes that it's her own phone. In the hand that had previously held her phone is a new phone with a black case and a cracked screen. "Put in yours, okay?"

". . . Okay. Sure."

Jia's wallpaper is a photo of her kissing Amber on the cheek, and Paige wonders if they are together. She opens Jia's contacts to add her number and finds that the only other person listed there is Ambie-Bambie, whose photo is a completely different person. Is this even Jia's phone? Is Amber's phone stolen, too? And if Paige puts her number into a stolen phone, is she somehow responsible for it?

She adds her name, but instead of putting Vitaly, she puts Vorhees, the last name of her virtual tutor from last year. Not that Paige had attended many of her sessions, but she can picture that name, Ginger Vorhees, listed over and over again in her inbox as she reminded her gently that she was *behind.* Mrs. Vorhees still likes to forward her college brochures, which Paige slips into her Trash folder along with the promotional emails of all the stores and coffee shops to which her mother has optimistically given Paige's email, as if they will ever be there long enough for all of those frequent buyer punches and points rewards.

"Vorhees." Jia nods. "Cool."

In Paige's own phone, Jia has taken a selfie and saved it as her contact photo. Her tongue is out, and her piercing is pushed upward by her teeth, so that the jewel looks like the raised fin of a shark. She has also saved Amber's number, listed as "Amber with the Good Tits."

"What?" Jia says with a smirk and a shrug when Paige looks up and blushes. "They are!"

The girls walk with Paige to the end of the alley, and then, with a salute, they go the other way. Paige waits until they have rounded the corner before she hurries in the opposite direction, turning every few steps to make sure she is not being followed.

Three lefts and she is back at the road where the caravan waits. Her mother is not in the back chair, but newly painted toys dry from strings hung from the wooden rafters. As Paige comes closer, she can smell the fumes, and she wonders if Petta remembered to crack the roof window. *You're going to give us chemical asphyxia.* But even Paige must admit that the dolls are even better than usual tonight—the little boy in the blue suit is particularly lifelike, with the brass buttons like silver plates on the polished blue table of his chest. Petta always does her best work after a move, as though her talent is a new tube of paint that she has only just begun to squeeze. Later, the tube will be flat, and the dolls will have shortcuts, and Paige will know that the breeze that lives in Petta has begun to blow . . .

But not now.

Paige opens the door—unlocked, of course—and kicks an empty food bar wrapper, which she can barely see in the dim street light glow coming from behind her.

"Mom?" she whispers.

"Hmm?" Petta asks. The voice comes from the bunk beds. Now that her eyes are adjusting, Paige can see the lump of her mother under the covers, and her face, which is just a shadow.

"Sorry. I got lost, and then my phone died."

"Oh, Paige." Petta rubs her eyes hard and then puts her hand back under the covers. "Are you okay?"

"Yeah. I met these two girls who helped me get back—but I lost the sandwiches."

"That's okay, honey. I'm just glad you're all right."

Paige kneels down on the floor beside her mother and puts her face close, so that she can smell the sweet wine breath. "Mom . . . ?"

"Yes?" Petta's eyes have closed again.

". . . Never mind."

Petta's breath slows, and then she begins to snore. Paige pulls up the covers and tucks them tightly around her mother's shoulders, and Petta does not stir, not even when Paige grabs two food bars from the basket and walks back across the caravan to the porch. The chair creaks hello under Paige's weight, and then she rocks onto the back legs of the chair and puts her feet up on the porch's railing, avoiding the dangling feet of the drying toys. The food bars are dusty in her mouth, and though Paige considers going back inside to get a drink, she does not want to wake Petta again. How strange, that her mother can sleep so early now, when just a few years before she would stay up so late to paint that the sun would already be coming up when Paige woke to the sound of her mother sliding into the creaking bunk. Paige wants to sleep, too; to forget everything, especially the thing that she does not want to name, which of course she is now thinking about.

Toy Palace.

As she sits back in the chair and lets the seconds slide past like cars on their side street, her mind begins to drift. Paige tries to recall any mentions of such a place, or of her mother's family, but all she can remember is Petta telling her that her grandparents had passed down the art of toymaking, and that her parents had both been dead by the time she left town. Whenever they came up, Petta would say, *We were very different.*

No.

Wait.

That isn't entirely true.

There was that one time, when Petta had kept them in the same town for far too long and the man she'd been seeing had started calling her Hun, that Petta had slipped. It was a Saturday, Paige remembers, and they only had a few toys to paint. Petta had a date that night, and Paige was going to a play at the high school—*Beauty and the Beast,* maybe?—with the daughter of the dry cleaner who let them stay in his spot. She was around seven then—old enough to help, but not old enough to understand that the life of a traveling salesman was not all vending machine candy and open road—and she was trying to decide between her only fancy party dress and a sundress with a t-shirt underneath. Behind her, Petta was working on a horse, and she kept messing up the lines, so that the unrealistic waves of the horse's mane looked like squiggly snakes instead of wind-tossed locks.

"Nonno would roll over in his grave," Petta said between clenched teeth, and then she threw the horse across the caravan. The head went straight through the window, shattering the glass. Paige froze, and then she looked at Petta, whose face was red with some blend of fury and embarrassment.

"Who's Nonno?" Paige asked, but Petta didn't seem to hear her. Instead, she grabbed the broom and yanked it from the hook.

"It's all this staying in one place," Petta muttered. "I can't work like this." She raised the broom in Paige's direction. "And you, always interrupting me to ask if you can do this or do that, making friends, giggling. You're going to have to leave them behind, you know? All of them. Gone. Like that." She tried to snap, but the broom was in the way.

"I know," Paige whispered.

"You don't know. If I can't make my art, then I can't live, Paige. I can't breathe." Petta clutched at her chest. "I might as well have stayed in Wintroster, feeding batteries into an animatronic gerbil. Do you know what I mean? Do you?" Her face was so red, and Paige wondered if she was going to pass out.

"Yes," Paige said, though she didn't, not at all. "I know exactly what you mean."

Petta had cleaned up the glass, and then she had calmly called her boyfriend and explained to him that she would be leaving for a short trip. *When will you be back?*, the distant voice asked, and Petta said, *Soon.* Then, without saying a word to Paige, Petta had begun to secure the tools to the wall, to fold up the chairs and hang them on the hooks, to roll down the windows.

"You want to point?" Petta finally asked, holding up a map of Florida, and her smile was the blank grin of a doll's.

"Yes," Paige said, smiling back.

Paige was still in her party dress, itchy pink tulle swishing at her legs, the zipper still unzipped down to her hips, when she climbed into the passenger's seat.

***

THEN I CAN'T BREATHE.

Paige feels that tightness in her chest now, eleven years later, as she lets the chair fall hard on the porch. She should have spoken up. She should have told her mother that she wanted to stay that day—on any day. She should have forced the words through her painted mouth.

But what about me, Mom? What about what I want?

Paige puts her fingers in the center of her chest, that river between bone, where in the portrait her mother's star hung familiar and yet strange on the wall of Toy Palace. But instead of the familiar flatness, Paige feels something strange there—something new—that makes her lift her sweatshirt away from her body. There is a strange, raised surface there, with grooves and lines, like the bundles that Petta buys at the store and keeps piled under her desk for carving.

A wooden surface.

A shard.

CHAPTER SIX

GENERAL DORIEL

General Doriel perches on his post, a flat sheet of beams that at any moment might loosen a nail and slap him down to the underbrush of the transition zone between the forest wall and the open deadlands of the Land of Toys. The dry dust whirls and settles in the strong wind, but thus far, he has not spotted any threats. His eyes sweep the coals of the fires, put out in the morning and soon revived for the afternoon, and then a stick crackles, darting his gaze back in the opposite direction.

"Calm yourself, Doriel."

The words are his own, but his voice is strange and low in his ears. He has not spoken since the morning, will not speak again until he returns to the hideout to report on the day's events. Deaths. Close calls, so that the ghost of himself lingers for hours in the empty air. In his mind, the ghost wears his royal uniform, the cap he's long-since lost, the buzzed cut neat at the neck and a trim beard instead of this uneven shave. But he cannot think too long on the image, or he might consider it a viable alternative to the endless hours stretched before him.

Snap.

Soundlessly, General Doriel secures his palm on the hilt of his sword. His senses alert the scent of old fabric, moldy and damp, and the metallic rust of old nails. There is a toy here, but how close, and moving in what direction, he must determine.

Snap. Snap-snap.

She comes into the thin tree line like a wave. Her bottom half is the culprit of the smell, each stuffed squid leg dragging debris along its fuzzy bottom, where little tentacles of skin and wood drip blood collected from the dirty pools of the deadlands. On the top, a doll's body, porcelain, covered sparsely in the top half of a nurse's blue uniform. Someone has cut her hair short, like the jagged wave of a piece of broken glass. Her arms chop in stiff and perpetual motion. Her eyes glare the red of the possessed. The metal belt at her waist was once a soldier, or a sword, or a little iron dog with a leash no one ever held, melted down and then formed, again, into this new grip of possession.

He waits.

Once, he would have leapt from the tree and drawn his sword, thrust the end, dead metal that should glow with the lost power of the Flare, into that stiffly turning midsection. Once, he would have known that others would protect the survivors. But he is all that remains, one young soldier made General by his own Commander with only the blessing of the dead Fae around him to witness it, one young soldier who still had so much to learn about this world, about the toys who inhabited it, toys who'd soon be dead or worse—

The doll spins her head to survey the forest and then slides her tentacle body forward, like a many-footed slug. Thrust, pull. General Doriel holds his breath, holds his sword hand tight against the empty setting where once a jewel from their own world sat, long lost in the harsh strikes of metal on metal, metal on stone, metal on everything that should not move but does with the magic of the Deathsprites in their veins.

The doll shoves her tentacles through a break in the trees and is gone, a whale over the red dust of the deadlands.

General Doriel sits back against the trunk and releases his grip.

PART TWO

CHAPTER SEVEN
PAIGE

Paige tries to take a deep breath, but her lungs feel trapped beneath that unfamiliar plane. *I'm finally going mad,* she thinks, clutching her hands to her chest. But after a few seconds, she finds that she can actually breathe, and so she takes a few inhalations and exhalations, appreciating the crisp coldness of the late-night air.

Again, she lifts away the sweatshirt.

Again, she finds the wooden shard intact.

Paige takes out her phone and sees a text from Amber: *Let's meet tomorrow.*

Are you still out? Paige replies before she can think too much about it.

Yeah! Jia texts back a pin, and then a wink emoji. A few seconds later, Amber texts, *Let's go!*

Jia says that they'll wait for her at a place called Pocket Seven, so Paige stands up and begins to walk. By now the lights of the storefronts have all dimmed, their blank glass facades like the unpainted faces of so many carved figures. The streetlights guide her path, trapped souls shining shadows of themselves against the neat branches of the imprisoned trees. She walks in the street, and the paved road plays valley to the buildings walling her in place. No one else passes. When Paige's GPS tells her to turn, its voice a cheerful echo against the hollow groove of the empty street, she mechanically crunches her heel and marches into the wind that has found her again in this new and terrible direction.

The pool hall, Pocket Seven, appears as a single door with maroon letters sandwiched between a boutique and a sushi shop. When Paige enters, the few patrons inside stop and stare at her from the row of green tables on her right, their backs hunched and their cues angled toward victory. The sound is the sharp crack of resin against resin. The smell is fry oil mixed with cologne. "Right with you, Sweetie," says the bartender to her left, a woman with wavy red hair and sleeve tattoos of playing cards, and there is Jia, hopped up on the rail with her weight on the bar, sweet talking.

"Hey," Paige says to Jia.

Jia nods but does not turn. "Jess, baby, just one more plate—"

"Run away, little fox." The bartender takes her dish towel from her shoulder and throws it in on the bar. "You've had enough."

Jia gives Jess another pleading look, but the woman turns away and busies herself cleaning the glasses. Jia shrugs, hops down, and puts her arm around Paige. "Women, am I right?"

"I heard that," Jess says, still not turning.

"She'll change her tune in an hour or so, you wait and see," Jia whispers loudly to Paige, and then she grins.

Amber is in the back, holed up on a stool perched above two black backpacks. The backpacks are in bad shape—one is missing a strap, and the other has a broken zipper. Paige can't see much, but there is the distinct underwire of a bra, a belt, and the heel of a shoe. Amber has changed her clothes, and now she is wearing a lace tiered skirt over the fishnets and an oversized band t-shirt tied at the waist.

"I like your shirt," Paige says.

"You know the band?" Amber lifts the shirt away from her body. "Well, technically, it's a collaboration. One Girl, Thirty Fists?"

"No," Paige says, looking down at her own chest. "I'm coming to realize I don't know much of anything."

When she looks up, Jia and Amber are both giving her concerned frowns. Jia puts her hands on Paige's shoulders and steers her to the chair next to Amber, where a plate of half-eaten mozzarella sticks and French fries tempts Paige's empty stomach.

"Go ahead," Amber says, nodding her chin toward the food.

Paige eats, and the food is salty and warm on her still-chilled mouth. The cheese sticks in her throat, but she forces it down in a hard gulp. "Water?" Jia asks, offering her own glass, but Paige shakes her head no and bites down on another French fry. When her stomach is full, she leans back against the hard chair and sighs.

"Better?" Jia asks.

"Yeah." Paige slumps. "I don't even know what I'm doing here."

"You're here because you need a friend." Amber leans off her chair to embrace Paige, pushing her head into her chest. Up close, the white letters of the "One Girl, Thirty Fists" logo look like sloppy lines scratched on a school chalkboard. Paige can barely breathe with her neck crammed up like this, but at the same time, Amber's heartbeat has a soothing effect. "Or two."

"Buy one, get one free," Jia confirms. She slaps Paige's back a bit too hard, so that her captured head slides up into the silver chains apparently hanging under Amber's shirt. Why is she wearing so many—and how many did she steal? "We're going to take care of you."

"Tell her the story," Amber says. She releases Paige's head, and Paige can finally breathe freely again.

"Of course I will." Jia stands and pretends to take a microphone from a stand; then she taps the invisible microphone three times and clears her throat. "Once upon a time," she begins, to enthusiastic applause from Amber, "There were two girls named Jia and Amber."

"Not really," Amber whispers in Paige's ear, so close her hot breath tickles. "But it's nothing against you—we just left that life behind, you know?"

"Stop getting ahead," Jia scolds. She waves a hand theatrically in the air, and then continues: "So these two girls went to different schools, and they were both strangers. But one day, their GSA advisors—"

"GSA?" Paige asks.

"Quiet in the audience!" Jia demands, but then her frown turns into a delicious grin. "I'm just kidding. These days, GSA stands for Gender and Sexuality Alliance—I'm surprised you've never heard of it."

"I didn't really go to school," Paige says. "It's a long story . . . "

"Well, put a pin in that," Jia says, feigning sticking a pin in the air. "For now, we're about to close-up on two girls, both being forced to work on a community project called the Pride Garden, sweltering under the late spring heat, sweat just dripping over their very hot bodies—"

"The hottest," Amber says with a wink.

"—one holding a shovel and the other holding a rake." Jia makes a shoveling motion. "These girls were not exactly gardener material, and so they got to talking, among the rainbow flower beds, which were sort of cute and sort of way too on the nose, you know? Anyway, it turned out they both had pretty bad home lives, but we'll skip all that boring stuff—"

"So boring," Amber says, feigning a yawn. "I mean, what queer hasn't been bullied by their peers and shamed by their parents and become a human so dead inside that they almost miss a true connection when it comes around, am I right?"

"Uh—"

"But we're done with all that, right?" Jia says, and Amber blows her a kiss. "Back to my story: these two girls decide to take matters into their own hands. They sneak into the principal's office, take his keys, and drive off in his car into the sunset. Well, before they take the keys, they may or may not have found incriminating evidence about the principal and emailed that evidence to the whole school—"

"But don't worry," Amber says, taking Paige's hand. Her palms are warm and smooth. "He was a terrible dude. Like, the worst. He once called Jia a—"

"Never mind that," Jia interrupts. "So anyway, after they spread the truth, the girls stole the car, ditched it on the highway, hitchhiked a ride, almost got murdered by a sketchy dude in a van, fought their way out, almost starved to death, got lost in some random farmland, and finally, when all hope was lost, they made it to Wintroster, where they stole just enough to buy some hot clothes and a few hot meals and maybe, just maybe, get to Washington, D.C., where the most attractive of the two—"

"Oh, please," Amber says, flashing her lace skirt up to reveal her thigh.

"—has a friend willing to take them in and get them jobs bussing tables. And in the meantime, if they find any baby queers along the way—"

"That's you," Amber whispers loudly, raising her eyebrows at Paige.

"—then they take care of them as though they're their own flesh and blood. No, better than flesh and blood—those people suck—but like a new family, a found family, the best kind of family."

Amber stands and hugs Jia hard, and Jia wraps her arms around Amber's waist and lifts her up. Paige can't imagine what it's like to have a friend like this—someone who has a shared history, who knows what you're thinking before you say it, who would do anything to take care of you. She'd settle for a good acquaintance at this point—anyone with whom she could talk to about the insanity that is her life.

Finally, Jia and Amber separate, but they are still holding hands, even as they take their seats on the stools. Paige feels a tug in her chest, or maybe that feeling in her chest is something else—something hard, a sliver of wood, impaled into her body like a nail hammered into a tree and left there until it slowly kills her—

"So, what's your story, Vorhees?" Jia asks.

"What?" Paige asks, and then she remembers she gave them a fake last name. "Oh. Well, I don't really have a story like that to share . . . "

Jia pulls Paige up to standing, and then she takes her stool. Their faces are watching her, expectant. Paige needs to say something.

"It's just that . . . My mom . . . We are always traveling . . . "

Paige's face is hot and sweating. She wonders if she should take off her sweatshirt. She doesn't want to embarrass herself in front of Jia and Amber, but she also can't seem to find the words to express anything she's feeling.

"Why don't you start at the beginning?" Jia suggests. Now she pulls her own stool out a little and motions for Paige to sit down, so that they can form a tight triangle. "And don't leave anything out. We want to help you, Paige—the way we wish someone had helped us."

"Okay . . . I'll try."

Paige runs through the events of the day, starting with her sleep-deprived arrival in Wintroster. She tells them about Toy Palace, and the familiar portrait on the wall. She almost tells them about the shard, too, but then she closes her lips and busies herself with playing with the discarded sleeve of Jia's straw.

"This is a real mystery," Amber announces.

"We *have* to investigate," Jia agrees.

"What do you mean?" Paige looks back and forth between them. "Like, some kind of secret operation or something?"

"That's our specialty." Jia waves her arm with a wild wave. "Remember the principal and the incriminating evidence? And, by the way, what do you think we're doing here?"

"Here . . . ?"

"In this pool hall, silly."

Paige follows her hand, and then, finding no answers, says ". . . Playing pool?"

Jia and Amber giggle.

"She's so sweet, isn't she?" Amber asks Jia.

Jia nods and laughs harder, until she is almost falling off the stool.

"What, then?" Paige's lips press together hard.

Jia bends down to the backpack with the missing strap and unzips it. There, in a pile, are wallets and phones too plentiful to be anything but stolen. "Just one or two from them," Jia says, her eyes drifting to the pool players. "Most we lifted earlier today."

"It's how we get by, remember?" Amber says without a hint of remorse.

"But the phones aren't why we're here." Jia leans in and whispers, "We think this pool hall is a front for something darker—specifically, the gang the police are looking for and offering a reward for any evidence of their whereabouts."

"The gang," Amber agrees enthusiastically, her voice too loud, and then hushes as Jia puts her hand over Amber's glossed lips. She continues in a whisper, "And lucky for Wintroster, we have a unique set of skills to find them."

"And lucky for you, too," Jia says, "because we can help you get to the bottom of this secret. We promised we would take care of you as one of our own, and we meant that—oh, and now that I'm thinking about it, I think we could go out the fire escape." Jia taps her chin thoughtfully with one chipped black fingernail, and her eyes drift past Paige, as though she is mapping things out in her head.

"Here?" Paige asks, confused.

"No, silly." Amber leans close, and Paige feels herself blush. She can see the red lines of lipstick in the grooves of Amber's thick lips. "Toy Palace."

"I don't know . . . "

But like two birds set loose from their cages, Jia and Amber have already lifted off from the perch of uncertainty and flown straight into the winds of action. They flutter around

Paige, throwing out suggestions, with words like *latch* and *key* and *let's go tonight*. That last one pulls Paige straight out of the hurricane of their beating wings, and she asks, incredulously, how they could possibly break into Toy Palace and get to the bottom of her family secrets before morning.

"No time like the present," Jia says, and her thin-lipped grin stretches wide at the thought of it.

"But—"

"Come on, sweet Paige," Amber says, her voice a low whisper in her ear. Her arm slides over Paige's shoulder, drawing her closer. Her lips are a kiss on Paige's cool cheek. "Let us take care of you."

"Let us slip off your leash and set you free," Jia agrees, sliding her arm over Paige's other shoulder and intertwining it with Amber's. "It's the least we can do."

"I . . . "

Jia and Amber do not wait for her to answer, but take up the backpacks and push in the stools with a long squeak on linoleum. They head for the door, an orderly line of stomping boots, and Paige wonders if they would even notice if she left. She slides a finger over the wooden shard, which seems, now, to be larger, and tells herself *I'll just go home and forget all about Toy Palace.*

But she doesn't.

Instead, a moment later, she has joined Amber and Jia in their purposeful walk toward those bright red columns and their deceptive golden ties.

***

THE FIRE ESCAPE IS AT THE back of the building. They reach it through an alley, which makes Paige think about how just a few hours earlier, she had pressed her hoodie against just such an uneven surface and met the two girls currently winding their way around dumpsters. Amber whistles a low tune under her breath, which Paige doesn't recognize. Every few steps, the wallets and phones in Jia's backpack clatter.

"What song is that?" Paige asks, trying to distract herself from the little voice in her head telling her to turn around.

"You really are the sweetest little thing." Amber stops and puts her hands on Paige's cheek. "Stick with us, and we'll get you all educated."

"Yup," Jia agrees. "You'll be a whole new Paige."

The alley is dark, so Jia takes out her phone—or maybe it's someone else's—and shines her flashlight ahead. After a few identical fire escapes, there is the familiar Toy Palace sign painted on the wall. Jia hands over her phone to Amber, and then she tells Paige to turn around and give her a little boost. Paige lifts Jia up like a child for a piggyback ride, and then she feels Jia's right leg on her shoulder and hands gripping hard against her scalp. There is the left leg on her other shoulder, and then the miraculous balance of no hands as Jia's feet latch under Paige's arms and around to her back.

"My little acrobat," Amber says with a mock swoon.

Now Jia strains her legs, and Paige fights the urge to look up, where she hears hands slapping on metal. Jia seems to grab hold of something, for her weight lessens as she pulls herself up onto the escape, but then more weight as Jia pushes up on the fire escape ladder to release the hook. Even more weight, still, as the ladder comes loose and threatens to push them both down into the ground, and then Jia lets go, allowing the ladder to slam down the track to the ground. *Smack.*

"Think someone heard that?" Paige whispers.

"Let's not find out," Amber says as she circles the ladder and begins to climb.

Jia follows her, and then Paige last, once the other two have reached the second story. The rungs are freezing cold and small, so that they bite into Paige's palms. She tries not to look down, but then she does. The ground looks further away than she expected, helped by the swallow of darkness there.

"Eyes ahead," Amber advises from the landing.

"Right," Paige says, wrenching her eyes away.

A few more rungs, and then she is at the landing, where she throws herself over the side and lays her back flat against the uncomfortable lines of the platform. Upside-down, she watches Jia slide a credit card from one of the wallets between the door and the frame, then tilts the card in the direction of the frame and swipes down. Next, Jia removes a hammer from the backpack and hits the deadbolt lock hard until it comes loose from the door, then uses a screwdriver to pry the deadbolt out.

The door opens.

Amber whistles in appreciation.

The little voice inside of Paige has begun speaking louder. *What if you get caught? What if your mom finds out? What if you have to leave again, just as soon as you've made some—*

No.

Don't say it.

She knows that whenever she feels this gripping inside of her, this pull *toward* something, she also feels the panic of the impending loss. But not speaking the words doesn't make them any less true. They might not quite be friends, but they are something to lose.

"Come on," Jia instructs from inside the door. Amber is gone, too. "We've got work to do."

CHAPTER EIGHT
PETTA

ROSA MOVES SURPRISINGLY QUICKLY FOR A woman who barely leaves her house, and Petta has to struggle to keep up with the short and rapid stride of her grandmother. They pass the sandwich shop, the toy shop, the candy shop, and now they are at the edge of the downtown strip, then crossing over into the streets where Petta is not permitted to walk alone.

"Where are we going?" she asks Rosa, but Rosa hums to herself, a strange song that Petta can't quite make out. She hears *naso* and *sorpreso* and *menzogna*, but how noses and surprises and lies tie together, Petta does not know. She wonders if she should call her mother, but decides that she'll see where they're going first, in case it's a clue to Rosa's apparent madness.

The street is residential, and then empty blocks between modest homes, and then strips of trees and uncleared brush. Then, at the end of the walk, a gate, behind which many storage units sit in rows like gray Lego blocks, newly painted but still showing their wear in the cracked cement of the drive.

"Here?" she asks Rosa.

Rosa taps on the buzzer. A voice cracks over the intercom, "Name and unit number?" and Rosa scoffs and waves wildly toward the camera set above the gray box.

"I changed your grandmother's diapers, Valentino. I'd hope you know me, still."

"It's protocol, Rosa," Valentino teases. Now Petta remembers him—he has been at some of their holiday parties, a bearded man with a hearty laugh that always fills the room. *A perpetual bachelor,* her father says; *a womanizer,* says her mother. "Come on in. It's been a while."

There is a high-pitched beep, and then the door by the side of the gate clicks unlocked. Petta holds the door for Rosa, who, now that they have finally arrived, seems to have tired almost instantly. She holds Petta's arm, and Petta wonders if they'll need to take a cab home, or call her mother. She checks her watch—half an hour until her shift starts.

"This is more important," Rosa says.

Rosa seems familiar with the lines of storage units, and she shuffles left, right, left again. Her breath is a steady pant. Her eyes are wild. She ends at #34, then slips a finger under her collar and pulls out a metal chain. Her chest heaves under the blouse, and Petta worries she'll faint, or worse.

"Take it," Rosa says. "It's yours, now."

Petta unhooks the necklace and uses the plain silver key to unlock the door of the storage unit. Then, before she does anything else, she places the key securely around her own neck. Maybe this is some strange hallucination, but clearly, what's behind the door actually belongs to Rosa, and Petta will be blamed if it's lost.

"*This is the lie,*" Rosa says, her voice a strange and unfamiliar monotone.

Petta lifts the door.

CHAPTER NINE

PAIGE

JIA HAS FOUND A LIGHT, AND inside the door is a bright, polished hallway with wood panels on the sides and hardwood flooring below. She unlocks the door on the right, and here is an office, with a royal blue velvet couch and an enormous banker's desk and chair. Behind the seat is a painting, not of the younger Camilla Vitaly, but of an older woman with a brown bob and a sharp chin beneath smooth cheeks. She wears a trim wool suit in a dark blue color, with the tied white bow of her shirt pulled tight at her neck and two big diamonds in her ears.

"That woman is Botox on a stick," says Amber. She pouts her lips to make them look larger. "I would be, too, if I had Vitaly money."

"You know the Vitalys?" Paige asks.

Jia snorts. She is behind the desk, unlocking it with an ease Paige has already learned to expect. "Everyone knows them. They're like the royal family of Wintroster, you know?"

"But I thought you aren't from here?" Paige asks.

Neither of the girls answer, and soon papers are flying like the leaves Paige had seen that morning—not drifting, but thrusting themselves wildly into the wind. Paige tells herself she should help, but then she moves to the small table beside the couch and picks up a vintage gold-framed photograph. The man there is dapper, with a fitted black suit and a whiskey glass balanced on his knee, and his sharp chin and long nose look so familiar. *My grandfather,* Paige thinks, putting the photograph back. *The legend.*

When Paige looks up, Jia and Amber are opening drawers and removing wooden boxes, inside of which are all kinds of keepsakes. Letters. Notebooks. Bracelets. Bobby pins.

"Won't we have to put this all back?" Paige asks the stacks of objects. They do not answer, and neither do the girls.

Amber slips a gold chain around her wrist and asks Jia to secure it; Jia does the clasp and then kisses the place inside Amber's wrist lightly.

"I'm not sure we should . . ."

"We're just having fun," Jia says. "We'll put it all back when we're done, we promise."

"Okay, but—"

"Hey, look at this." Jia rips a page from the back of a leather planner. Amber pulls the paper closer and squints, and Paige wonders if she should be wearing glasses.

"You found it!" Amber squeals.

"What?" Paige comes closer, trying to get a look at the writing on the lined notebook page.

Without answering, Jia and Amber turn to the portrait. At first, Paige worries they might destroy it—with the screwdriver, maybe or the silver letter opener Jia has lifted from the desk. Instead, they swing the frame away, revealing a safe so large the expanse of the picture must have barely covered it. There are two locks there: one a keypad with letters, and the other a traditional dial with numbers too small for Paige to read.

"Are we still looking for—"

Amber turns suddenly and gives Paige one of her charming smiles. The dim lighting glows off her alluring lips. "The evidence you need will be here, in this safe. But we're going to need the password, Paigey. Any ideas?"

"I don't know . . ."

"Just think on it," Amber says. Now Jia is staring at Paige, too. "But think hard."

Paige doesn't even know Camilla—how could she possibly guess her password? And the shard in her chest is pressing into the middle of her ribs, like the worst acid reflux in the world—or maybe that is just her imagination. "Do you know how many letters?"

"Five," Jia says impatiently. Then she turns back to the safe and puts her hands on the keypad there. "So, what do you think?"

Paige's mind is blank. She doesn't know this woman, not at all. Five letters. One word. Not Camilla, nor Vitaly, and certainly not—wait.

"Try Petta!"

Jia types the letters, and then the keypad's light turns green. Then the girls consult the page in Jia's hand and begin to turn the dial, until with the final number, the safe clicks open with a satisfied beep.

Oh, the stacks of green.

"Do you think she could be part of the gang?" Paige asks. Of all the secrets she expected to find, a crime boss aunt was not one of them.

"Gang?" Jia asks. "What gang?"

Amber squeals and draws the top stack out so that she can fan herself with it. Jia removes another stack and thumbs through it, as though she could count, so quickly, the hundreds or maybe thousands of dollars there. *They don't care about my family history at all,* Paige realizes, the shard in her chest burning, *and I don't think they care about me, either.* On cue, there are the backpacks, which the girls dump out, leaving a pile of discarded wallets, phones, clothes, and toiletries, like garbage from the deluge of a broken bag. The money disappears, then reappears as a sea of green and white inside the seam of the zipper.

"What about the truth?" Paige asks weakly over the yips and shrieks. "What about my family?"

Amber and Jia put on their backpacks. "Sorry, sweetie," Amber says as the weight settles onto her back. "This isn't personal—it's karma. Camilla Vitaly is the devil herself, incarnate and brought to Wintroster to ruin the lives of every poor soul who asks for a little bit of help."

"I don't understand—"

"She's the one pulling all of the strings." Jia's voice is hard and furious. "If we had time to tell you about what growing up in this town was like . . . Well, you'll find out for yourself, soon enough."

"But I thought you said you weren't from here—"

"You can come, if you want." Amber's voice is hesitant, or maybe guilty. "We can teach you . . ."

But Paige can tell by the way Jia is glaring that they cannot, indeed, teach her. And she does not want to learn anyway, not if this kind of betrayal is the result. Paige shakes her head, and Jia nods and leaves the room without a backward glance.

"Sorry, Paige—" Amber starts, but Jia's voice interrupts sharply from the hall.

"Let's go," she says, "before we miss our ride."

Amber leaves, and now it is just Paige in the center of the chaos, discarded documents and dropped bills like fallen snow beneath her feet. She walks around the desk and to the safe, where folders lie unopened and waiting in a neat stack. After lifting them so that she can read the tabs, she is surprised to find one with Petta in perfect blue cursive. When she opens the folder on Camilla's desk and sits down to read the contents, she finds a photograph of her mother from maybe ten years ago, along with a detective's report on his findings.

I found her, and I can assure you, Camilla, that Petta Vitaly is of no threat to the business of Toy Palace. She moves around the country in some kind of caravan, carving and painting wooden toys that she sells for much less than they're worth. I can see why you don't want her involved—she's a terrible businesswoman. Her current location seems to be one she likes—or, perhaps, her stationing herself here has to do with the man she is seeing.

The only other interesting thing of note is that she has a child with her—this was not expected. The child appears to be somewhere between five and seven years old. She looks like Petta, and seems to be Petta's daughter. I have enclosed a photograph, which I secured with great difficulty. I believe that Petta spotted me, for she went back in the caravan and began to shout to the girl about "Nonno" and leaving and some other things that I could not hear. Soon after that, they left.

I await your next instructions.

Impossible.

Paige reads the note, and then reads it again.

Nonno.

Leaving.

It's all this staying in one place.

Gone.

Paige's vision spins. She cannot understand what she is reading, cannot comprehend how the pages in front of her can be anything but a cruel joke. She slips the page off the desk and allows it to drift to the floor, then reads the next note:

I have tried to determine the father of Paige Vitaly, but to no avail. I await your next instructions.

Only when Paige reads these lines does she realize that this is what she has come here to discover. She doesn't care about Toy Palace, or the fearsome woman in the painting, or even the man in the photograph, who teases the viewer with cocky assurance. These are lines of her life that Petta has cut like a web from a dusted corner, and Paige cannot retie them, not even if she wanted to.

But him? The man who made her?

That is a question she wants to answer.

As though something inside her has settled into place, Paige suddenly becomes aware of herself. The sound of a siren in the distance. The cold chill in her hands from the open door. Her chest, which has begun to ache.

Her fingers graze the surface, finding its borders already at her armpits.

You need to run, Paige.

She bolts for the door, then stops at the hallway. To the left, the fire escape. To the right, a dark hall . . . No, not dark, for there is a strange glow there, a blue light, like a TV screen that someone left on. Paige knows that she should go back the way she came, slide down the ladder, but that light is like a hand pulling her hoodie in the direction of its making. Now she can hear music, low, a hum, vibrating through the door. How had she not noticed it?

"Hello?" Paige whispers.

"*There are two kinds of lies, you won't be surprised, short legs and long noses—*"

Paige takes two steps. "Who's in there?"

"*—but no one supposes that there is another much worse than the others—*"

Paige tries the handle and finds it unlocked. The door swings open, revealing a mostly empty room, but there, at the door's full opening, is a chair and its occupant. He appears to be a young man, though his head is hung low to his chest. He has tangled strands of pale blue hair, like tinsel has been threaded through the locks. He wears no shirt, so that the flat plane of his chest glistens over the ridges of his bones, and short pants that show his ankles. Someone has bound him with a heavy chain, which is tied around his waist. When Paige squints, she can see the end secured to the wall behind him.

"*—and this is the lie—*"

The young man lifts his head. His face is angular, just a chin and a sharp nose, but with bright blue eyes above the deep grooves of his sleepless shadows. His expression is blank, like the hollow flatness of a doll painted by a less skilled hand. He has no pupils, so Paige cannot tell if he is looking at her or through her.

"*—of a toymaker.*"

Paige considers shutting the door and fleeing. Perhaps he has not noticed her. Perhaps she might still escape this terrible place.

"Hello, Paige," the young man says.

She is suddenly aware of the chill from the back door. "You know me?"

The young man stretches out a hand. On his moving, the glow coming from his body pulses and then settles again into the same dull light.

"I know all of you."

Paige takes a deep breath and steps into the room, allowing the door to close behind her. The temperature increases immediately, so that she finds her forehead sweaty to the touch.

"Who are you?"

The young man shakes his head. "First you must swallow your medicine."

"My . . . ?"

The young man moves quickly. One moment he sits in his chair, the next he has risen and taken Paige's arm. His touch burns. His grip is tight, too tight, but she cannot wrench her arm free. "Paige," he says again, though she cannot tell if he is trying to ask her something or tell her. "*This is the lie. This is the lie. This is the lie—*"

The room explodes in a furious blue light.

CHAPTER TEN

PETTA

THE STORAGE UNIT IS A HOLDING space for a vehicle. Petta tries to take in the wide face of it, but she can only take it in parts: the dusty wheels, the dented bumper, the flat glass windows where little wooden butterflies hang from twine strung on the rearview mirror. She feels that the object in front of her is important, and very, very old.

"What is it?" she asks, touching the flat wood front of the vehicle's face.

"Our caravan."

Rosa leads around the side, where in red letters missing most of their paint, the words Rosa's Traveling Toys announce that her grandmother really is the vehicle's owner. Then she squeezes in the back, where a small porch attached to the caravan houses a wooden chair and a dusty red bottle of wine half-drunk and certainly turned to vinegar by now. Rosa steps onto the porch and unlocks the door with the same key she used to get into the storage unit, and there are the beds, the workbench, the window. Petta inhales the familiar fumes, then approaches the artist's station, where someone with a true talent for woodwork has been crafting an ark.

"You like it?" Rosa asks.

"It's beautiful." Rosa lifts the boat, feels its heft, and then returns it to the bench. Next, she takes up each of the animals, painted in delicate light blue hues. A gift for a baby boy, most likely. "Grandpa Arnaldo made these?"

Rosa smiles proudly.

"Really?" Petta shakes her head. "I didn't know—"

"These are the lost arts of the Vitaly family," Rosa says, indicating the rows of old toys lined on the shelves next to the window. "Your grandfather had talent, but he was all ideas—no actual craftsmanship. I was the one who brought his creations to life."

Petta has never seen such careful work. The painting is particularly meticulous, and Petta understands, now, why her grandmother always tells her to watch her lines. She has been learning from the best, albeit unknowingly. Why didn't Rosa ever tell her?

"Your father had different visions for the shop," Rosa says. Her eyes tear, and she sits down hard on the stool by the bench. "With him, our family's destiny was diverted, but hopefully not ended. That is why you're here, Petta: so you can take up what he abandoned."

Petta does not understand. Rosa knows as well as she does that Petta will never run the company, or even be allowed to make the toys they sell there. She might not even be allowed in the top-secret Maker's Room, from which the toys seem to magically appear each day.

"I'd love to learn," she admits. "But we'd need to keep it a secret."

"Oh, child." Rosa reaches a hand up to touch Petta's cheek. "I won't be here to teach you."

"What?"

"You don't need me, Petta—toymaking is in your blood."

"But—"

"One more thing." Rosa steps carefully across the room and sits on the bed, then pats the blanket for Petta to join her. The mattress squeals from their weight, and Petta hopes the bunks are as well-made as the ark. "There is a room on the top floor of Toy Palace—the one that is always locked."

"The antiques," Petta says, nodding. "Dad's afraid someone will steal them."

"I'm sure he is." Rosa takes Petta's hand, and her palm is wrinkled and dry. Then she squeezes Petta's hand firmly in her hawk grip, and Petta's fingers ache. "And they're going to . . . because that somebody is you."

CHAPTER ELEVEN

PAIGE

"WAKE UP, PAIGE."

Paige opens her eyes. Above her, a fresco is painted to give the impression that she is staring into a forest of golden leaves, and at the edges of her vision the tall headposts and footposts of the four-poster oak bed on which she must now lie. She turns her neck to find a high window, through which she sees not the grand forest of the fresco, but the dead limbs of many trees, shaped like actual arms and legs tangled together to form a wall of brambles. In the other direction, a pile of deep blue pillows blocks her sight.

"You're awake."

Paige sits up quickly, and the room spins. She puts her head in her hands, takes a deep breath, and tries again. Now she can take in the young man standing before her, this time not naked but adorned in a grand blue velvet jacket with gold piping and a matching golden crown. His hair, tied back in a low ponytail, is gold too, and his eyes are blue with gold flecks.

"Someone changed your settings," Paige says, closing her eyes again.

"Changed them back, you mean." She cannot see him, but his footsteps draw closer. "It was your touch that brought us here again."

"Again?"

"But we are not here—not really. We are inside my mind. Now we must hurry, for we only have a few minutes, Paige." The young man takes her arm and guides her out of bed. "The chain they have around my waist tethers me to their realm so that I cannot leave—and drains me so the stone they use to travel can stay powered. How mad it is, to move between realms with the power of the Flare, when it was the Flare itself that kept me from ever trying to leave my realm before. I was content. I wanted nothing. And now, though I might travel realms, because it amplifies my own internal strength, mine flickers weakly."

"What are you talking about?" Her legs shake from her weight, and she leans on the man harder than she'd like. Only now does she realize that she, too, has changed her clothes, so that instead of her hoodie and jeans, she finds a loose blue gown with gold stitching in the shapes of many interlacing dolls.

"I must admit, I dressed you like a Flarewhisper from this land . . . ," the young man says, raising his hands innocently. When he lets go, she almost collapses again, and he has to take her by the elbow and pull her back up again. "When you come across, you'll look quite different . . ."

He leads her to the window, and they look out on dense, disturbing brambles together. "I have not seen this place in many years. Look what has happened to it . . ."

A golden droplet wells in the man's eye and runs down the side of his nose. When it falls from his lip, the liquid splashes on the windowsill, leaving flecks of gold behind.

"Don't cry," Paige says. "We'll figure it out."

The young man draws a golden kerchief from his pocket and dabs at his eyes. "You've always been so caring, Paige. It's almost—"

The young man's head snaps up, and then he tilts it, as though he is listening.

"What is it?" Paige asks.

The young man turns and puts his hands on her shoulders. "I'd hoped we would have more time. There is not much I can do for you, little one, except to set you on the path to which you must now dedicate yourself. For when you reach the end—" He listens, and then his face suddenly slackens. "*This is the lie, this is the lie, this is the lie, this is the lie*—"

"But who are you?" Paige cries, loosening herself from his grip. "And what path are you talking about? What is going on—?"

She feels wrenched from herself, as though someone has put her through the spin cycle of a washing machine. Everything is a blur, all light flashes and frightening shadows consuming them. The young man's hum haunts her—*This is the lie, this is the lie, this is the lie*—and she cannot tell if the echo is in her ears or in her head.

***

A YOUNG MAN WITH HIS HEAD hung low.

The chill of a cold night's air.

Sirens.

***

THEY ARE BACK IN THE DARK room.

"Run," the young man says blankly. "Or you will never discover the truth."

She opens her mouth to argue, but then she hears footsteps on the stairs. Back through the door she runs, down the hallway that once seemed so long but now takes only a few quick strides, and over the platform of the fire escape, where she slides down the ladder and takes the last few rungs in a leap. The alley is dark without Jia and Amber's flashlights, and Paige stumbles as she runs over the uneven road.

Wait.

There, up ahead, are two beams dancing on the walls.

At first Paige thinks the lights belong to Jia and Amber, and she feels a sudden thrill at the idea that maybe they did wait for her after all. But on closer inspection, she realizes that the lights are the high beams of a van, into which several adults holding instruments are piling. They all wear straw hats, button-up flannel shirts, and cropped jeans that end a few inches above their lace-up leather boots.

"Let's go," a woman's stern voice instructs from the front of the van. Paige cannot see her, cannot see anything in the burn of the beams' brightness. "We need to get on the road pronto if we're going to make it home by midnight."

The musicians grumble, but soon they are all in the van. Paige reaches the side door just in time to stop it from closing, and a middle-aged woman holding a violin gasps in surprise at the sudden stranger in front of her face.

"Take me with you," Paige asks through desperate breaths. She holds up the bills she took from the safe. "You can have all this. Just get me out of here, okay?"

The woman leans backward, and a voice from the front of the van utters something almost undetectable. The woman nods, and then she says, over the growing sound of the sirens, "All right, kid. Get in."

The van door closes, and Paige catches only a quick glimpse of the red and blue lights playing on the alley walls.

Then there is just a blank white door, and around her, the warmth of strangers, all silent as they listen to the rise and fall of sirens.

CHAPTER TWELVE

PETTA

THE PARTY IS IN FULL SWING when Petta slips from the house into the dark streets. Behind her, through the wide window, she can see her mother perched on the arm of the couch talking with Lorenzo. Camilla is at the dining table, her back a rigid stem beneath the perfect petals of her blue suit, probably telling the neighbors on the other side about the day's sales numbers. Petta's friends from her studio huddle by the doorway, demonstrating some kind of technique with wild hand gestures—or maybe they are debating the merits of a certain artist. All Petta knows is that they all look engaged in their conversations, and happy, and completely unaware that the entire world is falling apart around them.

And then there is Rosa. Her grandmother sits at the window, in a rocking chair she gave Petta's parents when she downsized, staring right at Petta across the lawn. Petta nods; Rosa raises her glass of wine in a farewell. She has told Petta she will not be here the following morning, should she decide to return with her mission incomplete—and strangely, Petta believes her. She lingers on the view of Rosa's strong jaw, the determined press of her lips, the firm grip of her hand on the glass, and then blows Rosa a kiss. Rosa's face cracks like ice under a pick, and then, without a backward glance, Petta turns and disappears into the darkness.

Downtown Wintroster is mostly closed for the night, with the exception of the bar, which will not lock up until after 2:00 A.M. Petta passes on the other side of the walk, hoping no one there will see her—especially not the bartender, who's a good friend of her father's. When she meets the familiar columns of Toy Palace, she goes around the back and sneaks up the fire escape to enter through the second story door.

Petta has been on this floor a million times, but it seems different now, in the dim lighting of the EXIT sign and her father's flashlight, swiped from the kitchen drawer on her way out of the house. Ghostly. She passes her father's office and imagines him there, eyes set on the pages in front of him, muttering numbers and grinning now and again at all that he has made. Here is the door Rosa mentioned, locked, as she'd told Petta, by three deadbolts—but now, strangely, absent of any locks but a standard door handle.

That's impossible, Petta thinks.

She enters the room and stops cold. He's here, just like Rosa promised, the same blue hair and pale hue and that eerie glow around him.

"You've come," the fairy says softly.

"How did you move the locks?" she asks, though what she wants to say is, *I'm so sorry for all of this.*

"I didn't. I moved us."

Petta blinks in confusion. Surely this is the same room, with the same empty walls and same metal chair and same perfume Calvino insists is one of his store's greatest secrets wafting from below.

"That makes no sense," Petta says.

"Indeed." The fairy smiles thinly. "I don't understand it myself. My enemies forced me to come to this dimension—but I could also send myself back, if I could gather enough power. I have done it before." He shakes at his bonds, which clank behind him. "But I am too weak, Petta."

She has not told him her name, and she feels uneasy in his knowing.

"But you could have at least opened the door before," she says. "I've been here every day for all these years . . ." She stops talking and looks harder into his eyes. "Wait. You did not want to go back, did you?"

"So many dead . . ." The fairy's eyes go dull, and his body's glow dims. "I would not face them."

"And now?"

The fairy looks past her, at the dust in the air, or maybe something he sees there, floating. "She's told me I must."

"Who?"

"She says that it's now or in the next life—but eighteen years is so long to wait, sweet Petta, and I'm oh so very tired."

"I don't understand what you're trying to tell me."

The fairy shakes his head. He will not say more—maybe he can't say more—and it doesn't matter, anyway. Petta is going to free him—but she cannot do it tonight.

"I'll be back," she promises. "I need some tools. Maybe some help, too."

"Oh, yes," he says mildly. His eyes are still on some spot on the wall. "You said that before."

"No, I didn't."

The fairy's eyes close, or maybe lose consciousness completely. If he is still aware of Petta's presence, he doesn't show it.

"This is the lie," he mutters.

***

PETTA WALKS HOME SLOWLY. SHE DOES not want to see what waits there—not yet. She investigates the way the moon shines through the branches of the oaks. She inspects the perfect blades of grass in Mrs. Willis's newly planted lawn. She watches the cats sleeping on the hoods of cars, or under them, with just their eyes glowing.

Still, her feet carry her forward.

She meets the ambulance parked outside the door, flashing its lights in a silent song of a funeral.

"Where have you been?" Camilla asks, her voice a furious chastisement. How dare Petta not be accounted for? "Rosa's dead, you know. You missed it."

"Camilla!" Gianna says. She's been crying, and now she rubs at the red splotches around her eyes, worsening them. "Don't argue—not tonight."

"It's not my fault little miss air-for-brains went on a stroll. By the way, she was an hour late today—"

"Call your father, please." Gianna's voice is sad but firm. "Tell him he needs to come home."

"He won't leave until after his meeting tomorrow." Camilla is on her phone now, checking the calendar. "I'll ask his assistant to book him on a 5:00 P.M. from—"

"Tell him to come home. Now."

"Fine," Camilla huffs. "But this'll put it back three months, you know. Grandma Rosa would have wanted us to—"

Gianna waves Camilla away. Camilla is still ranting about their numbers as she goes into the house, probably to complain to their father without their mother there to chastise them, while Petta and Gianna sit on the front step and watch the emergency personnel strap Rosa onto the bed there.

They already administered CPR and AED. She isn't going to wake up.

"Where were you, really?" her mother asks. She presses her forehead to Petta's. "You can tell me, *piccola.*"

"I was thinking," Petta says. The doors of the ambulance slam, and then the lights are flashing, and the siren is wailing its funeral dirge. "About something Grandma Rosa said to me earlier, in her apartment."

"I'm glad you got to spend this day with her," Gianna says. She doesn't ask what Rosa said to Petta—doesn't even seem to care. Her mind is somewhere else, on someone else. "But tomorrow you're on time to your shift, okay?"

"Okay," Petta agrees, though she wants to say, *How can you worry about work right now?* If she had a daughter, she would never force her to do anything—and she knows, suddenly, that this is also part of what she wants. To create life, in many forms. To live.

Petta goes inside and passes Camilla, who is still talking loudly with their father about some meeting he's trying to pull together before he flies out. Petta feels sick to her stomach, or maybe she's hungry, and she lies down on her bed without changing her clothes or getting under the covers. On the shelf directly in front of her, a set of Russian dolls painted in a familiar hand line up like mourners waiting to shake hands with the grieving family.

"Five days," the littlest doll says, and Petta swears she really opens her mouth and speaks. Is she hallucinating? Is she dreaming? "Then set him free and leave."

"How can I hear you?" Petta asks, or maybe she just thinks it.

"I hope he'll make her strong, your daughter . . ." The doll's O mouth turns down. "But I'm not sure it will be enough."

"My daughter? What are you talking about?"

For a second, the dolls all glimmer a strange white iridescence. Then, they are wood again, lifeless and cold. Petta startles, and she finds that she is now opening her eyes, though she cannot remember closing them. It is morning, and the countdown has begun.

CHAPTER THIRTEEN

LILY

POCKET SEVEN IS A CACOPHONY OF noise as Lily rushes through the heavy door and allows it to slam the cold out behind her. The green tables are packed with locals in their team's signature green and gold, and Lily wonders if maybe there was a game that night—or whatever else happens in football. Celebrants raise glasses and slosh beer over the already-damp wooden tables, while others pass plates of fries responsible for the salty-sweet taste of the hot bar air. One woman with sweat dripping down her curly brown hair—or maybe it's slopped beer—cries, "No one can, no one can—," and the group erupts in a cheer: "—throw the ball like our quarterback can!" The woman collapses back into the mess of upraised glasses and shoulders jockeying for space around the tight circles of the tables, and soon she is just another identical head under a green-and-gold cap.

Lily's best friend Rashi has saved her a seat at the bar, and she waves her hand to usher Lily across the crowd. As Lily squeezes between two men arguing about some other man she's never heard of—probably a football player—the bartender, Jess, is practically sprinting parallel to her in the narrow lane on the other side.

"We're slammed," she calls across to Lily. "And Elza called out sick."

"I've already done a double shift," Lily calls over the noise, "or I'd come back there with you."

"Such a sweetheart." Jess gives her a wink, and Lily blushes and slips her gaze back across the room, to Rashi.

A few more steps, and there is the chair, already pulled back, with Rashi's knitted tote slung across the back to announce that it's taken.

"I thought you'd gotten lost," Rashi teases.

She is wearing a crown of woven flowers, and Lily reaches for the petals to find they are soft and give at her touch. Rashi's long, wavy brown hair is loose and flowing down her back, and her gossamer white blouse makes her look even more ephemeral than usual.

"The journey across the street from Toy Palace was an arduous one," Lily admits, feigning a swipe of her brow, "but I'd do anything for my best friend's birthday. You look beautiful, by the way."

"Thanks, *sweetheart*."

"Oh god." The warmth in her cheeks is back. "Don't even start on that."

"Can't a girl dream?" Rashi's face flattens into a serious line of the mouth and a drawing-in of the eyebrows. "I just want you to be happy."

"I am happy."

Lily peels off her purple blazer, remembering, too late, that she's still wearing her Toy Palace t-shirt underneath. Rashi raises her eyebrows and then laughs, and Lily joins her, giving Rashi a *whoops* shrug of her shoulders.

"I guess we can't both be the fashionable one in this relationship," Lily says. She gives a strand of her hair a flick, so that it soars gracefully over her shoulder to join her other curls.

"Hey," Lily defends, "I actually wear makeup now! Have you *seen* this golden eyeshadow?"

"Of course I have," Rashi takes Lily's chin and angles it up, toward the light. "I bought it for you, remember? I told you that one day *we'd need to start buying our shine.*" She releases Lily's chin. "That's a pretty good line, by the way—they should put that on a billboard or something."

"Oh, yes." Lily rolls her eyes. "What a positive message for girls of the world, everywhere."

They slip into their old routines for a while, updating each other on high school friends who have broken up, or dropped out of college, or left their parents' businesses to work at the gas station down the road. Rashi knows more than Lily, having stayed in touch with all the local state school people, but Lily offers the best gossip: Myers Landon, the "it" girl of their junior year—Lily's last year, since she graduated early—is pregnant.

"Shut. Up." Rashi takes Lily's hand and squeezes it hard. "How do you know?"

Lily gives a smug smile and sits back, so that she can cross her arms. "Her aunt came into Toy Palace today to buy one of those little blankets—the sheep ones. Said it's for her great niece—and Myers is the only option. She told me not to tell anyone—but you don't count, of course."

"Of course!"

Rashi has ordered them their favorites: spinach dip, French fries, and hummus with pita triangles still warm on Lily's fingertips. She's starving—double shifts always have that effect on her, and she scarfs down half of each plate in the few minutes it takes Rashi to eat a few fries.

"Make sure to breathe," Rashi tells her over the top of her wine glass.

"I—"

Lily's backpack vibrates from the chair behind her, and she takes out her phone and checks the caller ID: Camilla Vitaly.

"Whoa," she says, realizing, too late, that she sounds like a breathless groupie. She corrects her tone and says, with a business-like flatness, "It's Camilla. I'm just going to go outside for a minute—"

"Absolutely not!" Rashi grabs the phone out of Lily's hands and puts it on the bar beside her, past the plates and the napkin spotted with fallen wine droplets.

"What if it's an emergency?"

"You're off the clock," Rashi says. "And besides, it's my birthday, remember?"

"I'd hope so," Lily says, forcing the teasing tone she knows Rashi wants. "Otherwise, that crown you're wearing would look even stranger than it already does." Her eyes go to the phone again, and then back to Rashi's narrowing eyes.

"It's a headband!" Rashi says. "It reminded me of the one I wore for my senior prom, back when I thought maybe I was a word-I-can't-say, too." She tries to wink but ends up blinking both of her eyes by accident. They both laugh, and for a second, Lily actually does forget about the call.

"Speaking of young . . ." Lily says loudly over the din of the bar. Then she is interrupted by a patron demanding a drink, who leans too far over her shoulder to send over a credit card or withdraw a beer glass sweating in the warming air of the room. Finally, as he leans away, she finishes, ". . . I got you something."

"You didn't have to do that." Rashi smiles widely. "What is it?"

Lily rifles through her backpack and draws out a small red jewelry box with gold string. "Happy birthday, my dearest—and oldest—friend!"

Rashi eyes the red paper doubtfully. ". . . It's not a toy, is it? These colors look suspiciously familiar . . ."

"Can't a girl like red and gold?"

"Any other girl? Yes." Rashi shakes the box at her ear. "You? No."

Lily imagines she hears the rustle of metal on paper, though all Lily can hear is glasses clinking and people talking in a deafening murmur.

"Ever since you moved back, that store has become your whole life." Rashi places the box on the bar.

"I know." Lily tries not to think of the phone lying face-down on the bar near Rashi. Is it ringing again? She tries to see if the napkin next to the phone is vibrating, or maybe the present in Rashi's hands, but the pool hall lighting is too dim to tell. "And now you're going to tell me I need to go to therapy, aren't you?"

"Oh, you definitely need to go to therapy." Rashi unties the string. "But I'm more concerned that you're a twenty-one year old ivy league graduate who still can't tell her parents she's—"

"Don't."

Rashi's fingers play at the piece of tape holding the paper closed. "I wasn't going to say it."

Lily knows, and yet her pulse has already quickened. Her palms are sweating on her lap. Her eyes dart down the bar, looking for anyone her parents know—luckily, it's a line of young people unconcerned with anyone else's business but their own.

"I'll tell them . . ." Lily says, ". . . when it's relevant."

"Oh, we can only dream."

Lily pushes Rashi far enough that she almost falls off her chair, and Rashi laughs, the sound as wild and unencumbered as when Lily first heard it across the room back in third grade, when Rashi's family moved to the United States. Rashi had been Lily's first crush—a fact she still teases Lily about.

Rashi reaches the edges of the present's lid, which she removes with a hollow *thunk* on the bar. There is the titanium bracelet Lily ordered weeks ago, with a long chain of connected links and a circular pendant at the clasp with both of their names on either side.

"It's beautiful," Rashi says softly. She puts out her thin wrist, and Lily secures the bracelet around it. Then she shows Rashi her matching one, which she'd put in her pocket until then so Rashi wouldn't see it.

"Titanium is supposed to be one of the strongest metals," Lily explains, shaking her own wrist so the circle swings like a pendulum. "This way, even when you're off at graduate school becoming the most empathetic psychologist the world has ever seen, you'll remember me—"

"How could I forget you?"

Rashi leans all the way over their chairs to hug Lily hard. She smells like her mother's hair salon, a mixture of the sweet mist sprays and chemical dyes she steeps in all day, and Lily takes a deep inhalation. She'll miss the smell—and her friend—more than Rashi can possibly know.

"Oh!" Lily leans back to watch Rashi's expression. "I met a girl today!"

"What!" Rashi shrieks, and her hands clap so loudly the bartender turns sharply in her direction. "Like, a *girl* girl?"

"Shh, keep your voice down!" Lily whispers. Then she adds, "Is there a different kind?"

"I mean . . ." Rashi leans in to whisper, ". . . a girl *crush*?"

There is a joyous flush to Rashi's cheeks, and Lily realizes, too late, that she has told this story entirely incorrectly. Rashi will already be planning their future wedding, complete with the lilac purple bridesmaid dresses they saw once in a shop window and a speech revisiting all of their embarrassing childhood memories.

"Lower your expectations," Lily says. "I just talked to her, that's all."

"About what?" Rashi takes Lily by the shoulders and shakes her. "What's her name? Did you get her number? Are you going out?"

"Well, I told her about the history of Toy Palace," Lily begins, and the shaking begins to slow. "And then I walked her around a bit, and then . . ." Lily trails off, and Rashi drops her arms and purses her lips ". . . she fainted."

"She *what*?!?"

"Or, she sort of fainted. And then she got all weird and ran away. But I think you're missing the point, which is that I met a girl in this terrible town, and she was pretty, and I want to find out more about her."

Rashi sighs so long and hard Lily thinks she might pass out, too. Then she folds her arms and says, "Fine, I'll help you find her. First, tell me what she looks like."

Lily describes the girl: white skin; wild blond hair; a sweatshirt with some kind of stain on it; really tired eyes.

"She sounds . . ." Rashi lifts her eyebrows. ". . . homeless."

"She wasn't homeless!" Lily pauses, thinking of the way the girl was clutching her food during her tour. "Actually, maybe she was homeless . . . But still, there was just something about her that made me feel like I wanted to get to know her more. Something quiet and mysterious, you know?" Her words quicken and trip over themselves. "And you know how I sometimes imagine that the toys around me are all whispering, but I can't hear what they're saying?" She does not stop to check Rashi's expression—she already knows her eyes will be wide with doubt, or maybe even deep concern for her friend's mental health. "Well, when she came into the store, they all went completely silent, as though . . ."

Finally, Lily tries to meet her friend's eyes, but Rashi looks concerned with something on the bar.

"Rashi, are you listening to me?"

"Oh my god, just answer this thing already!" Rashi picks up Lily's phone and chucks it at her, hard. Lily fumbles it and barely catches it before it hits the floor. "It's been ringing non-stop since I took it!"

Lily checks her missed calls: seventeen from Ms. Vitaly, followed by five from the Toy Palace landline. COME TO THE STORE NOW, the follow-up texts demand over and over again. THERE'S BEEN AN EMERGENCY.

"I'm so sorry, Rashi, but something's happened—"

Rashi sighs again, but then her eyes go to the bracelet, and she takes a deep breath. "You're lucky you came with jewelry, my friend. Now go, before I change my mind and find another best friend who's as desperately in love with me as you are."

"Oh, please." Lily rolls her eyes and smiles, but then she remembers the calls, and her mouth turns down. "Thanks. I'll make it up to you, I promise."

"I know you will."

Lily puts on her blazer and gives Rashi a twenty-dollar bill for their drinks, which Rashi suggestively tucks into the low cleavage of her shirt. As Lily leaves the bar, she looks back to see her best friend already talking to someone else, a guy who vaguely looks like an older kid they went to school with back in the day. *If only it were that easy*, Lily thinks.

Then she lets the door close behind her.

CHAPTER FOURTEEN
PAIGE

THE MUSICIANS SIT ON THE FLOOR of the van with their legs crossed and their gazes locked on their visitor. Paige wonders if they should be wearing seatbelts. Instrument cases are everywhere, and at each turn, the cases slide across the floor and bump into the legs of the band members who push them away, just to have them slide right back again at the next intersection. A folk song plays from the front, though the notes are muted by the wall between them.

"So," starts the violin player. She has put away her instrument and is watching Paige with curiosity. Without her hat, she looks younger—early thirties, maybe—or perhaps it's the way she is sitting, like she should have a child perched in her lap. Her makeup is dark, with heavy eyeliner and dark red lipstick. She plays with a silver chain around her neck, on which two stones, emerald and sapphire, dangle.

"So." Paige opens her mouth, but then closes it again. What could she possibly say about the night's events that any of these strangers would believe? She looks down at her jeans, which have ripped at some point.

"What's your name, Hun?" The violin player puts her hand softly on Paige's arm. "Mine's Jenna."

"That's a nice name," Paige says softly. "I'm Paige."

The other three introduce themselves: Seth, a man with a beard down to his belly, is on drums; Elle, a blond with a lace tank top beneath her flannel, is on banjo; and Marcus, a clean-cut man with a swooped haircut, is on guitar.

"Your band doesn't have a singer?" Paige asks.

Jenna tilts her head toward the front, where behind the wall, an unseen driver carries them away from Wintroster and toward their next performance. "Sasha. Our fearless leader."

"Don't tell her that," Marcus warns. "It'll go right to her head."

With their names out of the way, the band asks her questions about what happened, and she answers them as much as she can without sounding completely insane. She tells them about coming to Wintroster to sell wooden toys, and about Jia and Amber, who convinced her to break into Toy Palace. She also confesses that her mother is Petta, and that Camilla is her aunt, though she suspects the family connection is more of a curse than a blessing in Camilla's mind. Two of the band members, Jenna and Marcus, are both originally from Wintroster, and they tell her that they've heard the fight over the family business and Petta's secret escape.

"Town legend," Marcus emphasizes. He leans forward, green eyes theatrically wide, and adds, "I was in high school when the family feud went public. They say that Petta inherited her grandparents' talent, and that when they died, she inherited some kind of family heirloom, too."

"Now I'm remembering," Jenna says thoughtfully. She sits back against the van wall. "A necklace."

"Wait." Paige sits up straighter. "Was it a star?"

"I think so?" Jenna shrugs. "I know more about Camilla, since she's pretty much run the town since her father's death.

Kids around town like to say she's a witch or something—but I think she's just blessed."

"Does she have any other family members?" Paige asks.

Jenna shakes her head no. Then, she gives Paige a kind smile and prompts, "What about you? Is your dad from Wintroster, too?"

Paige's gaze drifts out the window, where the road is a bare landscape of tree shadows and road signs lit by their headlights. "I don't even know his name."

The band continues to ask her questions, but Paige's body has begun to return to itself, and she finds she can barely keep her eyes open. The van bounces her like a child, and she presses her forehead to the glass and allows her lids to close. Her thoughts drift to the man in the room, and the way he seemed so empty as he chanted his terrible song. She must rescue him, she thinks—but how can she, when she is heading in exactly the opposite direction?

This is the lie, his voice echoes.

Her cheeks blush, so she pulls her knees to her chest and lays her head on top of them facing the door. Her neck aches, and she rubs at the skin beneath her sweatshirt to find that it has turned hard and hollow under her fingertips.

"Rest, Hun," Jenna says softly.

Paige closes her eyes and drifts off to sleep.

CHAPTER FIFTEEN

LILY

THE NIGHT IS COLDER, AND LILY folds her arms stiffly over her chest as far as the tight purple blazer will allow. In a minute she is shivering, and she wishes she'd brought the scarf Rashi sent her last year for graduation. *It was supposed to be a Christmas gift,* the note read, *but it turns out I'm not fast—or good—at this hobby. I think this is my first, and final, attempt. Still, you can wear it when you come back home—Can't wait!—this coming winter.*

At least there had been one person excited to see Lily return her things to her old bedroom, which Lily's mom had already started converting into a sewing room. At least there had been one person who said congratulations when Lily said she'd taken the position of Manager at Toy Palace, instead of *You're wasting your talents* or *A college dropout could do that job.* Luckily, her parents would never have the guts to say something like that to Camilla Vitaly herself—even they were afraid of her—but they might mutter it out of earshot, one day, and cost Lily the job she'd tried, but failed, not to want. There was just something about that store . . .

And there it is. Red columns. Golden tassels. Lights bright, though they should be dim, so that the stillness of the animatronic toys looked almost creepy in the glow of the harsh bright bulbs.

There are no police in sight, nor anyone for that matter, but when Lily taps on the glass door, Camilla Vitaly's personal security, Mike and Len, appear from somewhere in the back of the store.

"Come in quickly," says Mike, who is wearing the usual black t-shirt stretched over his barrel chest and his matching black cap, which he probably thinks makes him look like he's still an army captain. *Isn't he freezing?*, Lily wonders, but then she thinks that maybe there is some amount of muscle that makes someone impervious to the weather.

Len is wearing a blue suit and matching blue-and-white striped tie, which means Camilla called in from his night off. He looks smaller than usual under the loose arms and broad shoulder pads of the suit, but his face is as mean as ever with its usual pinched frown. The pointed beard doesn't help—it makes him look like a fox, or one of those murderous husbands from a Grimms fairy tale.

"Talk to me," Lily says as Len locks the door behind them.

Mike fills Lily in: there has been a break-in through the back fire escape, which had not been properly accounted for in their security plans. None of the cameras were angled properly—or, they suspect, someone tampered with them earlier in the night. They're about to run the footage from the last camera, one to the far right of the store, but they doubt it will offer any clues.

Their voices seem eerily calm—much calmer than she expected after so many missed calls.

Have they changed their minds about wanting her to come in?

"What did they steal?" Lily asks. Her eyes slip down the aisle, across the rows she can see from where she stands. Nothing seems out of place—not even the boxes of their most expensive electronics.

"Nothing," Mike says. He and Len look at each other, and then back at her. "Weird, huh?"

"Nothing?" Lily looks at them hard. "Not even the money in the safe under the register?"

"Nada," says Len.

"Zilch," says Mike.

Lily has that bad feeling she gets whenever something doesn't add up—the same one she used to get when she'd be doing Algebra II and she'd know, suddenly, that she'd missed a step, or when she was counting the register and could tell, before she'd determined the total, that the bills were off. And while she was on the subject, where were the police? She'd heard sirens as she was running toward the store, but now, the night was silent. Didn't they want to get to the bottom of who would break into Toy Palace?

"So, what can I do to help?" Lily asks, ignoring the feeling of her bar fries rolling around in her stomach.

Now it's Len and Mike's turn to stare.

"We thought you might know something . . ." Len says slowly.

"That maybe you'd seen something suspicious . . ." Mike agrees. "Something out of the ordinary."

"Like what?" Lily asks, furrowing her brow.

"Oh, I don't know." Len looks up at the ceiling, as though he's thinking hard. "Say . . . a girl? Or, say . . . someone who might bear a resemblance to someone who'd want to threaten Ms. Vitaly's place of business?"

" . . . A girl?" Lily's heart thumps hard in her chest, and she tries to take a deep breath before she starts sweating again. "You think a girl is responsible for this?"

"We saw you talking to her—" Mike starts, but Len elbows him hard in the ribs.

"What do you mean?" Lily asks. Her voice is harder than she means it to be. Her thoughts go back to the blond girl who looked like she'd seen a ghost. "I thought you said you didn't have any footage?"

"He means nothing," says Len, elbowing Mike again even though the other guard hasn't said anything. "Guess we're back to square one."

Len gives a mock drop of his chin to indicate disappointment. Or maybe he really is disappointed, and she's reading more into the situation than she should? After all, they couldn't possibly think she'd aid a criminal in breaking in… could they?

"Guess we'd better let you get some sleep," Mike says. He takes her arm and guides her toward the front, even as she tries to argue that she should at least count the inventory—what if the thief took some of the more expensive dolls to sell online, or what if they are still there, hiding in wait until the store is empty—

"Yes, you should get some sleep," Len says. The two men take her arms again, and now they are shoving her out the door, gently but firmly, so that she cannot even turn to give the room a backward glance.

The door slams.

The lock slides closed.

Lily turns, as though to knock on the door, but there, again, is her watch: 12:01 A.M. Just six hours before she needs to wake up for her next shift—and she is tired, she realizes, so tired that when she gets home that night, she falls asleep in her Toy Palace t-shirt and name tag.

A girl . . .

Someone who might bear a resemblance . . .

Petta's Traveling Toys.

CHAPTER SIXTEEN

PAIGE

THEY ARRIVE WITH A SUDDEN JOLT and an enthusiastic honk. Paige falls into a pile of cases, and one hits against her wooden chest with an unsettling thumping sound. Her heart pounds wildly, and she tries to orient herself, remembering only a minute later that she ran away with a bunch of strangers.

"Let's get you sorted out," Jenna says, and she pushes Paige up to sit. When she looks out the window, she finds they are in some kind of heavily wooded area with no light, save for the stars and a single porch light left on at a distant door.

"Sasha said you can stay here for the night," Jenna explains. She gives Paige an apologetic shrug. "I need to get home to my kids."

"I totally understand," Paige says, trying not to let her voice rise to a panicked octave. She has not even met Sasha, and the last thing she wants to do is stay the night with her.

Someone opens the back doors to the van, and then they are all clamoring out in a tumble of arms and legs and stretching backs. The musicians yawn and disperse, so that, all at once, Jenna is giving Paige a hug and then disappearing into the night, where, a minute later, headlights bring the dense forest around them into sharp relief; Marcus is saying he's just down the road and then walking off with his cell phone's flashlight as the only guidance; and Seth and Elle are leaving in the opposite direction, where, again, the brief flash of two headlights brings clarity before the last plunge into darkness.

"Goodbye," Paige says, though there is no one left to hear her.

"And to think," says a low voice in the darkness by the front of the van, "I was the one who *didn't* want you to come along."

Paige turns slowly toward the voice and squints, but all she can see is a tall, dark shadow. The hidden figure walks right past her, sending a whiff of incense and sweet perfume, with some kind of fabric's rustling as the only other hint of the moving form. Paige feels something rise up in her as Sasha brushes past, but it isn't fear. Curiosity, she realizes, turning now to follow the swishing skirts, and a hint of anticipation.

The cabin to which they trek is the one with the porch light. As they draw closer, Paige can see more and more of Sasha, starting with her hair, which appears to be half red and half blond, and her dress, a corseted black sweetheart top attached to many layers of black tulle. Her boots are black leather lace-ups with pointed toes, like she has emerged from a Victorian portrait, and she steps hard, as though she is stomping out her own tune. As Sasha steps up to the door, she begins to hum a tune, which is low and sad and barely distinguishable from the wind blowing through the trees. Slowly, the words become audible, though the meaning is still far from Paige's grasp:

Please, Fire Eater, you mustn't burn me,
for I am a sorrowful boy, you will see.

Without unlocking the door, Sasha turns the handle and pushes.

Your wails give me such a strange feeling, a sneeze,
E-tchee, E-tchee, E-tchee . . .

On the last rise of the final note, Sasha flips on the living room light. Or, at least, Paige assumes it is the living room, though the decorations are nothing like the homes Paige has read about in books or seen on TV. Instead, over all the black-painted wooden paneling hung with matching black shelves, are lines of antique toys. Here a cast iron horse and carriage drawn by a lady in a tall hat; there a pressed steel duck on two wheels. Dolls with eyes drawn left above chubby composite cheeks, a wooden dog on a worn yellow string, a circus elephant cycling balls to a spiraling column. And of course, amongst them, the familiar work of a skilled hand, so that Paige drifts to the nearest shelf and presses her finger to the face of a sweet wooden boy with a realistic set of blue eyes.

"I thought you might enjoy that little collection," Sasha says.

Sasha finally turns around to face her, and Paige is struck by the realization that the lead singer is much older than she initially thought. Her face is done up in heavy makeup, with eyeliner flipped at the corners of her eyes and deep purple lipstick on her smug, pursed lips, but at the corners are deep wrinkles, as though she has been giving this exact same expression for at least sixty years.

"My mother made these," Paige says, though she suspects Sasha already knows.

"Lovely craftsmanship, that Petta Vitaly."

Paige nods and returns her gaze to the selection. Six of the wooden toys are her mother's, though one nutcracker has a few of Paige's signature moves.

"I wondered about that one," Sasha says as Paige's hand lingers on her work. "You're a lot like her, you know."

"Not as much as you'd think." Paige drops her hand. "So, you're from Wintroster, too?"

Sasha nods. She walks across the room to a wooden chair and perches there with her wrists outstretched on the armrests, like a queen. "You know those Toy Palace dolls that hum little tunes?

Paige shakes her head no.

"Well, anyway, that's my voice coming from the box."

She has not been invited to sit down, so Paige leans awkwardly on the back of another wooden chair. Her body is exhausted, but her mind is racing.

Do it, Paige urges herself. *What have you got to lose?*

"Do you know anything about a man who lives on the second floor of the shop?"

Sasha looks up sharply and locks eyes with Paige. Her pupils are so brown that they look black in the dim lighting. Her eyes never blink. "I might."

Paige decides to sit down anyway. The slats of the chair bite into her back, and she shifts uncomfortably. "Can you tell me?"

Sasha finally looks away, toward the fireplace empty of flames. "It's hard to explain."

"I'll believe you," Paige says. She leans to the side, trying to get a better position by putting her weight on her elbow. "I promise."

Sasha sighs deeply. "What do I care if a little runaway thinks I'm crazy?" She waves her hand in a dramatic flourish. "Forty years ago, I was working in a little pub in downtown Wintroster, and I started hearing this . . . Well, to call it a song is to misrepresent it entirely. The sound was more like an echo, sent down through the empty streets and into the door to my unsuspecting ears. From that night on, whenever I went into town to work a long shift, I would hear it again, any moment when I wasn't singing my own tunes."

"And the song," Paige says, leaning forward. "Let me guess." She clears her throat and then begins, wishing she had a better singing voice: "*There are two kinds of lies, you won't be surprised, short legs and long noses—*"

Sasha's eyes widen, and she inhales a deep gasp. "Yes," she cries, leaping up from her chair. "*And this is the lie of the toymaker.* You heard him, too?"

"I saw him." Paige's back sags over her legs. "But I left him there when I ran away."

Sasha stands up from her chair and takes two long strides to the shelves on her left. Her hand extends toward a plastic baby doll with a sweet, blank face, and then she presses one black fingernail into the soft stomach sewn to the plastic head. A tune begins, a sort of *ga-ga-ga-ga* that works its way up and down the scale. The notes are sweet, but Sasha frowns at the rising and falling of her own voice. She presses the stomach again, and the sound stops.

"I saw them advertising for a singer in the newspaper, so I showed up and auditioned." Sasha returns to her chair and leans back. "I didn't have a single performance under my belt, but I figured, what better way to get closer to that humming I'd heard?"

"Weren't you scared?" Paige cannot imagine auditioning for anything.

"Terrified. But I went anyway, and they brought me to an office and had me sing right then and there, in front of your grandfather."

Paige swallows hard. She can imagine the great founder of the modernized toy sitting behind his banker's desk like a great judge upon a bench.

"Miracle of miracles, he hired me on the spot." Sasha

smiles, and her gaze drifts past Paige, as though she has returned to those earlier days. "I only needed to come twice to get the song down, so, on the second visit, I told them I knew how to let myself out. But instead of leaving . . ." Sasha leans forward and puts her hands over her mouth, as though she is trying to keep back a secret.

"What did you do?" Paige whispers.

Sasha parts her fingers just slightly, so that the deep purple of her lips is just visible in the valley between them. "He was so beautiful, Paige. He told me to come to him, and I pressed my head against his thin little chest and closed my eyes."

Sasha closes her eyes, and for a minute, she is silent. Then, she takes up her story again, though her eyes stay closed.

"'*What do you wish for, Child?*' he asked me, though I was long from those years, and I said, '*For my voice to bring life to others, the way yours has for me.*'"

Paige leans forward and asks, ". . . And?"

Sasha begins to hum again, but this time, the notes are from the man's sorrowful song: "*There are two kinds of lies, you won't be surprised, short legs and long noses.*" Her voice rises, and now the notes are filling the room: "*—but no one supposes that there is another much worse than the others—*"

Paige feels a strange wonder growing inside of herself. Something about the notes is lifting her, as though she is a hot air balloon and Sasha's song is the propane. She straightens her back, and then her heels lift off the ground.

"*—and this is the lie—*" Sasha booms out.

Paige's muscles strain her forward, all the way onto her tippy-toes. A strange cacophony of movements are happening to her right, too, and, when she turns, she finds the wheels of the toy cars and wagons spinning slowly, like a wind has come through the window. The dolls' eyes shift left, right, left. The duck quacks its bill up and down.

"*—of a toy—*"

The room goes wild. All of the toys move at once, dancing and rocking and spinning wildly in newfound life. A metal horse falls from the shelf and clatters to the ground, where it kicks its legs in a frantic frolic. Paige is almost off the ground now, and she feels a warm sensation in her chest. When she lifts her sweatshirt, she finds the familiar flesh that should be there, across a rack of very human bones.

"*—maker*!"

Abruptly, the song ends. Sasha collapses in her chair, and Paige falls hard onto her heels. The toys collapse in their places, so that dolls are draped over dogs and cars are scattered at all kinds of strange angles. The chaos reminds Paige of a child's toy room, in which the owner has abandoned all of the beloved possessions in their places until the next day's romp. She checks her chest again, notes the grooved wood's hollow return.

"So, it's wishes he grants," Paige says, but, in her mind, she thinks, *But I have not wished to become a toy.*

Sasha doesn't say anything for a while, but she hums, over and over again, that silly little song. *Please, Fire Eater, you mustn't burn me, for I am a sorrowful boy, you will see.* She seems to be thinking, but about what, Paige has no idea. And in the meantime, Paige's guilt has returned; she wonders whether the man tied up in the toy shop hates her, and if her mother will hate her when she wakes to find Paige's bed untouched.

What am I doing here?

But she knows that she cannot go back, either. Not now, not when she knows that Petta will pack up the toys and lock up the doors and return, again, to the long stretches of highway that separate them from their town. If they leave Wintroster, Paige will never find out the truth—*But whose truth are you really concerned about?*

The man in the store, of course.

Don't lie, Paige—not to yourself.

I am most concerned about him!

Paige's shoulder aches, and she rubs at the muscle to find it hard, like a knot tied in a very thick rope. The wood seems to be spreading, and she wonders how long it will take to turn her entirely into hollow wood.

Fine. She crosses her arms, and Sasha is too busy singing to herself and staring at the empty fireplace to notice.

"I *will* go back to the store to save that poor man . . ." Paige says, sounding more forceful than she feels. "But, first . . . I want to find my father."

"Your father?" Sasha laughs for the first time. "So that's what this is all about?"

Paige's eyebrows draw so close together her forehead aches. She crosses her arms and hunches. "Why are you laughing?"

"Because." Sasha stands and brushes off her skirts, as though she is shaking off the dust of a fairy's persistent powder. "I know exactly where he is!"

"You do?"

"Yes. But we can't go now." Sasha shakes her head so that her fringe bangs swish back and forth. "The hour is late, and besides, he won't be there until tomorrow morning. We'll leave then—as soon as the sun rises over the trees."

"And when will that be?" Paige asks, but Sasha just shrugs in reply.

Sasha brings Paige to the kitchen, where there are no clocks anywhere, nor even a microwave to declare the hour.

Sasha puts a kettle on the mint green retro stove, and Paige sits in one of the red plastic chairs beside the glossy white and chrome table and rubs her forehead. Then she takes out her cell phone, which is almost out of battery, and reads the time: 2:05 a.m.

"Do you have a smart phone charger?"

Sasha shakes her head. "I'm still using my flip phone—good old Annabelle Gray."

Paige raises her eyebrows. "You named your phone?"

"I name everything."

How strange, this tranquil life, when Paige has spent every day she remembers with a dashboard clock or the crafted cuckoo of her mother's earlier days. Every moment was about the time—or, rather, the time until the next departure.

When the kettle whistles, Sasha removes two porcelain mugs from a stack beside the stove and pours water into them, then fills two tea infusers with what she calls "not-a-daisy leaves" and dips them thoughtfully up and down. One of the mugs has vintage-patterned orange and red birds perched on a green vine, while the other has blue birds secured to two sunflowers. In an amount of time Paige wishes she could quantify later, Sasha declares the tea "*Finito!*" and gives Paige her pick of the two.

"Blue is my favorite color," Paige says, and then her mind slips to the fairy. *I am going back,* Paige insists, and she must mean it, for her chest does not ache this time.

Sasha leaves Paige to her tea while she changes behind a door off the living room. Perhaps she is gone for a minute, or maybe twenty, for Paige finds herself drifting off to sleep over the steam of her mug.

"You need to sleep," a soft voice whispers.

Sasha has returned, this time wearing a long, white sleeping gown and a pair of black slippers decorated to the toe with black fur. Her hair has been pulled up by a black claw clip, though it is long enough to still reach down past her shoulders. She wears no makeup, which actually makes her look younger—or maybe it is just the dim glow from the single pendant light. Her tea is gone, and she refills the water from the kettle before sitting in the other chair.

"That's better," she declares. Then she inhales a whiff of the tea. "Should have changed out the leaves."

Paige takes a sip of the tea, which is hot and bitter. She wants to ask about her father, but Sasha seems to be preparing for bed, and she does not want to press her luck. Instead she asks, "Do you have any sugar?"

"Sorry," Sasha says. She gulps down the steaming liquid from her own cup. "I don't let that poison in the house. And no milk, either—but that's just because I'm on the road too much to keep it from spoiling."

What about my father. Does he like sugar?

"No worries," Paige says. She takes another sip and tries not to wince. "This is perfect."

"Good. And now you must sleep," Sasha says softly.

She leads Paige away from the table and toward the door where she changed, which turns out to be a short hallway with two bedrooms at the other end. The one on the right is marked by Sasha's name, written in black with a vine and a single red rose painted around the cursive letters; on the left, the wooden door turns out to be a guest bedroom, so plain compared to the clutter of the other rooms. The only decorations are a queen-sized bed covered in a tan fur blanket, white paneled walls, and a gold bench with flaking paint and a tan seat cushion that looks like it has never been sat on. Behind the bed, floor to ceiling windows reflect the two women and the blank white walls.

"No toys in here?" Paige teases.

"None but you," Sasha says softly.

"What do you—?"

But the door is already closing behind Sasha, and even though Paige knows she must have heard her, the singer does not return.

CHAPTER SEVENTEEN

LILY

THE FOLLOWING MORNING, LILY DOES NOT stop to say hello to anyone. She does not wave to the baker, to the man who collects the trash, to the florist, to the seamstress, to the grocer, or to the woman at 1203 Spicegood Road who always wishes her a blessed day. She does not stop for a bagel—her stomach is in knots—but rather rushes right past the white lettering and exclamation points without even a second glance.

There it is.

The caravan.

Lily takes a seat on the stoop across the street a few houses down and removes a newspaper from her backpack. She unfolds the paper with a soft flip of the pages, then brings the edge to the bridge of her nose, so that only the tops of her eyes peek out from the grayish-white paper. It smells like her mother's cooking, which makes sense, since it's yesterday's paper, previously read by Lily's father and then abandoned on the kitchen counter until that morning, when Lily snatched it up. Now, the smells of ink and pulp compete with the smell of the city roads and the clean morning air trying to wipe them away with every chilly breeze. At least she has a padded flannel jacket on today, with Rashi's scarf tied tight around her neck to keep her warm, she thinks, as her gaze drifts across the caravan and then back to the door. It will be a long morning.

***

FINALLY, WHAT SEEMS LIKE HOURS LATER—NO, she realizes when she checks her watch, what *is* hours later—a woman emerges from the back of the caravan. She wears a thick wool shawl, one of those where the wearer sticks their arms through the holes on the sides and then crosses their arms to keep the fabric folded over their chest, with a tight tan sweater and high-waisted jeans. Her feet are bare, and after she sits on the chair, the woman tucks them up into a crisscrossed pose. She rests her coffee mug on her right knee, and her eyes stare down the road, as though she is already lost deep in thought.

It's Petta, Lily thinks. *I'd recognize her anywhere.*

The woman's eyes burrow into the horizon. Her mouth is a long line of sadness, and she rakes her fingers through her wavy gray hair over and over again while she thinks. Even back then, in the portrait, she had that look—as though she knew so much more than she should have at that age. As though she knows so much more now than any human might.

Lily wonders if she should talk to the toymaker, but she can't bring herself to move—not toward the caravan, and not away, either. She's frozen there, on the stoop, with the concrete beneath her chilling her bones and the paper growing heavy in arms aching from holding the paper upright for over two hours.

"I'm waiting for my daughter," Petta says suddenly.

Lily looks around, but there is no one else to whom Petta might be talking. "Excuse me?"

"My daughter." Petta's eyes slide slowly across the line of buildings to meet Lily's. "Her name is Paige—and she's gone."

"Oh." Lily folds the newspaper and rests it in her lap. "I'm sure she'll be back soon."

Petta shakes her head. "No. She's far from me—and I fear that soon, she might be lost forever."

Lily wonders what she should say next, but nothing comes to mind, so she sits there, silent, until Petta speaks again.

"Want some coffee?"

And so, Lily ends up slipping through the back door and into the caravan, which is more spacious inside than it looked from the stoop. The smells are familiar, in a way—wood polish, paint, sawdust, the scents that still linger in Toy Palace, too, even now that most of the toys are animatronic. You can't get a smell like that out of a place, no matter how many years pass—and Lily has tried everything, even Rashi's suggestion of lavender and vanilla essential oils. There are two beds—one of them is made, and the other has just a bit of the corner folded back, as though Petta just slipped from inside like a bean from inside a tight green pod. The window on the right is closed, but Lily imagines this is where they take customers, since the old-fashioned register is perched on the ledge there.

"You should really get something more secure, you know."

"So Paige tells me."

Petta does not go to the stove, but rather perches on the edge of the chair at the workbench and crosses her legs. Then she puts her hands on her knees and leans forward. "Did my sister send you?"

Lily's mouth opens and then presses tightly closed again.

"If not her, then who?" Petta leans back against the ledge of the workbench. Her eyes burrow into Lily's, until Lily has to look away, at the worn wood of the floor. There is dust there, between the boards, and little slivers of chipped paint. "Ah. You've seen her, haven't you?"

"Who?" Lily's eyes trace the lines of the boards, returning to her own boots.

"My daughter."

It's not really a question, or even if it is, Lily does not answer. Instead, she sits down on the bed and loosens her scarf a little, so that she might ease the tightness growing in her throat.

"I bet she was quite taken with you."

Lily can feel herself blushing, and she rubs at her warm cheeks as though she might will her embarrassment away. Petta smiles, but then the expression disappears quickly to become the same faraway eyes and thin-lipped line of her distance.

"Did she meet my sister?"

Lily shakes her head no. She wonders how much she should tell this woman—after all, she doesn't owe her anything, and besides, her daughter might be the one who broke into Toy Palace. Maybe whatever she stole is right here, in the caravan. Maybe Paige isn't gone at all, but merely hiding somewhere in Wintroster.

"If I'm not here when she gets back . . ." Petta's voice catches. ". . . will you tell her that I'm sorry I didn't tell her about everything sooner?"

"Why wouldn't you be here?" Lily asks. She can't help the concern in her voice, even if Petta might be a criminal.

Petta rubs at the top of her chest, and then her arms wrap tightly around her body. The shawl is like a cocoon, from which Lily expects her to burst—or maybe it's more of a shroud. "My sister will be all she has. At least here, in Wintroster, Paige won't be alone."

Now Lily wraps her own arms around herself and squeezes. Her eyes burn, and she realizes, when she puts her hand to cheek again, that she's crying. "I'll tell her."

"Thank you."

Petta stands, and Lily knows that this is her cue to leave. She walks to the door, but something, a feeling that she can't quite explain or even fully feel, makes her say something out loud that she's never told anyone—not even Rashi. "I can hear the toys talking—but it's not their voices that I can make out in the constant noise of the shop. It's a man's voice—a haunting voice—and it sings the most forlorn song I've ever heard."

Petta's head snaps up. "Sing it for me, please."

"Oh, I couldn't—"

"Sing it," Petta says, and her voice is as sharp as a carving knife.

"All right," Lily clears her throat. "*There are two kinds of lies, you won't be surprised—*"

"It cannot be." Petta stands up so quickly that the chair beneath her falls to the floor with a loud bang. "You're sure you've heard it yourself? My sister didn't put these ideas in your head?"

"I've never even told her," Lily said. Her stomach clenches, and her fists ball tightly so that the nails dig into her palms.

"But he left years ago." Petta leans on the workbench for support. "I helped him leave years ago . . ."

". . . Who?" Lily feels like she is paused at the top of a roller coaster, and that whatever comes next will plunge her down, down, down into a life she is not sure she wants to live.

"The prisoner upstairs." Petta swallows hard. She shakes her head, as though even she can't believe whatever she is about to say. "The fairy."

That's impossible, Lily thinks, but she finds that she can't utter the words. She searches for that feeling she gets, her algebra equation feeling, the same one she relied on when she chose to come back to Wintroster a year ago despite what her parents would say.

The fairy.

Petta nods, as though she is responding to something Lily said out loud, and Lily nods back. Then the toymaker reaches out her hand, grips Lily's arm, and squeezes so tightly that Lily will later find prints of her fingers as small blue bruises. "You have to help me save him, Lily. We are almost out of time."

CHAPTER EIGHTEEN
PAIGE

DESPITE HER WORRY, PAIGE SLEEPS DEEPLY, pulled down by the physical weight of two days of restless deprivation. When she wakes, it is to the unseen bird trill of morning. The backlit faces of curious oaks peer down through her window, and when she moves her neck, the beams behind them shoulder their way to blind her. "I'm up," she grumbles, and then she covers her eyes with one arm.

"Paige?" Sasha's voice calls from somewhere past the door. She knocks, and Paige wonders if it was this rapping that woke her in the first place. "We're late. Wheels up in twenty, or we'll miss him coming in."

Him? Paige removes her arm and sits up in bed. *Oh. Right.*

She slides her legs across the bed and moves to standing, where she stretches out the tightness in her back and chest. She checks beneath her shirt, but there is no change. *At least I don't lie in my dreams.*

Sasha has given her a change of clothes, and Paige unfolds the University of Wintroster hoodie and holds it up to find the washer-worn fabric is just the right size. The yoga pants, too, though when she actually slips into them, she finds the waistband a bit tight around the hips.

Her stomach grumbles, so she follows the noises of the house back to the kitchen. Sasha is wearing a new dress this morning, a white mini dress with a crocheted front, which she has paired with floral stockings and black cowboy boots with white flowers sewn on the sides. Her hair is damp, and there are new waves in her white and red hair. She stands at the stove heating water for instant coffee, and when she catches sight of Paige, she tosses Paige a package of biscuits.

"He comes in after the morning catch," Sasha says, as though they are picking up a conversation.

"Catch?"

"For the fish, silly." Sasha stirs in tablespoons of black granules.

"Fish?" Paige takes the mug and drinks quickly. The liquid burns her throat, but almost instantly, she feels more alert. "So, my father is a fisherman?"

"Of sorts."

Sasha grabs a brown saddle bag purse from a hook by the back door and shoves her keys, wallet, and a few food bars into it. "Want a water bottle?" Sasha asks, and Paige nods yes, realizing at the same time that Sasha will probably expect her to leave later that day. Will she drive Paige back to Wintroster?

Is she even going back?

Of course I'm going back, Paige thinks, and there is that ache again, this time on her right bicep. She rubs at the skin there and finds it flat and hard, her toymaker's muscles replaced by the plank of wood. When she flexes, nothing moves.

"To the van!" Sasha announces, raising one arm like a conductor. Her sleeve slides backward to her shoulder, revealing a sleeve of toy-inspired tattoos. There is a little monkey banging on a pair of cymbals; there is a set of two warring robots; there is a Barbie, though her head is held under one arm beneath the nub of her naked neck. Paige wonders what else covers the canvas of Sasha's body, but she feels it would be rude to ask, and then Sasha is out the door and stomping her way across the front yard.

Goodbye, Paige tells the old stove and the matching mint green fridge. *And thanks for—*

Paige might have waxed sentimental some more, but folk-rock music suddenly blasts from the van speakers. Paige scurries out of her seat and out the door before Sasha can try to leave her behind, and in fact she looks like she might, poised powerfully up on the high passenger's seat like some kind of mad queen. Birds fly from everywhere, frantically diving away from the threat of the music. Paige feels the strange pulse of a new energy in the air.

"Ready to meet your dad?" Sasha booms like she's yelling into a concert mic.

"Ready," Paige says, and throws herself up onto the passenger's seat.

***

THE DRIVE IS SHORT—JUST OVER TWENTY minutes—but the change in scenery is startling. Gone are the oaks and pines and shadows between sunny beams; here are the flat and open grasses of an impending beach. The smell comes first, salty sand, and then the whip of sea air through Sasha's open windows. The water is a long line on the horizon, the ripple of waves, and then, in the parking lot of the cantina, a booming crash. It is too cold for many visitors, and the wind rides through Paige's borrowed sweatshirt and chills everywhere but her wooden chest and upper arm. She shivers, and her teeth chatter.

"Here." Sasha throws her an old puffer coat, green with fake brown fur at the neck and around the hood. The size is too large to be Sasha's, and Paige wonders if it belongs to one of the band members. "You're going to need this."

Paige slips into the sleeves and feels instantly warmer. "Thanks," she says, zipping the coat up all the way. Then she tucks her hands into her pockets and raises her shoulders to her ears. "I'm not used to this weather."

Paige follows Sasha through the mostly empty lot and past the boarded up walk where ice cream stands and hot dog shacks have already shuttered for the winter. *We'll be back April 1,* signs in the windows announce, with the exception of one coffee stand and a persistent barista who is scrolling on her phone behind a dirty pane of glass. Past the walk is an empty stretch of sidewalk, and there, at the end, is the marina.

There are not many ships tied up at the docks, and Paige wonders, as they draw closer, which of the bobbing vessels might belong to her father. The bright white yacht? The sleek blue sailboat?

"He's back," Sasha confirms, her eyes on a ship to the left. "See? It's that blue one there at the end."

Paige finds the last ship, though to call it "blue" is to ignore the grime on the hull and the peel of the paint so that the brown-white surface beneath peaks through like a dirty fingernail. Paige thinks that the ship is a fishing vessel judging by the nets slung over the side, and the little room on top, too, where dirty curtains over the portholes and front windows block any passengers from view. *The Tunny* announces the side of the ship in terrible handwriting.

"That one?" she asks skeptically.

"It just needs to float," Sasha says with a chuckle.

They approach *The Tunny* to find music playing under the sound of the wind and waves. Some kind of old country music, Paige thinks, though she has never lingered on a country station long enough to hear any of it. The smell of fish gets stronger as the ship nears, and then it is overpowering her, so that she struggles not to heave at the gutty flavor of the air in her nostrils.

"Hey, Tom," Sasha calls out, and the music stops. "You've got company."

The door of the boat opens, and there he is. Paige knows immediately that he is her father—they have the same long nose, the same flat face, the same blond hair the color of dry sea grass—and she feels a strange mix of knowing him so certainly and yet feeling nothing toward him at all.

"Who'd you bring, Mom?" he asks, pulling in one of the rope nets as he talks.

"Mom?" Paige turns to Sasha. "What does he mean, Mom?"

"Well," Sasha says, and then she shrugs. "I'd have told you if you'd asked."

"Why would I have asked?" Paige says incredulously, but Sasha only shrugs again and gives her a little smile.

The man looks back and forth between them, and then his complexion darkens into an embarrassed red. "Wait a minute . . ."

"I was quite surprised myself," Sasha says. She crosses her arms. "Anything you want to tell me, Tommy? Maybe something about a certain Petta Vitaly and *a child you secretly had together?*"

"It's not like that," he says, his cheeks getting even redder. "It's . . . complicated."

"I'll bet." Sasha waves her arm up and down over Paige, as though showing off an auction item about to be bid on. "A whole human amount of complicated."

Tom and Sasha look at each other for a long time without saying anything, and Paige looks down at her zipper. She doesn't know what she expected during this meeting, but it certainly wasn't this. She wants to know what he means by complicated, and why he never told his mother about her, and why he never called or sent a letter or even a smoked fish . . . but at the same time, she isn't sure she wants to know more after all.

"Come aboard," Tom finally says. "I'll tell you as much as I can."

Getting onto the boat involves an unsteady plank of wood and a lot of rocking that makes Paige feel like she is about to fall into the marina at any second. She wants to clutch for a hand, but no one offers one, so she makes it across and tries to land gracefully on her feet, even as the boat rocks with their added weight. Paige's stomach sloshes, and she feels almost immediately ill.

"You'll get used to it," Tom says, his eyes on the net in his hands.

They go inside the door and then down to the below-deck room, which actually smells less fishy than the exterior. When Paige looks up, she finds the answer: seven pine air fresheners dangling from the bare rafters. The room is depressing: a bed and bench built into the wall, a map of the world with a bunch of pins stuck along the edges of the continents, and a single green wool blanket with moth holes in it. Paige wonders if Tom has a house somewhere else, like Sasha's hidden cabin, or if this is his whole life, right here on the sea.

"I'll start at the beginning," he says, taking a seat on the bed and indicating the women should sit on the bench. His wide chest heaves under his button-down flannel. "But it's going to sound completely crazy."

CHAPTER NINETEEN

LILY

AT EXACTLY NOON, LILY TELLS THE cashier at the front that for once, she is going to take a full hour for lunch. "I have a headache," she says. "A little rest up in the office will make me feel so much better."

"We can't go upstairs—"

"I got permission from Camilla, don't worry."

The cashier, who goes by Pippa, looks unsure. She is new, a college freshman who just moved to Wintroster from upstate New York, and she's probably still trying to remember to hand over the receipt every time the register spits a tongue of white tape through the slit in its top. Lily just trained her only the week before, taking her through what she calls Lily's School for the Best Cashiers in Virginia, which mostly involves lessons in smiling, working one's voice to its highest possible register, and gift wrapping. Not just paper and a bit of tape—that was amateur stuff—but enveloping a toy in a bed of soft red tissue paper, fanning a stiffer golden sheet, and arranging both inside of a thick paper Toy Palace bag made to look exactly like the columns at the front. Now, the new cashier is confident in her counting and the way she joyfully clicks the register drawer into place. But this—one of the five unbreakable rules

Lily shared at the end of their session—has requested the kind of critical thinking Lily's program was supposed to have drilled out of her.

"I . . ."

"Catch!" Lily tosses her keys to Pippa, who almost drops them as her long, skinny arms flail under her oversized Toy Palace t-shirt. *We need to order more smalls,* Lily notes, and then she remembers that she will probably never put in another order for the store ever again. Her stomach clenches, and she bends over and gives a wail that is only partially contrived. As soon as she leaves this register and ascends the steps, she will be a traitor to everything she holds dear—everything that has saved her, for all these years, from the life her parents think she deserves. "Now I feel like I'm going to be sick."

"Should I—?"

"Listen to me." Lily looks up from her hunched position. Her voice drops to an even more serious note. Her eyes meet the wide, lemur eyes of Pippa. "For the next hour, you have to pretend to be Lily Jones, okay? Can you handle that?"

"Yes, sir," Pippa says, standing up straight. "I mean, ma'am. I mean—"

"It's okay." Lily wonders if this girl will still be working the register in a month, or a year, or four years, when college has ended and the world has descended upon her like a weighted blanket slowly filling with lead. "You're more than capable."

Then Lily is climbing the stairs—the forbidden stairs, the prohibited stairs, *Oh god, what am I doing, trusting a complete stranger instead of the woman I've worked for the last five years?*—and arriving, for the first time, on the second floor.

***

The hallway is too dim for the hour, as though someone has set a shade on top of the bulb of the sun trying desperately to beam through the window at the other end. Dust drifts, bringing scents of wood and Camilla's powdery perfume and something else—or maybe it's not a smell, but a feeling, like the air here is thicker.

"*There are two kinds of lies, you won't be surprised,*" a voice whispers, as though the singer is crooning right into Lily's ear.

Lily crosses the hallway and unlocks the back door, where, not long ago, Paige and her accomplices entered Toy Palace and learned whatever truth Lily must now face. A few seconds later, Petta comes into view, still wearing the shawl and carrying a leather bag that clanks with the sound of metal on metal.

"You planning on doing some woodworking while you're here?" Lily whispers.

"Locksmithing," Petta says. "I wasn't sure I could rely on you."

"Thanks for the confidence."

Lily ushers Petta inside and then closes the door behind her. Somewhere outside, a camera will be capturing every move they make, sending it to the tapes where later, Camilla Vitaly herself will probably watch her manager allow this break-in. *I'm so sorry,* Lily thinks, and she tries to block out the rest of her emotions—especially the deep disappointment of a vanishing future at Toy Palace. And, of course, there are also the disappointed faces of her parents, who now will have a daughter who does nothing at all instead of a job that any college dropout could do, and Rashi, who will finally be sure her best friend is completely and utterly unhinged.

"You're too good for that store, Lily. How many cashiers do you know who got a perfect math score on their SATs?"

"I'm not a cashier, Dad."

"Manager, then? Hah! A staff of five college students and a few shelves of toys isn't exactly a big job—you should be running a company, or at least shadowing in my footsteps. Do you know how lucky you are? Do you know what it took for me to get here—to give you this life?"

Lily tries to make her mind blank, but the thoughts come like a tide, washing over and over again through her busy mind.

"Did you hear about poor Mrs. Thomas down the road? Found her son with that boy who used to sell candy bars for his camp tuition—remember him? Joey? Jesse? Anyway, the two of them are apparently—why, I can't even bring myself to say it—and now she's been to church praying for him night and day ever since."

"You mean he's gay, Mom?"

"I said I couldn't say the word, Lily."

"Sorry."

". . . You don't know anyone like that, do you?"

". . . Why would I?"

"Well, if you do, you should pray for them tonight, and for every night afterward, for as long as they do not act on their perversions, the Lord will forgive them on the day of judgment—"

"Hearing voices?" Petta asks.

"Yeah." Lily shakes her head. "Is that normal?"

"He tends to have that effect on people." Petta removes her phone from her pocket and scrolls through her contacts. "But no need to worry—you'll have plenty of time later to regret everything you've done once we're tied up by my sister's henchmen. For now, we need to focus on our work, okay?"

Once we're tied up? Lily thinks, and then she realizes that she never asked Petta to tell her the rest of the plan—the part where they escaped and drove off into the sunset, or whatever happened in heist movies after the criminals pulled off the theft.

"Wait—"

Petta presses a name on her phone, and then she says something softly into it, though Lily cannot make out the words, not now that "*There are two kinds of lies, you won't be surprised*" has resumed in her head. She considers abandoning Petta before the alarms go off and the key holder calls security, but she knows that it is too late—the tapes have already recorded her face, her words, her unforgivable betrayal.

"*Short legs and long noses, but no one supposes—*"

Petta's gaze shifts down the hallway, and her eyes narrow. "You can hear his song now, can't you?"

"Yes." Lily's mind abruptly quiets. "At least I could, a second ago."

They walk softly down the hallway, to where a new light, blue and soft, beams under the bottom of the door. Lily swears that light was not there before—or maybe it was, but she just hadn't been paying attention? Now, a humming comes, growing louder and louder like someone is turning the knob on the volume to the maximum output.

"*—that there is another much worse than the others—*"

Lily tries to bring herself to open the door, but she finds her body paralyzed from the noise. Petta, however, seems to have no trouble continuing their mission, and her hand lifts easily to the knob and turns. The glow is blindingly bright, and the humming like a rattling of Lily's brain, so that she would crouch down in a fetal curl if she could will her body to move.

"*And you're quite familiar with that lie, aren't you?*" a young man's voice says flatly.

"Hello, old friend."

The man is beautiful, in a haunted way. His angular face reminds her of an old portrait she found once leaning in the corner of a thrift shop, a layer of dust unable to obscure the high cheek bones and wavy hair and piercing stare of the bright blue eyes. Or maybe it's not his look, but a feeling—as though he carries time itself in his bones. As though he might press his long-fingered hand over her eyes and she might find herself sitting at a long table lit by candles and covered by gold platters, or croon her a song that could carry her to the childhood she wishes to forget, all of the lessons, all of the pressures, all of the girls she never talked to and the words she never spoke to her parents and—

"Lily," Petta's voice says sharply.

But she cannot cling to the driftwood of her name, not when there is so much pulling her under the waves. Not as the entire building begins to shake, and at the end of the hallway, the door rattles against the frame.

"He's pulling me down," Lily says, though when she actually does look down, she finds herself upright and bathed in a bright blue glow. "I can't—"

"Come on, Lily. You need to tell them."

"You don't understand, Rashi. They'll disown me—or maybe kill me, bring me back to life so that they can disown me, and then kill me all over again."

"You're just being dramatic."

"Fine. Maybe, instead, the news will kill them—yes, that sounds more likely. They'll both die from a combination of grief and disappointment, if it's even possible to be more disappointed in me than they already are—"

The light fixtures loosen, and one falls to Lily's left, in the periphery of her unwavering gaze.

"We've come to rescue you," Petta says. "If I'd known . . ."

The man drops his angular chin to his chest and closes his bright blue eyes. He looks asleep—or maybe dead.

"But Petta," he says, the sound audible even under the violent quaking of the chains and the walls and the entire Toy Palace building. "As I told you last time, I do not want to be saved."

"Help," Lily says, but the voice is in her head.

Petta bends down to whisper something in the fairy's ear. He smiles a little, as though he is satisfied with something, and then he presses his hand to the place above Petta's top button of her shirt—the place where the toymaker often puts her own hand, though Lily does not know why. There is a glow, much like the blue glow under the door, and Petta steps back and puts both palms in the place where the man's hand once pushed. Her shoulders seem to broaden—or perhaps she is just standing straighter. Her arms seem to thicken—or perhaps she is just shifting in the strange blue light.

"Help," Lily says again, this time out loud.

Then, she loses consciousness.

CHAPTER TWENTY

PAIGE

Tom tells them that he and Petta never dated. They met in downtown Wintroster, and they became friends, albeit temporary ones. Tom was about to leave again for a trip around the world, and Petta was already planning on leaving her family name behind. Friends-for-a-day, they called each other, though they met up for four nights straight before they started to realize that maybe there was something more between them than just a conversation at a coffee shop.

On the fifth night, Petta said she had something to show Tom. She took him to Toy Palace and brought him to the room on the second floor.

"I know where this is going," Sasha says, leaning toward her son. "You saw him, didn't you?"

"You've seen him, too?" Tom asks, eyes wide. "All this time, I thought you'd never . . ."

Sasha puts her hand out, and Tom takes it and squeezes it hard.

"Anyway, I could barely comprehend what I was seeing." Tom drops Sasha's hand and wraps his arms around himself. "Petta told me that when she left Wintroster, she was going to free him, and that her family would come after her. She'd have to stay on the run, she said, and I told her that on the run wasn't an all-bad way to be." He smiles a little, seeming to remember something, and his eyes are somewhere past Paige. "She had such a pretty laugh, and she laughed then, though I could see the pain behind her eyes. I told her I'd help her, as best as I could, and that we should free him the next night, together."

Tom's eyes tear up. "So, we did it—we went back, and we set him free. It actually wasn't hard—I'm not sure why Petta didn't do it before that, to be honest. Maybe she was afraid of upsetting her family? Maybe she knew she couldn't go back?"

"It's hard, having no one," Sasha says. She puts her arm around Paige, but Paige can barely feel anything over the numbness of her anticipation.

"Actually, now that I think about it," Tom continues, "she also showed me this key she had. She told me she had just gotten it. That ring any bells for you?"

Paige nods. She feels like she is no longer on a boat floating on the water, but sinking quickly into its unknown depths. How has Petta never mentioned the man in the room, or the other realm, or anything, at all, about any of this? And why not? Did she think she might save Paige from ever knowing the truth, when instead she has only left her daughter tied with the anchor of eighteen years of lies around her ankle?

But then why come to Wintroster? Paige wonders again. *Why now? Why ever?*

"After the chains dropped," Tom continues, "he didn't move or anything—he just sat there, singing his haunting little tune. Then, finally, he turned his strange eyes up to us and said, very softly, *What do you wish for, Children?*"

". . . And?" Paige asks. She finds she has moved to the edge of her seat. "You asked for a baby, right?"

"Oh . . ." Tom turns red again, though it's less obvious this time in the darker light of the room. "I see why you'd think . . . No." His voice goes softer, as though he wishes he could not speak his next words. "I asked for a fishing empire. And I got it, too—have you ever heard of Empire Fish?"

Paige stares at him, eyes wide.

"You know, with that catchy little jingle?" His voice returns to its normal volume, and in fact, the thrust of his chest implies he feels pride at his words. "Everyone's heard of it: *Empire fish, the fish you wish for when you wish for fish?*"

Paige's lips press hard into a flat line.

"It's not that I didn't want a kid or anything," Tom says, seeming to realize, far too late, what he has said, "but I just wasn't ready yet. Or, I guess, I honestly didn't really want a kid at all, since I never had one with anyone else or anything, and—"

"Just stop talking." Sasha shakes her head. "You're embarrassing me."

"Sorry." Tom takes a deep breath. "Anyway, I wished for an empire, and Petta wished for a child. She said that she wanted to start a new family—one that was honest, and that would bring honor to the Vitaly name."

Honest? Please. Seems like that part of the wish didn't get granted, did it?

"You're here, aren't you?" Sasha says, as though she's read Paige's mind.

"I guess," Paige says, but she's not convinced.

And there is something else she doesn't understand. "If you set the man free, then why did I see him yesterday in the same chains again?"

"What?" Tom shakes his head. "That's impossible. He granted our wishes, and then he vanished," Tom snaps, "just like that."

Paige doesn't understand any of this. If they set the man free, then how did he get trapped again? Where is the room in the brambles? Why hasn't anyone ever mentioned any of this to her? And why—

A sudden *ding-ding-ding* of a cell phone ring interrupts her spiraling thoughts. Tom feels around in his pockets, and, finding nothing, searches the sheets. There is the phone, an old model with a cracked screen, which he presses to his ear.

"Petta?"

Paige's mouth drops. "How did she . . . ?"

"Paige?" Tom says to her mother, and when he looks at Paige, she shakes her head *no*. "Yes, she's here." He mouths *sorry* and then turns his attention back to the phone and nods enthusiastically. "Yes. Mm-hmm. Okay."

"What is she saying?" Paige asks. "Tom, what is she saying?"

Tom puts up a finger, as if to say, *I'll be with you in a minute.* "She's ready for all that? I mean, she's just a kid—"

Petta talks for a long time, and Tom nods again. Paige can make out every few words, especially the ones she's already heard: *man, brambles, wood.* Then Petta's voice goes quiet, and Tom hands the phone over to Paige. "She wants to talk to you."

Maybe I don't want to talk to her. Maybe it's too late for us to talk about any of this.

But Paige takes the phone and puts it to her ear. "Mom?"

"So, you've met him." In the background, the loud squeal of metal on metal, and then a strange thud. "I thought we'd have more time."

We've had eighteen years.

"You can trust him," Petta says. Now Paige thinks she hears the sound of footsteps. "He'll get you where you need to go."

"What do you mean?" Glass breaks in the background, and Paige stands, as if she can somehow see Petta through the porthole window. "Mom, where are you?"

"*There are two kinds of lies, you won't be surprised, short legs and long noses—*"

"Mom? Mom, are you in Toy Palace?"

"*—but no one supposes that there is another much worse than the others—*"

Paige hears the hammer of metal on metal, and then something breaking. A sudden pain blooms between her eyes, and the whole room lights up in a blinding blaze.

"*—and this is the lie—*"

Petta's breathing is slow and steady in the receiver. "I asked you to make her strong," she says, and her voice is the higher pitch of a conversation with a stranger. "Did you do what I asked?"

Paige's entire body burns under the heat of the light. Then her skin begins to heal itself into a hard surface, as though her skin is a shell under which she must hide her soft interior. *Wood,* she realizes when she pushes up her sleeves to face the grainy surface of her arms. *All of me. It's—*

Now she can see him there in the corner, as if the ship is in an adjacent room and the young man is tearing his way through the wall. He is just sitting there, though, with his head hung low and his eyes dully blazing. Behind him is the strange shadow of another person, and when Paige squints, she can see her mother waving. Then Petta turns, as though to respond to someone else, and a girl enters the vision: Lily, the manager from Toy Palace, who is on the ground, but trying to work herself up to her elbows. Paige tries to wave back at them, but she cannot get her wooden arm to move properly.

Only seconds, and then there are more people: Camilla Vitaly in a high-collared coat and a pillbox hat and some men with broad shoulders wearing black t-shirts that say *Security*.

"Mom!" Paige yells, and her scream draws Petta's attention back across the strange divide.

"Don't let them break you," Petta says softly into the phone.

The young man lifts his head and stares up at Petta with a benevolent blankness.

"*—of a toymaker*," he sings mournfully.

The room explodes into a blinding white light. Paige's vision blurs, and she falls, endlessly, as though she is hurtling through the endless void of the universe itself.

PART THREE

CHAPTER TWENTY-ONE

THE FAIRY

YOU ARE RETURNED.

And she is here, too—the little marionette—sleeping on the bed where once your mother sang you songs of your new homeland:

Over the many starry seas,
to the land of toys and pure belief,
where none of our wars could make their home,
so sleep, my son, and never roam.

Where *he* slept, too, with his golden trimmed tricorn hat still angled over one eye and the jaunty velvet coat discarded over a chair above the crumpled silk stockings. They are gone now, taken with him, while his hat remains on the cushion. Medoro, Medoro, Medoro. How he always fluffed his curly hair with a chocolate paw; how his gold silk tail made him so proud that he covered it when it rained. How he stood so straight with his chin held so high that you asked if he was trying to nose the stars. How he probably lay, on the Day of Death, with his mouth crooked wide like he went down laughing, laughing, laughing at the fairy who had turned him back to wood. All of them, heaps of them, bones of them, so that, when you look to the window, they are walled around you, tombing you, the one who lived in order to never live again. Locked in a room. Sucked dry of your fairy power. Unable to travel back to this world. Not caring, for what else waited beyond that for you? Or perhaps he is a devil now, possessed by their terrible powers, a fate much worse—

"What happened?" the little marionette asks.

She sits up and rubs her eyes, and then she removes her hands and looks down at the wooden palms in surprise. "Oh," she says, stretching her fingers. "I'm . . ."

"It was necessary," you say, your voice dull and hoarse. "If you want to stay here—"

"And where is here, exactly?"

You look, again, to the shrouded window. "This was the Land of Toys."

"The . . . ?"

You turn away from the window and sit down on the bed. "We came here for respite, and they welcomed us. We lived together for many years, with our magic and theirs sewn together like a rope." You entwine your fingers. "All the easier for them to hang us with it when they came."

She rises from the bed and puts a wooden hand on your arm, and your skin lights in a warm blue glow under her touch. "Who?"

You nod your chin to the window, where she walks and looks out on the limbs. Then, as though she can read your mind, she lifts the latch and pushes her weight against the glass. For so many years you did this, threw yourself against the panes, yet only those strong arms might swing the window open and dent the mountain of bones cursed to keep you in this tomb. Her mother wished her strong all of those years ago, and she is, though you doubt there is any strength enough for what's to come.

The marionette looks out on the world beyond and gasps.

You should stand beside her and face your fate—face what you and your people have brought here—but you turn away and look, again, to the chair. He used to say that you were his light, and that if you ever left the Land, it would be like the sun vanishing forever behind the horizon. But you brought nothing but darkness, nothing but death—

"I don't understand."

You imagine his hand on your shoulder, the fingers latching gently under your bone and creeping you up off the bed. Obediently, you rise to his touch, and he kisses your forehead. *All is not lost, Alexio.*

You walk slowly to the window, and he is there, beside you, holding you up. Standing with you as you look past the hole in the mound of the dead, as you look out on the burning fires of the wooden toys there who make fodder for this dark world's only light, as you face what you have done: metal melting from the bones in the giant cauldrons, great clouds of wood smoke, sparks like fireworks announcing the never-ending funeral. Many of the trees have been turned to charred stumps, but the ones that remain tower over the horizon, reminding you that in this land, you and the marionette are as small as you feel.

And there, flitting like hornets around the hive, are your enemies.

"They were once fairies," you whisper.

Now, their wings have been inlaid with metal, like terrible bats tipped with lion claws of sharpened steel. A younger fairy lays on the ground beside one of the cauldrons, screaming as the metal burns into his self-healing skin. Their clothes are metal and wood, chipped from the bodies of these same toys that lie just inches from your face. They have added accessories, too, which you have not seen before: mechanical glasses on their eyes that seem to zoom their vision, power packs around their waists, and machines on their feet that thrust them into the air to counter the weight of their wings.

"So many species of us," you continue, your voice full of longing for your fellow fae you never knew. "It is said that when they could not find the Great White Light, the Deathsprites drew Red Fire from the living things around them. Once ready to move on, they took Red Fire from the center of celestial bodies at work releasing energy and heat. What I mean is that they make them glow—and die."

"And those toys down there . . . ?"

"The Patched. They have been torn apart and pieced together, run through with Red Fire that controls their minds, and set to the Deathsprites' terrible work . . ."

They are made in their image, so that now, between the fires, run the giant creatures of this new realm, dogs so large they might take you in their teeth and clamp down until your light no longer shines. They have been cobbled together from stuffed toys that once danced in the center of the town, joyfully swinging their padded arms and legs and heads with yarn hair that undulated beautifully to the beat. Their eyes are mismatched goggles that roll in their wooly sockets. Their mouths house teeth made from wooden stakes sharpened from doll bones.

"I can't . . ." the little marionette cries, and she turns away and puts her head on your chest.

She has not even left the room, and she is lost in grief. How can you make her do this? Who knows what other horrors await you in the space between the castle and the other side. Who knows . . .

Your gaze slips down, across the bones, where, between gaps, you spot the wooden bricks they glued to make the walls, which now are cracked and flaked. Then you look up, above the mound, to where the plastic battlements they painted gold are topped with azure parapets. The fabric scrap flags, also bright blue with brilliant flares, speak of a wind that long ago was stilled into a stifling heat. You cannot see the wooden drawbridge, but you wonder if it's laid down in surrender over tin basins long since dried of their fake moats, or if the plastic links still hold their tight rejection of the Deathsprites they could not stop. At least the castle stands against the heat and smoke—and that is something that the toys would honor, if they lived.

"There, there," you say, and your voice is his.

"What am I supposed to do here?" she asks. Then she lifts her head suddenly to pat her cheek and exclaims, "I can't even cry!"

"You are a toy of this land now," you say. "There are many things you can do that are new, and many old things that are lost. Not forever, I hope—but for a time."

"How much time?"

You squeeze her shoulders. "Enough to determine whether we might separate this world from the other forever."

Paige sits down on the bed and pulls a pillow to her lap. "I don't understand any of this. How are the Deathsprites even crossing over in the first place?"

You look to the horizon, where somewhere far from here, you know the crossing place is well-protected. "There is a stone they took me through, which before their use was rumored to carry toys across this universe to another world. But the stone cannot transport fae—at least, not in the way the Deathsprites hoped. Can you imagine when they first awoke in that silly toy shop, metal bones and fiery blood replaced by objects your grandfather sold?"

"But you did not change into a toy—you crossed through as yourself."

You shrug and do not say, *I wish I hadn't. I wish I'd tried to cross the realms and failed, joined Medoro, all those toys now Patched or lost for good*— "It seems the Flare, which I used first to bring my people here, allowed me passage as myself despite the stone. Unlike their Red Fire, Flare is an inner source, as though we're pitchers for a wellspring of the soul. It's hard to comprehend . . . And even I am starting to suspect that maybe they are all connected. Perhaps the stone is very old—not of this land, but ours. Perhaps we gave it to the toys so very long ago that memory of such a gift is lost . . ."

Your eyes move to the rubble that was once the town, where bones and wooden bricks and splinters mingle with bent metal in great heaps, but then you wrench your gaze past it again and do not look back. Instead, you look to Paige, who stares down at her wooden arms around the pillow.

"Why do the Deathsprites keep going, if they can't cross over as themselves? What good is it to be a toy?" she asks.

"Oh, child." You cannot face her sadness for long, and you cannot see the town again, so you look up at the painting on the ceiling, *the garden where I'll meet you when you dream.* "Nothing is stronger than the bond of true belief. When the children of Earth press those fairy toys to their chests, they put all their hopes and dreams into them—and they don't even notice the Deathsprites feeding off them at the same time. Deathsprites come back from Earth much stronger, and once they figure out how to come through the portal without being turned . . ." You point weakly behind you, toward the column of red light in the distance and a lake you cannot see from here. "I do not know what work they do at that horizon, but I know that if they finish it, this world will be your fate, and that of every other planet in your realm."

"But why would my family help them do such a thing?" Paige cries.

"Oh, Paige." You shake your head. "Success. Fame. Power. These things don't just fall into a family's lap. The Deathsprites sent a message and a pendant, which for these years has hung on a Vitaly neck to bring the wearer power to persuade—a very human use, I'd say. First your grandfather, and then your father, and now—"

"I know it." She clutches her own bare neck. "But I still don't understand why they would risk their death . . ."

"Because they do not know what we do: that the Deathsprites never leave a world alive. And the Vitalys will never know it, not until they are the very same bones that pile this castle's walls."

She cries out, and her fingers go to her cheeks again, searching for some outlet for the pain you know so well it wraps you like a cloak.

"Did my mother know about this?" she asks wildly. "Did she know, and not tell me, for all of this time?"

"Your mother?" Oh, Petta, your sweet savior. "They would never think her worthy of such a prized necklace, nor even the knowledge of it. And remember, she thought she'd set me free. She thought I might return and fight . . ." How naïve you were. How hopeful. "But they found me almost immediately and brought me back."

Paige shakes her head. It's all too much, a plunge into the deepest waters of your failure, all the things you wish you'd known—*But it is not too late,* Medoro's voice reminds you, though you don't believe him. "So, you crossed the realms again—what next?" she asks, though you wish now to stop this dreadful tale. "You called for my mother?"

"I tried, but she was out of reach, slipping from my mind with every move. I still do not know what returned her, finally, to this place—and why she did not explain everything to you once she had set her mind on it."

The marionette is very quiet. She is always thinking, this child, and her thoughts are like minnows darting through your own blue waters. You might read them, but he is in your head, too, reminding you that to have the power of a prince is not the same as acting like one.

Finally, she squares her shoulders and says, "Maybe she just couldn't find the words."

You look out on the land together and listen to the roaring flames and their sparking tongues and the barks of the monstrous dogs as they bite at each other's heels. To leave this room is to say, *I shall throw myself upon this fire, so that I might be consumed.* And you would, without a second thought—but you have made a promise.

You can hear Petta's voice as if she is in the room, or in your very own head. *I wish for a child, Alexio—a child who is honest and honorable. And she will need to be strong—stronger than you, or me, or any of us.*

This I shall do, in return for my freedom. I shall make her as strong as a beam that cannot be broken. Strong as a tree that can weather the storm.

You sounded so confident, but deep down, you knew there was no such stuff from which to carve a human child.

Maybe a toy, though.

Now that you might do.

CHAPTER TWENTY-TWO

PAIGE

Alexio will not leave the bedroom—cannot leave it—and so, Paige opens the tinplate door herself and steps into the empty hallway.

As soon as she hears the click, she presses her back against the cool wall and takes a deep breath. When she first woke up, she was consumed by the reality of this land, its bones and smoke and terrible monsters, but now, in the silence of the dim and dusty hallway, there is only the strange feeling of air breezing down a wooden windpipe and into the central chest beneath her shirt, where, instead of two expanding lungs, the cavity fills and empties purposefully.

Does she even need air to breathe?

She exhales and then stops herself from inhaling; her vision swims, so that the plastic bricks that make up the interior walls make a kaleidoscope swirl. Apparently, she does need oxygen—but why would she, if she is a toy?

Next, she presses her hand beneath the University of Wintroster sweatshirt to her heart. There is something beating there, but it feels different, like a hammer tapping lightly on a wooden board. So, all of her organs are made of wood—whichever organs remain, that is. And even her fingers feel the sensation of wood differently, the way things feel through a thick leather glove.

After she excavates the evidence of her vitals, she moves to the surface of her body, which feels smooth and dry, like the workbench back home. There are grooves raised in the hull of her chest, the jutting hip bones under her pants, and the same angles of her face, though she will need a mirror to be certain. Her hair is the same long blond strands, but now they are strings, able to be braided or tied back but not brushed.

I'm still me.

Now she can move. Paige steps cautiously over the smooth plastic floor to a carpet woven from blue and gold strings, which seems to have been made on a larger version of a child's weaving loom. Paige had one when she was a kid, given to her at the only birthday party she ever had by a girl whose name she can't remember. It had calmed her, the pulling over and under of the nylon loops, but she had always needed Petta's help finishing the outside with the crochet hook.

Across the carpet is another room, and Paige takes a long breath into her strange lungs and remembers, again, that her body is a foreign land on whose shores she has only just arrived, before turning the handle to open the door.

Dust.

Stale air that she can identify as oak, warmed plastic, and the metallic tinge of blood—so she still has her senses, or at least some of them.

The room is darker than the hallway, and she hesitates at the door before plunging inside. Immediately, she recognizes that these are servants' quarters, with long tables where various items for the castle were left in various stages of preparation. A glass vase with plastic flowers arranged on one side, perpetually sprightly. A pile of linen napkins, some folded beside them in a neat stack. A dress hanging on a mannequin with a human form—no, a Fae form—which, on closer inspection of the thick blue velvet, appears to be a queen's formal gown. The style reminds her of the dress shop at the Renaissance Festivals where she and Petta used to occasionally sell their wares—if they could get on the artisan list in time and manage to be in the right state when the Faire began.

This must have belonged to Alexio's mother.

She cannot imagine what he is going through—what he has gone through for all of these years. Everyone he knew was either dead or patched into a demonic murderer. His planet, sucked dry and spit out into the hopeless universe. No wonder he sits on his bed and stares out the window, gaze turned inward, ears echoing the last words of everyone he loved. She would do the same.

But her family is not gone, and as Paige circles the room in search of weapons, she finally turns her thoughts to what she has avoided thinking about: her mother.

The lies of a toymaker.

What was her mother doing in Toy Palace? And how did she manage to help Alexio cross back into this world—unless, maybe, he never needed anyone's help at all? Maybe he did not want to come back? Maybe she forced him?

She has a way of getting what she wants.

And I have a way of letting her.

She wants to scream, to pound her fists against something breakable until it crumbles into dust, but what good would that do? This castle does not hold the answers of why Petta kept the truth of their family hidden from Paige for all of these years, or why, on a whim, she returned them to Wintroster without preparing Paige for what she would find there. And the bigger question: why is Paige suffering for her mother's deception by becoming the very object of her mother's making?

Why has she become just another silly wooden toy?

There are no answers here. Focus, Paige. Focus on surviving so that you can demand these answers when you see her again.

The objects of the room are an interesting blend of real materials—wood, clay, porcelain—and toy objects like plastic plates, bed frames, and drawers that are so light Paige accidentally rips one of them out of the frame and sends a collection of marbles and coloring pages flying in the air. The pages careen like birds, zipping first one way and then the other, while the marbles hit loudly and then roll under the other furniture, never to be unsettled again.

Quiet. Who knows what Patched toys are patrolling this castle, or worse, the Deathsprites—

Paige is so deep in thought that she stumbles over a body before she can realize what her boots have touched. Here are the bones of a Fae, long, humanlike, with nothing left around them but a blue stain. When Paige looks closely, she can see tiny shimmers of silver-blue sprinkled there, barely reflecting what light comes in from the half-covered window. And now that she is looking down, she realizes that this Fae is not alone—there is another body beside it, or rather, half of a body, this one the skirt and shoes of a ceramic scullery maid. At her waist are the jagged lines of her violent break, severing her in two and allowing whatever Deathsprite attacked her to carry her chest and head away for assembly.

How did they pick which half? Paige wonders, and then she feels bad for thinking it.

By the fireplace directly beside the maid is a third body, so small Paige almost misses it: the very tiniest nesting doll, cracked open like the maid but with neither half taken afterward. Was this nesting doll a child, as it looks to be, or was it a full-grown adult toy trapped forever into the stunted bowling pin form of its creation?

These are questions for Alexio, and she should go back, for she will need to convince him to leave his bedroom before she goes any further. And besides, there are no weapons in this room, unless you count a butter knife, sewing scissors, or wire cutters one of the servants had used to trim the plastic flowers' ends, but perhaps he will know where to find some.

"I'm sorry," she whispers to the bodies and bones, and then she turns away. Death will surround her from this point forward, but it's life that she must find—if not for this land, then for her own.

You'll have to be strong, she thinks, wrenching open the door.

The entire thing, including the metal hinges, comes off the frame in her fist.

CHAPTER TWENTY-THREE
LILY

THE SONG OF THE MAN WHO once sat in the metal chair rings in her ears as an absence, so that when Lily moves and rattles the chain hooked around her ankle, it seems to accompany the missing words—*the lie of the toymaker.* Oh, Lily knows all about lies now, doesn't she? She frowns at the welt on her skin, the chain, the matching silver links keeping Petta Vitaly captive on the other side of the room.

"I still can't believe I never even checked what was up here," Lily says.

"Don't blame yourself." Petta sits against the wall and leans her neck back, so that her silver hair cascades almost to her leather belt. She seems to be inspecting something on the ceiling—or, Lily realizes, drifting into her own set of regrets. "You couldn't have known. That's just the echo of his voice in your head—it will fade, I promise."

"I didn't even try." Lily's mouth is dry, and the words feel strange on her sandpaper tongue. "I didn't even ask what was up here—"

"Why would you have?" Petta drags her head upright and looks at Lily. Even in the dim lighting, Lily can make out the sternness of her straight-lined lips and the furrowing of her brow. "My sister has a way of convincing people they're on some kind of toy crusade, set on a mission to save the world, one animatronic puppy at a time. She's good at what she does—and she thinks that for her skills, she will be rewarded."

"By whom?"

Petta doesn't answer, and Lily knows that she has edged, again, toward the dark chasm in which the woman across the room holds the secrets of wherever—and whoever—is on the other side of that bright blue divide.

And Camilla holds them too. Lily saw it this time, as the security guards tied them up and Camilla watched from the door. The high ledge of her chin. The narrow, beady eyes. The thin line of her lipsticked frown, an arrow of red. The way she said, *Oh, Lily,* as though she was the one who had betrayed Camilla instead of the other way around. And then she'd just left them there, without another word, gone to do who-knows-what about the blue fairy disappearing to who-knows-where. That was how insignificant they were to her—like bits of dirt under her blood-red fingernails.

"At least your daughter seems to be okay," Lily says to break the silence. She thinks of the girl—Paige—looking up at her from where she'd fallen on the ground that day in Toy Palace, her face blank from confusion and fear and the betrayal she had only just glimpsed on the portrait wall but did not yet understand.

"Okay?" Petta laughs dryly, then coughs. "I've sent her to the most terrible place in the universe . . . And I didn't even tell her why."

"I'm sure she'll figure it out." Lily shifts to try to get comfortable on the hardwood floor, but her tailbone aches so badly that she shifts, again, to the other side. "She seems pretty smart—just a little lost, that's all."

"Well, she would be." Petta shakes her head. "I don't know why I didn't tell her . . . Not even when we were on the way, and this outcome was so certain I could see it the way I see a pattern of a toy so clearly in a piece of wood."

"The truth is hard." Lily thinks of her parents. Have they traced her to the pool hall? To Rashi? Has her best friend told them she went to work—and if so, have they demanded the police raid Toy Palace? Can they, when they apparently have no jurisdiction in this store?

And while she's thinking about it, has anyone broached the subject of *with whom* she might have disappeared?

But Rashi would never tell them . . .

Would she?

"You like her, don't you?"

Lily's face scrunches up, and her nose wrinkles. "Rashi?"

"Who?" Petta shakes her head. "I meant Paige—my daughter. You seem to have developed a fondness for her."

"I've barely spoken to her." Now Lily's cheeks are burning, and she is grateful for the sparse light.

"Sometimes you just know." Petta closes her eyes. "She never had the chance to stay in one place . . . to get to know anyone. I regret that the most."

"Why didn't you just stop traveling, then?" Lily asks, trying to change the subject. She presses her cool palms to her cheeks. "Give her a chance at a normal life?"

Petta looks like she is trying to decide how to answer—that chasm, again—but instead of speaking, she taps her ears. Lily listens for footsteps in the hallway, but she doesn't hear anything—nothing but that eerie silence.

"You can't hear them?" Petta asks.

"Who?"

But now she can hear it—engines, many of them, revving somewhere far in the distance, like an angry hive of bees.

"It's time to go," Petta announces, as though she has just finished tea at a fancy party and has placed her napkin delicately on the table next to her plate. Then, she rises from the ground, stretches her back, and ties her hair into a low ponytail with a band from her wrist.

"Uh, I'm not sure if you've noticed, but we're prisoners here . . ."

Petta bends down, puts her fingers around the chain around her ankle, and pulls. Lily expects her to grunt, or even whimper as the metal links bite into her skin, but instead, the chain breaks off like it's made of plastic—cheap plastic, at that.

"How did you just . . . ?" Lily shakes her head. Is she hallucinating? Is it the thirst? The hunger? "That's impossible."

"You'd better get used to it, Lily." Petta crosses the space between them, and then she is there, at Lily's ankle, releasing her bond. There is no strain in her face as she does it—just a mild determination, as though her mind has already left this room and drifted across town to whoever is driving those cars. Once the chain is off, Petta puts out her hand to help Lily to her feet. Lily's legs ache from the sudden strain, and she feels lightheaded, like she is going to pass out.

"Easy." Petta puts her arm under Lily's to hold her up. Her muscles are hard under her shirt, and Lily wonders how she could be so strong. "Do you know how to fight?"

". . . Fight?" Lily shakes her head no.

"That's okay." Petta slowly releases Lily from her hold, as though she is testing whether she can stand. When Lily stays upright, Petta takes a step back and rolls up her sleeves. Then she puts her hands squarely on Lily's shoulders, the palms just a light touch through the padding of the blazer, and looks deep into her eyes. "What you're about to see might shock you—that's normal. Just remember that you just watched a man and a girl on the other side of town disappear through a break in space to another world—and set the bar for reality there, okay?"

". . . I . . ."

But Petta does not wait for her to answer. In one quick move, she pivots her body, puts her hand on the door handle, and wrenches the entire piece of wood off its hinges like it's a prop in a movie instead of a heavy slab. The door flies across the room and hits the wall, where it smacks and then falls backward with an echoing boom.

Guards yell from somewhere down the hallway.

Petta steps through the doorway in a flash of her gray ponytail.

Lily closes her eyes.

Somewhere out of sight, there is the heavy thud of fists hitting bone and the fall, fall, fall of bodies.

CHAPTER TWENTY-FOUR

THE DOCTOR

FINTAN WAKES TO A SQUARE OF gray sky through his cell window. No birds—never birds, anymore—but a toy plane passes and then doubles back on patrol. *Close enough,* he thinks, and throws off the thin wool blanket that passed, in his dreams, as the Flare's delicate embrace. His feet meet the ridges of the stone etchings carved into the plastic of the toy floor, and his toes wiggle. His pants look dirtier than before, as gray as the sky, and he wonders again if the whole kingdom has lost its blue glow under its occupation.

Is there even a kingdom left at all?

Then he notices the smoke in the bottom right corner of the thick plastic window. *The castle,* he thinks, and a small smile plays at his lips. *So, the Prince is finally back.* Everyone said he was dead, but no one knew what Fintan knew—what he had earned to know, with the work he did.

Don't think of it, he thinks casually, but he cannot fool himself. Not when he saw the smoke from the castle the day it happened, not when he was here in this very cell just breaking through a rough piece of dried meat with his teeth like a dog, like he had all the time in the world.

And he did—twenty years, fifteen for good behavior, but

let's be honest, he never knew how to behave. Then, all of a sudden, the descent of the ship, like a great red cloud storming over a clear afternoon, and the smoke, everywhere, like the whole world was on fire.

"What's happening?" he called to his guards, but they never responded. They had left to fight—to die—at the side of the Prince.

For three days, no one came. No food passed through the door. Prisoners died—many prisoners—and the smell that drifted through the hall and into his room was worse than Fintan could even describe. He lay on his bed and thought of his hideout, dug under his backyard and covered in grass he'd stolen from his neighbor for its dense and protective thickness, and how, if the Deathsprites discovered it, they would ransack his poor creations.

Well, they did discover it.

And then they came for him.

The door at the end of the hall's slam was the first clue that the prisoners were no longer alone. Fae screamed for something to eat, for a bit of water. Toys banged their metal and plastic and wooden fists on their doors. Languages blurred, the high-pitched chatter mixing with the low hums of the Flaresong.

Shoes tapped down the line.

The sound stopped at Fintan's cell.

He sat up, and the world spun. He clutched at his bed, and the sheets came with him, a tangled mess of stale blanket and Fae. By the time the Deathsprites got the door unlocked, though, he had managed to sit up and prop his leg in a cocky *you-don't-scare-me* stance.

The Deathsprite who entered was as tall as the ceiling, with a terrible grimace face more dog than Fae. He had wings that he shook open like a bat, if the bat had inlaid metal on his mammal bones, and sharp talons at the ends that still dripped with the blue blood of a now-dead Fae. His clothes were scant, just a red cloth tied around his waist and smaller kerchiefs at his elbow and knee joints, some long-forgotten Fae custom Fintan couldn't place. Impossible, that they had all come from the same single Fae line, splintered so many centuries ago that they were as dissimilar as Flare and fire.

"Fintan Blake?" the sandpaper voice growled.

"At your service," he said, giving the newcomer a little smile. *I'm about to die,* he thought, but he was less scared than he imagined he would be.

"We found your workshop."

Fintan couldn't help smiling a little. "Incredible, isn't it?"

The Deathsprite gave a *Hmph.* "The experiments you did there . . ."

"Ah, my Patched. No one liked those very much, did they?" Fintan waved a hand to indicate the cell. "They couldn't see my vision."

"I can."

Fintan cocked his head. "What is it you want me to do, exactly?"

"Whatever you want." The Deathsprite flexed, and all of the metal pieces along his wings snapped in a sharp *clang.* "But no Flare magic—only Red Fire. I want to see the delicious glow of their eyes. Understood?"

"Quite clearly. Only . . ." Fintan stood, even as his legs threatened to collapse him back on the floor. His back straightened and cracked. "I'll need a bigger room."

"Room?" The Deathsprite laughed. "This whole building is yours. Use the survivors—or kill them, if they're no longer of use. But be sure to drain their power—we cannot afford to waste a drop."

"Thank you," Fintan said. His fingers itched, feeling, already, the proximity of his creations. "I look forward to our partnership."

***

Now, he swings open the cell door and leaves his room. Fintan passes the brown plastic beds where his employees sleep fitfully under their own wool blankets, wondering if they will see the smoke and know what he has now realized. Will they speak of it?

Probably not.

They'll be too afraid—and they should be.

At the stairs, he listens for the heavy steps of Deathsprites. Only two or three patrol the halls now, and they're weak, the runts of the pack. Most of the Deathsprites are at the mines, digging at the key to their salvation. And better they are distracted—for Fintan has more important work to do.

Finding no obstacles, he ascends to the basement, where the interrogation chamber has become his other home. His second hand, Gwynn, stands at attention at the door, a clipboard in their hands. They wear the required uniform—a blue prison suit with a white apron on top—and a pair of magnifying glasses tied with blue ribbon around their neck. Today, they have braided their hair in rows, tied at the ends with twist ties probably swiped from the kitchen two floors up, but such petty steals don't bother Fintan—and Gwynn knows it. There have been other *collections*, too—a wrench here, a few nails there—but Fintan knows that this is just part of Gwynn's character, the way that Fintan has his own small quirks . . .

"Doctor." Gwynn hands over the clipboard, and Fintan surveys the charts printed there. "Everything is as we hoped with the newest patient."

"Good." Fintan returns the clipboard. "Today, we add the Red Fire."

"Yes, Doctor."

Fintan enjoys the excitement in Gwynn's face. Long ago, Gwynn was just a reluctant worker bee, trudging metal slabs back and forth, carrying patients to the various testing rooms. And now, look at them—pure anticipation. They follow Fintan to the operation table, where a music box sits with its side removed and its silver heart connected to the wires that lead to kegs of Red Fire lined along the opposite wall. Amazing, how the Deathsprites can replenish their source, a death juice wrung from the citrus skins of their enemies and the lakes of their worlds and even the very core of a conquered planet, to drink themselves and fuel their ships, while the Flare just fell away from the Starsprites and was gone. *Don't think of it,* Fintan tells himself, *or you'll drift again—*

But he is drifting already, and his skin prickles at the warm feeling of his memory. Floating. Absorbing. How he'd do anything to get that feeling back—*and that's what you are doing,* he reminds himself sternly. He takes up a pair of tweezers and secures another tube to the music box. *Focus. Focus on your work.*

Other workers drift in, sleep still there in their glowing blue eyes. They've all dreamed of it—always dream of it—and on waking, have had to wrench that world away. He must earn them, each morning—but he's more than capable, and they want to live, of course. Then there are those who have sampled Red Fire, who take less swaying to participate in Fintan's vision—but they are prone to violence, harder to control. Day by day, their numbers grow, and lines between the Fae grow blurry . . .

"Listen up," Fintan says, his voice filling the room. "Today, another new creation will be born."

He looks, again, at his lovely child, which is already so much larger than him. The music box, and above it, the melded head of a stuffed rabbit, where the mouth has been inlaid with over one hundred carefully stitched fangs. Delicate work, those sews, but as Gwynn always says, Fintan has the slightest touch in the kingdom.

"Begin the awakening."

Gwynn nods curtly and walks to the switch. With a strong pull, the power shifts from OFF to ON, and the red juice flows through the tubes. Like a determined rivulet, Fintan thinks, and again, he is drifting on a sea of memory. *Not now. Not here.* He focuses, again, on the silver box, which has begun to play a sad melody of slow and uneven notes. Red liquid fills the cavities. It absorbs into the metal, the head. The music grows louder, more untuned, like the wild fists of a child are banging on the keys of a grand piano. The rabbit's mouth chatters.

"Enough!" Fintan announces. With a clench of his fist, he signals Gwynn to shift the power switch to OFF again, and then he points to one of his workers to remove the tube.

The Patched rabbit-box is silent.

Everyone waits.

Finally, the stuffed head begins to shake, not violently, but like anyone who's just been woken from a deep and lengthy sleep. Its mouth opens and closes, finds itself unable to speak.

The lids flutter open in surprise.

"You've done it again, Doctor," Gwynn whispers proudly.

From the head of the operating table, the red eyes glare.

CHAPTER TWENTY-FIVE

THE FAIRY

THE CASTLE IS A TOMB.

The marionette—*Call me Paige*—has returned and is standing in the hallway, while you stand at the precipice of the door, the smell of burned wood on your nose, the sight of the stripped blue wallpaper like gauze from a wound in your eyes, the sound of nothing but dust drifting to the empty wooden chairs where merriment once rose from the toys and fairies who gathered there. You reach for the Flare that once ran through the castle like water through pipes, that should rise up the walls to enter your feet and your hands as they stretch for the power your people create. Joy into joy. But nothing is there—only the bit of the Flare left inside of you, given the day you headed the crown, that winks like a star so distant it can barely be seen. Yet it brought you here, didn't it? It brought you home.

Paige puts out her hand, and you take it. The wood is dry and firm. She seems more confident now, like the wood has carried to her very soul, and you hope that she will be strong enough to carry you when your own light fades.

"Come," she says, tugging you on. "We can't stay here."

You look at Medoro's hat on the chair, but you cannot bring yourself to take it. You tell your feet to move, and they do.

One step. Two. The sound is the soft echo of leaves falling on frosted ground.

"If they are the Deathsprites," she says, "then what are you?"

On the right is your mother's door, the largest, made of gold and gemmed in blue-colored glass, with figures carved by the finest makers in the Land of Toys. *I need nothing so fine,* she said, but the door brought her joy— and joy from a queen of the fairies means joy for them all.

"We were once called Starsprites, when we lived in our own kingdom. But now we are called Flarewhispers. Or we were, when there were any of us to be named."

You drag your eyes from the door and move on, ignoring the temptation to just go in for a minute, an hour, to lay on her bed and weep until the Deathsprites come for you.

"I don't get it—"

"Imagine the sun," you say, your mind awash in the bright blue beams. "If you were to live there, you would always be bathed in that glorious heat."

You take a right and pass the servants' quarters. Their beds will be empty, their plain white covers still thrown where they left them when in the night the Deathsprites came. *Don't think about it,* you tell yourself and continue to walk.

"But if you left," you say, "and the beams were put out, and all you had was the magic that you, yourself, could make, then it would not be a star, but rather a Flare, whispered in the dark of a universe that seeks to blow you out."

"Starsprites," she repeats.

You nudge her down another hallway, and there are the steps, where the banging metal outside echoes up and back again.

"But you don't have wings like them."

"We did not need them," you say, leading the way down the steps, trying not to think of the time when you used to touch the banister and feel the echoes of the Flares others emitted as they jubilantly made their journeys. "Not until we had to leave."

Your mind drifts to home. Not this home, but the one where you nestled into the warmth of the never-ending Flare, which ran over your realm like a river. How you lay in it, letting the sweet joy of its water drift you into blissful oblivion. If you close your eyes and concentrate, you can trick yourself into believing you're back there, and that your own weak heart is beating in rhythm with the great blue might. Then you remember how you brought your people here, how, when you looked around, your home was gone, and in its place, this Land of Toys . . .

You'd thought it was a coincidence, yet now you wonder . . .

The sudden blink . . .

The change of worlds . . .

"I feel so sad when I think—" Paige stops and cocks her head.

You listen, and now you can hear what her wooden ears have already detected: reverberations on the lower steps.

"Something is coming," she says. Her voice is soft but high. She is scared, and you remember feeling this way, before you had nothing left to lose.

"Run," you say, and you shove her back the way you've come. "Run fast—"

But the steps are coming faster, faster, faster, and you know that you will not make it. You reach the landing and give Paige another push, and then you turn, your Flare beaming in your chest, to face whatever terrible beast this place has made.

What comes first is the lights, gray-white beams through the dust of your people. Then the hood, clapping at the body, revealing, in each yawn, hundreds of teeth. Then the windshield, its beady red eyes, its wiper lashes, wide and raging at the intruders in its hall.

"Is that a car?" Paige asks, and you realize that she has come back to you.

"I told you to run—"

No time. The Patched car bumps its wheels over the last of the stairs and lunges for you, so that the great hood mouth should swallow you in a bite. But Paige pushes your shoulders down, your whole body down, and she is so much stronger than you knew, so that you find yourself lying flat on the ground and the metal underbelly of the car in the air above you. On the bottom of the car are pieces of other toys, stuck there during their own demise, and you put a hand up as though to pick the bones from the frame.

"Do something," Paige says loudly in your ear. "Remember who you are."

Who you are.

Are you?

With the hand that is already raised, you reach for the Flare and find it, again, in yourself. Blue light beams from your palm, and the car, in midair, falls apart. The pieces rain down the hallway—wheels bouncing, frame sliding, lights smashing into puddles of glass like raindrops on a sidewalk.

"Whoa," Paige says. She stands up and pulls you with her. "Why didn't you mention you could do that?"

The Flare in your chest blinks weakly. Paige sees it, too, and her face falls.

"It's dying out, isn't it?"

"And me."

Paige opens her mouth again as if to speak some comforting word, but there is nothing she or anyone else can say.

You are the last, the only, and all you can see, when you look at yourself in the mirror of the hallway, is a ghost.

"You're not dead yet," a little voice cries out from the wreck.

Paige startles and takes a step back, but you stand still as stone. You know that voice. You have sat with that voice in the quiet hours, when the chain felt heaviest, and allowed it to give you hope.

"Cricket?"

There she is, the little darling. Plastic body small as a teardrop diamond, plastic legs like oars dipping into the water of the wreckage. She hops to a headlight and shakes off the dust that has gathered like a frost in an early morning field.

"But I tell you, Prince Alexio, that you will be dead soon if you don't remember the gift you have been given."

"I don't understand," you say. You look to your chest and its fading star.

"This." Cricket leaps to your chest and settles over the Flare. "You fairies think the Flare is a spring, and that one must sit close to it to absorb its powers. But the truth is that the Flare lives inside of you, like a battery waiting to be charged. And you might charge it, Alexio—and live. If you want to."

"Of course he wants to, silly little cricket," Paige says.

Cricket does a quick jump to face the marionette. "Don't even get me started on you, Miss Paige. Your wooden appendages say enough, anyway. Lying to your mother. Lying to Alexio."

"To me?" you ask.

"And lying to yourself. Oh, that is the worst of it—to not even have the fidelity of your very own soul." Cricket shakes her head in disappointment.

Paige leans in and whispers loudly, "I don't think I like her very much."

"Don't even—" Cricket cocks her head and listens. Then she leaps, again, like a clock hand wound backward, and says to you, "There is something else coming. We must move, Alexio. There are no slow hours here."

Cricket pushes her feet through your shirt, so that you feel the little pins of her feet. You take Paige's hand and run, again, down the hallway, and to the stairs, which this time do not light or echo. You do hear the sound that Cricket heard, though, as the castle door slams shut somewhere down on the first floor.

"Should we—?" Paige asks.

You descend, still, for you have no choice—this is the only passage to freedom. The sound downstairs is louder, a sort of chaotic rolling about. A glass shatters. Something falls from a wall.

"I don't want to—" Paige tries to say, backing up, but you pull her off the stairs and into the hallway, where you put yourself between her and whatever you will face.

At first you don't see them, for they are something that is hard to look at, an abstract painting of various shapes and colors. Then they move, whirl rather, and you see that they are penguin wobblers who have been painted over as clowns. The mouths move in animatronic gnashing of cherry-red lips, and their hair, rainbow twirls of wire, spark electric threats in the dark hall. They settle as one, move as one, like someone is flipping their switch. Now they stay still; now they tumble down, their heads almost to the floor, and then swing up again into their same position.

"I hate clowns," Cricket says.

The painted white eyes of the clown wobblers all stare at her above their cheeky grins. The pupils, under the heavy liner, flash back and forth between you and the marionette. Then they swing forward again, this time staying angled to the side so that they can roll right toward you.

"Alexio, can't you—?" Paige asks.

And you could, but rather you can't, for the Flare is still flickering lowly. You put your hand out, but no magic leaps.

"Cricket?" Paige asks uncertainly.

"I am nothing but a plastic bug," Cricket says flatly. You feel her dig in deeper, as though walling herself for the coming storm.

The first clown is almost to you, and this close, you can see the penguin paint beneath. The wide, innocent eyes. The perky beak. Can he still feel what moves his body makes? Or has his form been revived without his soul, which, like a hermit crab shell, holds only the only living piece of the dark magic of the Deathsprites inside?

"Goodbye, little Cricket," you whisper.

And this should be goodbye, but a wooden fist crashes through the green collar of the clown and pulls out a mechanical heart. The wobbler stops moving, and the others, confused, crash into each other like train cars stopped suddenly on the track. *Crack, crack, crack* go the fists of the little marionette. The wobblers in the back try to roll away, but Paige is faster, and soon they, too, are like eggshells discarded from the mechanical yolks.

Now she stands in the wreckage of the wobblers, staring down at her hands as though they are gloves borrowed from someone else.

"Well done, Alexio." Cricket's grip loosens. "You made yourself a little warrior, hmm?"

Paige drops her fists.

"Let's go," you tell her, though you know you should say more—say anything. You remember how he reached for you, that first night, and how you pulled away. All you knew was the solitary life of the fairy, reborn again in the Flare, and all you wanted was to drift in the waters of it until your time came. Eternal peace. Eternal solitude. *But you are in our world, Alexio. It is in our bonds that we find life. Allow others to wind you up, and you might just find the music that plays from your soul is much sweeter than the one-hand notes of yourself.*

But now the other hand has gone. Now your notes are flat and slow, so that at any moment the hand will withdraw, and the end will come—in relief.

***

You pass the grand entrance to the Hall, pass the kitchen, pass the lower servants' quarters, all while sustaining a single thought: *do not think at all.* Medoro's voice is there, in the silent rooms, like the flicker of a candle, but you do not follow the light. Move, move, move, you urge, and your feet obey. Around you the cricket and marionette argue—something about lies and wood and a mother's desire—but you understand the undertone of friendship is building there, and so you do not bother to interrupt. All that matters is that, when you are gone, Cricket will comfort the girl, and she will not be alone.

Here is the armory, and now you do turn, quick on the heels, so that the cricket leaps from your shoulder to your head in anxious anticipation.

"We need weapons," you say.

The room is mostly empty, ransacked during the final stand and never replenished. You imagine the great weapons of your ancestors scattered over the Land of Toys, buried under bones like proverbial needles in haystacks no hands will ever touch.

Instead, there is dust, and empty metal hooks, and wooden cases with velvet interiors that smell of the tang of blood, and a few weapons so useless even the dying fairies thought not to bring them into battle. And even if you could find a use for them, how to arm the girl when she has no flare to power the swords and bows that are otherwise useless sticks of metal and stone?

You are dizzy with defeat.

Your head is heavy and old on its ageless neck, and you find yourself sinking onto the wooden bench along the wall. You place your chin between your palms and feel him there, holding you up, whispering: *There is a whole world that is made between two people—a world that cannot be destroyed, for it is always there, as long as one exists to call upon it.* But what if you are a ghost? What if you do not want to call upon that world, for to do so would be to remember all you have lost?

No, you think, throwing your hands from your face, he knew nothing of what was to come—

Wait.

Impossible.

You lift your glowing palm to find an ornate letter M carved in wood. "It cannot be," you say, turning and dropping to your knees to inspect the mark. But you would know it anywhere, for you have read it at the bottom of the notes he left for you whenever he would go to Council, notes that sung the heart words you could only feel. M for Medoro. M for your love. You slide your hand along the bench, then under, where the tips of your fingers meet the familiar phrase that ended every correspondence:

Until we meet again, in this world or the one that we have made.

And there is something else, something large, something that glows toward you now from the dark with the strength of a Flare that one cannot imagine could be destroyed. You pry the sheath away from wood and raise the weapon you would know without your eyes to tell you.

"What is it?" Paige asks, leaning over you to see.

"Starshard," Cricket whispers. "But how . . ."

You raise the glowing sword the way your mother used to lift the symbol of your kingdom high above her head to cheers from Fae and Toys and all who thought the Flare would keep them safe from harm. Seen from any place on land, the glow was so intense that warnings would go out the day before to stop poor sailors from drifting to their deaths or motorists from crashing in the blinding light. Fairies looked, of course, for your eyes had been made to weather such a sight, and many more, a glowing star of them, an endless overwhelm.

But now, Starshard is but a shadow of itself, a flicker of the flame, so that the marionette reaches her hand to run a wooden finger on a dull side of the blade.

"It isn't sharp," she says. "What good is that in battle?"

"It is not a sword," you say. "This piece was carved from home, and carried here, like us, to die."

"But it's not dead," the cricket says, "and you, my prince, aren't either. I hope that you remember, when the time requires it."

You nod, but if you were like Paige you'd find a little shard of wood inside your hollow chest. Then you add the belt around your waist and slide the shard into the sheath again, where thickest leather hides the treasure of your land.

"And me?" Paige asks.

You look around, reject the bow, wave off the shield that needs the Flare to power it. What can you give her, when you know that nothing can be used? Your eyes slip over daggers, finding an axe, which rarely met the hands of Fae who favored delicate designs and swift defeats.

"This one?" Paige lifts the axe and leans a little at its weight. A small adjustment of her back, and now she swings the weapon swiftly, so the whoosh of air feels like it echoes through the caverns of your mind. No, that is not the blade, but memory, as sharp as blood drawn from the wound she has not made.

Cricket cocks her head. "Who wielded it?"

You slide in time, and suddenly the breeze of open-air cools hairs along your cheeks. Your partner, someone high in rank, takes up the axe, while you raise up a sword the trainer recommends.

"That silly thing?" you mock, your feet like cat paws finding flatness in the grass. "What use is force against the Flare, my friend?"

"My prince," your partner says, respect not just in words but also in the eyes that bow below you, "to rely on power we cannot replenish is to make a weakness we do not possess. We once were Starsprites, can be yet again, if we start shouting and not whispering our end."

His words are like a blow, and you are so caught off your guard he swings the axe mere inches from your chest. The blade holds there, caught quickly before it cuts, while in your hand your Flare sword halts its useless flight.

You say, surprised but trying not to be, "You speak a truth I shall consider."

"My prince." He pulls the axe away and bows over the handle, deeply bows, the kind of bow that shows you've earned more than what you had in loyalty, and then he disappears.

That night, Medoro listens as you voice the doubt you did not know you had. What if the Deathsprites find this land and bring their darkness with them? What if they finally blow you out? What of the toys who house you, who have shared their home—and what of him? You used the Flare once to escape them, not to win—and there is so much less of it, and so much more to lose.

"I mark your words," he said, and brought lips down to yours. Then, thoughtfully, he added, "I'll figure out what to do. Should that time come—"

"I hope it won't, but fear it will—"

"—I shall prepare a plan."

And oh, he would have, for his word, under the laugh of joyful pleasure, always had the strength of truth. He never lied. He'd tell you if he disagreed, or if he thought you silly, or if something that you did offended him—though he rarely needed to. If Deathsprites had arrived a few days later, had not come that night to steal you from your bed and kill the queen, had not left these bones, and his, the hat, the wooden sticks, you're sure he would have saved you all—and now you wonder at the words of him, the Fae who warned you they would come. Maybe he knew? Maybe he was one of them? Maybe many were, and since have joined the ranks of those who stitch the dogs and make the metal frames and search for how to break the portal bonds and free their death upon the human world?

"Alexio?" the cricket calls from somewhere else. "Alexio, can you hear me?"

You blink.

You're in the armory.

The marionette is sitting at your side.

"Where did you go?" she asks.

"It holds a different strength," you say, tapping the axe, as though to finish what you'd said so many minutes earlier they've probably forgotten. "I think it suits you."

She nods and hoists you up. Cricket takes the post upon your shoulder, and together, with these bare accouterments, you leave the room and find, again, the endless hall. The carpet dusts the air. The portraits ghost your mind, but you find the strength to leave them in their frames. You have no time for ghosts now, not so close to when the fight will end. *He'd want me in it,* you remind yourself. *He'd want me to be strong.* As strong as he was when he stole this shard, for treason was the call of such an act, especially from mother's own collection. Are there other clues around the castle you might find, if you should look? Is it worth dipping down again, where you might soon be lost?

"Should we go out?" Paige asks, and you are at the door, so tall the top is in the shadows of the entryway.

"We must," you say. "We have no other choice."

"You have a plan?" the cricket asks you softly.

Plan.

He promised one, and you must think of what he would have done.

"A plan of sorts," you say. "Now let us go and find it, if we can."

Paige turns the knob and swings the door.

The burning death smell floods the room before the sight of all the broken toys.

I've changed my mind, I can't—

You turn away and close your eyes.

You must. You have no other choice.

You open them and take a single step.

We once were Starsprites, can be yet again.

Your stomach clenches tight.

Stop whispering, Alexio. Start shouting.

I cannot—

You meet the grim light of the fires.

This is the lie, this is the lie—

You feel the ghosts of toys around you, hear them in the crackle and the hammering of limbs. What good are you to them? You could not save them once, and weaker now, you cannot save the girl, the marionette—

Of the toymaker!

You turn away, but then you see the girl go past, her axe alert, her eyes so wild, a different girl than you met just hours ago, just days ago, just years ago when you created her and granted Petta's wish.

The toymaker, you think again, but this time, you understand what he's been trying to tell you in all of your endless songs.

The toymaker.

The toymaker.

The toymaker.

CHAPTER TWENTY-SIX

THE DOCTOR

THE PATCHED RABBIT-BOX IS MOVED TO the training side of the prison, a place which Fintan mostly neglects to visit and which, today, holds absolutely no interest. It is only the birthing that truly excites him, the time when the creation on the table belongs only to its maker. After that, the being is like a baby bird thrust from the nest, left to fly or fall to the wings of the Deathsprites as they wish. And besides, he has already moved his mind to the next project—a carousel, onto which he imagines he might attach the heads of broken dolls, or maybe jacks, or what about a few shark heads, now that would be interesting—and barely notices as the workers clean the operation table and put away the tools.

One line does catch his attention, though, and now he is pulled up quick from his creative reverie.

"Did you see the smoke?" one of the workers is asking another.

"Yes," the Fae beside him says, "I wonder if it's who we think?"

"What difference does it make?" Gwynn says. "He'll only be found and returned, anyway."

"Just like last time."

They act like they know Prince Alexio, like they personally helped harbor him for the mere hours he managed to come back eighteen years ago, but Fintan knows that even before he was taken, their ruler was as withdrawn from his subjects as any Fae craving the Flare would be. *Prince in name only*, he thinks. *Too busy playing with toys to care that we're all miserable here.*

"Who cares if he's back," Gwynn says. Their face is stone cold. "Wasn't it Prince Alexio who let the Deathsprites take our world in the first place?"

Exactly, Fintan agrees. *Wasn't he the one who wrenched you all away across the universe without a single thought of fighting?*

You think you'd have won? another voice in his head asks. He hasn't heard from this one in a while, and it catches him off-guard.

Of course not. But we would have died valiantly.

And that's better? the voice asks. The voice is like the sound eyes would make when they roll.

Go away.

You'd like that, wouldn't you? He doesn't remember her being so sarcastic. Does time work on voices in your head the way it works on real people? *You'd like it if I left you to your pointless excuse for a creation—when you know exactly what you should be doing with your time.*

Fintan shakes his head. *Shut up. Shut up, shut up, shut up.*

You shut up first. The voice is laughing at him. He wants to slap himself, but that will draw too much attention. *Don't you have some silly carousel to glue?*

Fintan's blood pumps angrily through his arms, which want to hit something, or pull something from the wall, or smash something with the hammer lying too close to his elbow. But he doesn't—he doesn't even twitch.

After all, he's had years of practice.

Yes. He is completely in control.

CHAPTER TWENTY-SEVEN

THE FAIRY

"FIRST, WE NEED A SUBJECT."

You are in the shrubs beside the castle, tucked there with the marionette and the cricket and the weapons stuffed between limbs of the bushes.

"And I'm supposed to . . . ?"

"Yes." You wave your finger quickly, as though bringing down an axe. Then you dip the finger up and down like a needle through the air. "Destroy, and then create."

"Simple as that, huh?"

You like this new Paige, one who speaks her mind.

"Simple as cake, as they say in your world."

Cricket bounces up and down. "It's *easy as pie*, and this certainly doesn't qualify."

"I actually agree with her," Paige says. But her hands grip the axe tighter. She is strong enough. "Which one should I go for?"

You survey the landscape, make eye contact with the creatures you've been trying to escape. How terrible they are, how hard to look at, like someone vacuumed up the bones and spit them out as bundled fur and wood and metal fiends. To the left, a dog, that fierce devil, guarding the garden. In the center, the fairies and their fiery work, which you must, at all costs, avoid, until the very end. And to the right, a wooden soldier, flat and at attention, with the bottom half of him a spider body of bayoneted arms.

"I think the soldier would be best," you say.

"You're sure?" Paige's voice is steady, but her eyes are wide. "Isn't he a walking arsenal?"

"The dogs are worse," Cricket confirms. "They're vicious beasts. And toothy jaws—"

"All right." Paige grips the axe again. "I'll do it."

"And while you work, we'll gather tools," you say, "and find the bottom half."

"And if you can't?" Paige asks.

"Then he shall die," the cricket says, "and finally be at peace."

Paige doesn't say another word, but hugs the trees and meets the right side of the battlefield. On cue, the soldier shuffles his rifle legs, all eight of them impaling dusty ground, until he faces Paige directly. You can't see her face, but you imagine that she looks upon her foe with fear and bravery both.

"Run," the cricket says, and you recall you've promised tools and hopefully a soldier's other end. You leave the bushes, turn again, but there's no interest in you now. The soldier darts a foot ahead, and Paige removes it swiftly with the axe. Another foot, but carefully this time, so that Paige swings the air and almost hits her shin.

You wish that you could help, but you must go inside the castle, while the cricket bounces all around, inspecting death's remains for white pants pressed together at attention, and the turned-out shoes. Medoro loved to mock them, put his own feet at attention, press his arms against his sides, but it was more their manner that he mocked, the stiff expressions of their duty, and the way they said *Good day, Sir* even when they met a lady or a little child barely older than a newly planted tree. You liked them, liked their formal ways, liked how their accents sounded when they said those words, but you laughed anyway, for how he had a way of making everything a joke—except the way he felt for you, said in the tone that lived behind your bedroom door alone. Medoro loved to mock them, even—

There's no time, he whispers, pulling at your hand.

The tools.

How quickly you've forgotten.

Now you're running down the hall again, and to the closet where the groundsman kept the box of hammers, nails, and measuring tape, kept washers, screws, and coiled wire taped in silver circles at the bottom, kept the things he used whenever something sprung a leak or lost its power, silly problems only of this world and those without the endless Flare. The box is heavy, heavier than you thought, or Flare has drained you weaker than before. Maybe a few more times, and you will sputter dry and dark forevermore, or once—

There's no time, Alexio.

Tools. Right.

You lift the handle with both hands and run, so that the front bangs at your side, will leave a bruise, a dark blue hole that may not ever heal. You're glad you never saw your mother that way, never saw her bleed or blow out like a candle flame, and oh, now you are thinking of her, and you wish to go up to her room, the door you passed, and lay upon her bed—

Alexio, there's no time!

You meet the door and kick it open, throw the tools out on the grass, and there is Paige, with five of eight legs off and those remaining kicking at her like three stabbing knives. The soldier's furious brows lean tight together, and his mouth is popping up and down, as if he's shouting *Sir! Sir! Sir!* Off come the other three, and now he's just a body, bobbing madly, hot potato on the ground, drawing dust up like an angry cloud.

"Cricket, you find it?" Paige calls out, and Cricket squeaks a happy "Here!" from somewhere not too far away.

"I'll get it," you would say, but when you turn, a dog is grinning wildly in your face. The eyes roll terribly in their globes. The mouth chomps air and spits fluff drool down to the dust. It's sniffed you out, and probably all will do so when they catch the scent of Flare that lives inside you, yes, of course, you should have known this end would come, and sooner than you thought.

"I'm ready," you call up to those sharp teeth, and spread your arms to hug the end that finally has come for you.

"Not yet," a little voice calls out, and then the cricket launches from your shoulder to the eye.

What can you do? The dog rears up, so you can see the stitching of its belly, and, as though inside a dream, you draw your sword and give the shard a thrust. With one dull push as far as it can go, the lightless blade finds something it can power down, so that the dog collapses in a pile of fabric, cotton, teeth, and loosened threads, so red and fiery, copper wires that are slowly cooling into lifeless string.

"Nice work," the cricket says, and then you turn together at the final ring of metal close behind your back.

The soldier falls, but Paige takes up the half and carries it to where the legs lie lifeless on the ground. "Give me some nails," she says, and gets to work on hammering the pieces back together, so that the soldier is his normal, stiffened self. "And now the Flare," she says. "Put out your hand and send it through."

And send it through . . .

Away from you.

You look upon the fingers of your hand and will them forward. This could be the end, you think. The last time that you feel its sweet and calming flow. You press your hand to that long forehead on the ground, and in an instant, blue light lifts the eyelids.

"Good day, Sir!"

You fall upon the ground, and up the soldier hops. He gives a little trial bounce, and then another, hop, hop, hop, his legs still stitched together in their perfect posture. Then he is gone, to somewhere he must hope is safer than where you stand. Your own eyes flutter, and you feel a faintness overwhelm you, so that the world goes quiet, senseless, smell-less, like the floating nothing of the Flare.

I'm spent, you think. *Medoro, I am ready—*

Someone's arms are on you. Wooden. Strong. They lift you up and carry you, step, step, step, while Cricket's voice is in your ear. *Not yet, Alexio. Not till we are done, and we have saved this place, or stopped them, if that's all that we can do.*

I can't, you think, and drift up to the mural on the ceiling.

The garden where I'll meet you when you dream.

The wooden arms give way to the soft flesh of someone new. They press you against their chest, and you can feel it there, small and pulsing—the Flare.

Impossible.

Nothing is stronger than the bond of true belief.

I cannot—

Believe, Alexio. Please believe.

CHAPTER TWENTY-EIGHT

GENERAL DORIEL

The prince is heavy in his arms, but General Doriel does not waver as he steps a worn leather boot surely over the scorched vines that were once the royal garden. The land here smells of burned greenery, like the leaf fires of the fall season, or like the smoke from the buildings from which all of the metal toys were produced back when there were workers enough to man the lines. The marionette is by his side, firing questions. A cricket hops angrily on his shoulder like the incessant taps of a training sword when he was first learning to battle. "Where did you come from?" they are asking, "And how did you escape the Deathsprites?," and "Who told you we were here?" They don't trust him, don't know him, but he knows this Fae in his arms, for how many times did he square off against the prince in the training yard? How many times did he allow the prince to land a blow, just to see the confidence it brought him? And there was that final conversation, which General Doriel thinks of now as his arms begin to ache. He was too late—or at least he has told himself this for the years since the prince's disappearance.

Now, he will get his second chance.

The garden paths are interrupted by fallen toys and felled trees. General Doriel steps over a thick trunk, while the marionette struggles to sit on top and then swing her stiff legs over. Giving up, she hands a fisty punch to the middle of the tree, which shatters into shards of dry wood to leave a passageway in its center.

Alexio, what were you planning?

He considers taking off his army jacket, but without the thick blue wool, he will wear only a stained white shirt. How unprofessional. So, he leaves on the jacket, the high collar, the brass buttons. So different from the gauzy dress he wore on his own planet, so many years ago . . . But he must not think of the Flare now. He must not remember.

As they leave the garden and move to the remaining forest that circles the ever-widening industrial wasteland, the questions continue—little annoyances, like bugs in the face of a soldier waiting to charge into a battle to the death. What bother has he for a few bites on the cheeks, a few nibbles at the arm? He has faced death, has looked it squarely in its burning fire eyes, and in the terrible tooth mouths of the dogs, and in the bayonet legs and the cursed whirling knives, and he has stopped flinching for anything, even as this new development of the realm shifts. Well, perhaps this has made him flinch a little, for if Prince Alexio could slip between worlds like a man slipping from a river into a stream, then it is only a matter of time before the Deathsprites finish excavating their vortex's final piece and gain enough power to do the very same. No more traveling in their terrible ships. No more slipping through stones. No more biding their time as they collect new power, quench their thirst for death with the thick red liquid they pour from their canteens, dip their swords in barrels of blood wrung from his people until they glow like coals—just death, everywhere, until the entire universe falls.

Yes. That is enough to make even a seasoned general flinch just a little.

"—and before you just carry Prince Alexio to wherever we're walking, young man—" the cricket demands.

"I am much older than you—" he corrects.

"I need you to stop and tell me—"

"Do you know how he did it?" General Doriel stops and turns his head to his shoulder. "Did he tell you?"

The cricket folds her legs. "I presume you mean shift realms?"

"Of course I do." General Doriel resumes his quick stride, and in his hurry, a branch snaps back and hits the marionette in the face. She shakes her head, but seems unbothered. "Such a move should be impossible. And yet he's done it many times—and not just planets, but across whole universes, too."

The cricket is bouncing again, but this time, thoughtfully. "It is the Flare. The Great White Light, for Red Fire could not follow him without the change—"

". . . At least for now," adds the marionette.

None of this makes any sense. So, they sent the prince over to power their work—that much is clear. But how did he stay in his true form? And why does the marionette seem like a human girl, anyway? Did Alexio create her himself? And, again, *why*?

He could ask these questions, but he supposes they have no more information than he does. Alexio has always been a strange Fae, prone to the kind of emotional swings one associates with toys or humans. A dreamer. But dreams can haunt you, and emotions can turn sour, and oh, how these sentiments got the better of him on the training field. One could always count on Alexio to grow frustrated or angry, and then he would miss, and miss, and miss.

Yet clearly, there were benefits.

Love.

General Doriel still wonders at it. A relationship with a toy? How unusual. And Alexio's incessant talk of the Flare? Unequaled. The rest of their people had moved on, had accepted their fate, but Alexio still carried that torch of desire inside of him, so that when one touched his burning skin, one felt a kind of quickening in one's own chest.

It'll do you no good, General Doriel reminds himself. *To rely on power we cannot replenish is to make a weakness we do not possess.*

They pass through the forest without incident. General Doriel has cleared these lands of most of their demonic inhabitants, and besides, the refurbished toys do not like the difficult tightness of the trees. They prefer to roll and whirl and dust up the central region, so that, from a high branch, with binoculars at his eyes and the keen sight of a Fae, General Doriel feels the whole world is a machine made up of these vicious cogs. The smell here is better—just a little smoke, mixed with damp, mossy sweetness. But the scent is changing as the forest grows narrower, carved at its side like the cheeses they used to serve in the Great Hall, winnowed and winnowed until now it remains just a few acres across and about twenty long. Still, it is enough for his purposes—and for theirs.

"The moss berries are safe to eat," he tells them, then remembers that they are a marionette and a cricket. "Anyway, just in case, don't touch the red tree berries—they are not native to these lands, and they will probably kill you as soon as their poison touches your tongue."

The marionette swings her axe to clear a few branches out of the way. "So now that we're in slightly less mortal danger, you ready to tell us who you are?"

"Not in the slightest." General Doriel smiles a little. "You are persistent, though, I'll give you that. You speak your mind."

"It's a new thing," the marionette says, and frowns. "A little late."

"No such thing, Marionette," he says, though he doesn't really believe it.

"It's Paige, by the way."

"And there's no such thing as 'slightly less danger,' either." He stops and listens, and the others do the same. A stick cracks not far from them. Perhaps it's nothing—or perhaps they are being followed. He continues walking and whispers, "Here, there is only danger, everywhere, all of the time—even with the Fae busy with their mines. We must be alert, for if we are killed, there is no one left."

He stops abruptly, and the marionette digs in her heels and sways.

"You hear something again?" she asks quietly.

He finally allows himself to gaze on the familiar steel, and the wooden handle, which once brought him so much comfort. "Just the sound of that axe. It's mine, by the way—and I'd like it back."

The marionette tightens her grip. "Prince Alexio gave it to me."

"Hmm."

General Doriel does not say another word for the rest of the trip. He is thinking. He is trying not to feel the burning of his arms. He presses the prince tighter to his chest, but this only makes the stinging worse. Sweat beads at his forehead, and he wipes it away with his shoulder. His feet grow hot in his socks.

"I could carry him—"

"No." General Doriel presses Alexio closer. "This is my duty."

Finally, they arrive at the familiar mouth of the cave where General Doriel has spent the last twenty years of his life. He is both calmed and repulsed by the view of it, its hungry mouth, its protective shell, and he thinks, for a second, that this time he will turn away and be free of the obligations inside. No, he knows himself better—he has never released himself from responsibility.

"Prepare yourself," he says grimly to his guests. "There are horrors inside."

The marionette steps behind him, and he leads her and the cricket into the darkness. He knows the way, and he finds the familiar grooves he once carved into the stone and follows them. Once, he had a lantern for his passage, but it has long since broken—and besides, light was the way many of his fellow fighters were discovered. Better to live in the dark, like the ghost one will become, than die in the warm light of a final lamp's glow.

The air changes, and then he tells the marionette, "There are steps here." Slowly, he carries Prince Alexio down seven uneven steps, while the marionette follows with her hand on his shoulder. Her fingers feel the way a branch would—light yet firm, and the temperature of an inanimate thing. Another grooved path, another set of turns, and now they are finally here, the door, where Starsprite markings carve the way in:

Follow the Flare.

This is a trick for the Deathsprites, who know the Flare as a burst, so bright and powerful. Their fingers would go up, to the top of the door, where they would set off the spikes that would shoot through their holes to find their unsuspecting victim. Deathsprites would not understand that what burns so brightly comes from within, so that to "follow the Flare" is simply to dig one's fingers in the center of the door and find the handle hidden there.

Now the door clicks open, and finally, there is flame and light. The smells of turpentine and wood. To the right, a bunny puppet, all white head and just the plain pink sack beneath, where no one's hand controls the cloth-y fist that hammers nails; in the center, drinking birds, a pair that, when they dip their beaks, strike knives upon the sharpening stone; on the right, the wood stick horse, who holds a paintbrush in his mouth and paints the surfaces that then will dry upon the hearth. There are others, dolls with magnet dresses, miniature accordions, muscle men, and kites that dip and weave to lift weapons up and carry them precariously across the cave to sheath them. All of the toys wear leather belts around their waists, from which makers' tools dangle and clank with their rapid movements. General Doriel takes a deep breath and exhales slowly, allowing himself to feel joy that, thanks to his efforts, none of these toys are patchwork demons—and none of them have red in their eyes.

"What is this place?" Paige asks, and the workers there all turn to stare, openmouthed, at the strange new addition to their ranks.

"This, my marionette friend, is the Land of Toys." General Doriel sinks to his knees, finally spent, and places Prince Alexio carefully on the cool stone floor. "Or, at least, what remains of it."

The toys surround them, and they cry out, together, *The prince! The prince!* They have such hope, already, when it is clear that Prince Alexio is no more able to save them than he has been to save himself. *He must rest!* they cry, and then he is carried, with Prince Alexio, to his bed. His duties fall away. Sweet comfort. Sweet release.

When he wakes just a few hours later, Alexio is gone.

CHAPTER TWENTY-NINE

THE DOCTOR

FINTAN IS BENT OVER THE PLANS for the carousel, working by the flickering candlelight the workers have replenished on their way home for the evening, when he hears *her* voice. Not the sarcastic railing of the annoying voice from before, but the other one—the one he cannot ignore. He hears her as he thinks of the other prisoners, who probably play cards in their cells, or play tricks, or just lay back on their beds and imagine that they are home again. *Terrible work ethic,* Fintan has just been thinking. *No wonder I'm in charge.*

But then, she comes, as she always does, when the night falls.

No, you're not, a sweet voice whispers in his ear. *I am.*

Fintan refuses to turn his head. His hand moves on the page, creating circles where the attached heads will be drawn in by Gwynn's more artistic sketching.

Oh, Fintan. She puts her hand out to cover his drawing. The brown skin glistens like a star. *Why do you waste your talents on such evil designs, when you could make something beautiful instead?*

My Patched toys are beautiful. But even as he says it, the drawing below becomes ugly, the scribbles of a child who thinks they have brought to life a family instead of a set of stick figure nightmares.

He turns to the fairy, but no one stands by his side. No, wait, she *is* there, the little cricket, perched on his shoulder. She chirps her hello, and he puts out his finger to touch her head. His hand moves through the body, onto his own thin shoulder. She is gone.

No, he corrects. *She was never here, remember?*

CHAPTER THIRTY

GENERAL DORIEL

General Doriel finds Prince Alexio in the place he expects: the jail, where they keep the demonic toys they have captured but not killed. Each has their reasons: the partner of a toymaker, or the child, or the neighbor, or some other sentimental attachment that has long since died in the fiery eyes of the wild and deadly beasts before him. Now, they are wild at the sight of fresh meat, and they beat their awful heads and thrash their teeth furiously at the bars.

"He's not here," General Doriel says softly.

"I know." Prince Alexio turns from the cages, and General Doriel is astonished to see how weak and pale his leader looks. He had assumed that with some rest, the prince would be much improved, but the sleep seems to have only served to bring him consciousness. "I had hoped . . ."

"You misunderstand me." General Doriel steps forward and places his hand firmly on Prince Alexio's shoulder. Once, this touch might have been like the loving hand of a sea captain on the deck of a ship, which could no more love him than the water could notice his journey over its surface—but time has stripped away anything but duty. And besides, even then the way General Doriel felt was just an echo, a longing for the kind of feeling Prince Alexio had found with Medoro. Maybe things were better, he'd thought. If only he could find it within himself . . . General Doriel shakes his head. A few hours of proximity, and he is already losing himself in the secondhand Flare. "He is in his own cell. For the safety of the other toys . . ."

Prince Alexio's eyes are wide, and then he sways as though he might faint, like a leaf snapped from its branch. "You tell me truly that Medoro is here? In this very place?"

"Not Medoro," General Doriel corrects. "Not anything like him. But the body is here, split in two and sewn to two halves of a bull, the one the other toys would ride for sport at the yearly celebration."

"That does not sound too—"

"You will see." General Doriel removes his hand. "Steady yourself, my prince."

They leave the jail and go through the door on the opposite side of the room. There is the cell, split in half by bars, with one half of the demon Medoro on the right and the other on the left. The right houses his body, unfamiliar in its four-legged posture, while the left side hosts the doggish charm of the poodle face made ugly by the snarl of a vicious beast and matted chocolate curls. Drool spits from the long, sneering mouth. Teeth chomp at the cage. Now that they have been activated, the bull's stuffed bottom bucks its cushion hooves, and the bull top beats the bars in even time, first one, then the other, with its tan horns inlaid by Deathsprite silver. This kicking, rearing, wild toy once let little teddy bears lie upon his back. Now his horns and hooves fall and then return, fall and then return, soon bruising the bodies of both creatures and still coming back again for battle. The seam's metal staples spill stuffing like so many foaming mouths. Both dog head and bull head glow red from the eyes, marking their possession like the speeding headlights of a car that wants nothing but to ram you dead. They will destroy themselves to do it, and this is why they have been taken away. No contact. None. This is the only way to keep Medoro safe—if he is even in there, at all.

Prince Alexio steps closer, but the bull halves beat and beat him away again with their lower and upper hooves. There is blood, now, and it drips on the floor in dark and glowing droplets of red. "You could not fix him?"

"Fixing him is not the problem. It's changing what's in here." General Doriel taps his temple.

"But your Flare?" Prince Alexio touches General Doriel's chest, and again, he fights the urge to slip his own hand over the one that resides there. *You are not that young boy anymore,* Doriel reminds himself, though on the outside he has aged only a few days.

"I have no Flare." General Doriel's voice is flat and emotionless. Good. "No one does, anymore."

Prince Alexio shakes his head. "Respectfully, General Doriel, you are wrong about just this one thing. I have felt it when you carried me, and I feel it now, inside of you. Perhaps you cannot use it—but that is an entirely different matter."

General Doriel doesn't say anything for a while. He is thinking—thinking about all the Fae he has lost, and how they put their swords up and waited for that lovely blue Flare that should have sharpened their weapons to strength. If there was any of that sweet river left inside of them, why would it not emerge to save them from their fates? Why, when the Deathsprites can hold and call upon such terrible power from their own husks?

"No Flarewhisper has ever known the source of our power," Prince Alexio says, seeming to read General Doriel's mind.

Then he perches on the small bench carved from stone and watches Medoro sadly. "Nor do I understand why I could use it before, but not now, when I so desperately would call upon it."

"It would kill you."

"Yes, I know." Prince Alexio opens his mouth and then closes it again, but General Doriel knows what he would say. That he would gladly save Medoro, gladly give his life, but he would merely pass this echo of grief along to someone else—and he cannot, the way General Doriel could not pass Alexio to the marionette, even if he fell along the way. One's duty was everything—it was all they had left.

"Please get Paige," Prince Alexio says. He has not taken his eyes from Medoro, not once since they entered the room. "I would hear from her—"

"A marionette?"

"A toymaker." Prince Alexio shakes his head. "Perhaps she will see what we cannot."

***

General Doriel finds Paige and the cricket in deep conversation with the toys. They have formed a circle by the tools, and they are explaining something to the marionette in a technical jargon that General Doriel has never tried to understand. He is a Fae, and they are the toys—end of story. Perhaps he might have learned . . . But he finds himself in the blade, and the axe, and the bow. That is what he knows, and what he is, and what he will always be. The prince is a fool to think that there could be a seed of the Flare left in such a brute as him . . .

"General Doriel?" The marionette is looking at him with earnest curiosity. "Is the prince awake?"

"He calls for you." General Doriel shakes his head to clear it. "He is in the back cell, with Medoro."

"Medoro?" The cricket leaps to General Doriel's shoulder, and he fights the urge to flick her free. "He's here?"

"In a way."

They follow him to the back, and the toys come, too, though they stop at the door of the jail and twitter there nervously. Born soldiers, General Doriel thinks, but not leaders—not a single one. They like to have orders, and to stay here, in the cave, embraced by its dark safety. Then again, what point would leaving be, when they would all be slaughtered soon upon their exit? He fights the urge to sigh, for how many years has he made himself accept these limitations? *The toys are better than the Fae,* Prince Alexio used to remind him, even when there was no foe to necessitate their help. *They cannot lead because they have no need for it. Every toy is just a note in a greater melody, and they have been happily playing it for longer than we know. We are the problem, General Doriel, for without the heavy hands of Fae to fall them out of tune, these sweet beings would be better off, I'm sure.* General Doriel was not sure that he agreed with this sentiment, or anything the Prince said for that matter, but then again, he knew his place. Not until that conversation with the axe had he—

Doriel, you are circling the drain.

So he is.

When they reach the back room, Prince Alexio is still sitting in the same position, still staring down the beasts, and they have pooled their wounds below them like the shuddering waters of a disturbed lake. *This is the lie,* Prince Alexio is muttering, and General Doriel raises his eyebrows toward Paige, who shrugs. "He says that a lot," she says, taking a seat next to Prince Alexio. "I think it helps him think."

"Or the opposite," Cricket suggests. "Snap him out of it, Paige."

The marionette gently puts a wooden hand on Prince Alexio's arm. He blinks, goes quiet, and then says, without turning from Medoro: "I cannot feel him."

"That doesn't mean he isn't there," Paige says, but she does not sound sure. "You want me to fix him?"

"You must," Prince Alexio says, "but I fear it won't do any good. Without my Flare—"

Paige's eyes widen. She leaps from the bench, startling Cricket right off of General Doriel's shoulder and sending General Doriel reaching for the hilt of his sword, but Prince Alexio does not dart his eyes from the bucking bulls. The marionette approaches the bars with an assurance General Doriel would normally admire but in this case finds utterly irresponsible, and though he calls for her to stop, she takes a keyring from behind her back and unlocks the door before he can even move.

"How did you—?"

She is inside the cell, and everything becomes chaotic. The bull is kicking at her, batting her against the bars. Then, Medoro is biting wildly at her arms, so that at one point he gets her bicep in his mouth like a stick and is shaking it. Paige merely bats at his nose until he releases her, and he slinks away, glaring at his prey.

"I'm sorry," she says, and then she has the axe in her hand and is sweeping it cleanly through the central line of Medoro's waist. Off falls the top half; down falls the legs.

General Doriel expects her to exit the prison cell and unlock the other door, but instead, she pulls at the bars between the two until they form a hole large enough for her to walk through. "What is this power?" he asks, but no one answers—no one even breathes. Now, it is the bull head butting at her, and the dog legs scrambling their nails to leave gashes in the wood beneath her ripped shirt. She does not bleed, does not even notice, and again, the axe swings true. Down falls the bull head, still snarling; over tips the dog body, like a shoddy chair.

"Give me the Starshard," she calls, and now General Doriel understands what is happening. He moves to stop the prince, leaps to do it, but he is not fast enough. His feet leave the ground just a second after Prince Alexio sends the dull shard flying through the air, and when he falls, his hands are empty.

"Don't!" General Doriel cries. He scrambles to his feet and then rushes the cell. "That is an heirloom of *our* people, not his! Do not waste it! Do not put it out!"

"I'm sorry," Paige says softly.

Then she stakes the bottom of Medoro with one end of the Starshard and impales the top of Medoro on the other end. The pieces meet, and then there is a blinding blue light, so close to the sweet release of the true Flare, the star Flare, the life Flare that birthed them and held them and carried them again to be reborn. General Doriel has tears in his eyes, but they are sweet and sad, knowing that this will be the end of his people for good. All for this world's silly infatuations. All for the fickle feelings of toys. He should have never brought Prince Alexio to this room, not until the very end, when all hope was lost for good. He should have never—

The light burns true, and then it dims, sending the blue glow up and down inside of the dog's lifeless body instead of outward. The whole creature shakes, and then the front legs are rising, finding the sides of the body, as the eyes open and the nose sniffs at the air. The irises have changed, and now they flare a wild blue.

"Alexio," says the mouth in a sweet whisper. A paw reaches for his hat but does not find it. "You found the gift I left you!"

"It was not yours to give!" General Doriel screams.

He leaps for the dog through the open hole in the side of the cell, and then they are tussling, so that he has Medoro by the ears and the dog has him by the shoulder. Paige yells at them to stop it, and she claps, as though they really are dogs and not two beings with decades of frustration and jealousy and oh, no, he has let it all overwhelm him again.

"General Doriel, that is quite enough!" Prince Alexio says quietly.

General Doriel releases his grip, and Medoro does the same, shaking his teeth free of the Fae's fragile skin. He bows low to the prince, who nods his head briefly in return.

"The Starshard is mine alone," Prince Alexio says, "and I have gladly given it. Just like Medoro once convinced the toys to give us a piece of their land so that we might find safety from the Deathsprites—or have you forgotten that grand gesture so soon, General Doriel?"

"I have not, my prince," General Doriel mutters. But he has—of course he has.

"Good. And I'd hope you'd know I had my reasons for this selection—reasons beyond just personal attachment?"

General Doriel rolls his eyes. "Oh, Prince Alexio, even I cannot pretend this was no more than an emotional—"

"I'm glad we are in agreement," Prince Alexio interrupts. "Now Medoro, my love, why don't you show them all what you can do?"

CHAPTER THIRTY-ONE

THE FAIRY

Believe, Alexio.

And there he is, your love, as jaunty and as lovely and alive as ever. He leans his elbow on the cell and presses weight there, gives a cheeky smile, saves his seriousness for later, for when you are alone and whispers in your ear, you'll hear the true Medoro call down to your soul. For now, he's there, so cocky, irritating Doriel, and you are here, just staring at the one you thought you'd never see again.

"Alexio?" he's asking.

"Yes?"

"You're sure . . . ?"

"I am."

You walk into the cell with his top half attached and take his paws. They feel familiar and so strange, like you are dreaming, and you fear you'll wake. His eyes close, and the pulse begins, so bright, so blue, and you can feel it too, it floods you, bathes you in the glow of Flare you haven't felt in many years. You feel your power coming back, not just the Starsprite strength, but something else, a well that you might draw from every time and never dry.

"Good job," the cricket says reluctantly.

Paige says it's nothing, but she smiles, and you feel her pride the way you feel Medoro's easy company.

"It cannot be," the general says, but you can tell he already believes again. How to deny what he can see with his own eyes? And you suspected, for the toys have something that you don't, so pure, complete belief, despite the odds and facts and rules and many ways that things go wrong. They always have believed—that's why the Deathsprites use them, why they turn the toys' eyes red while Fae are only felled beneath their sword. The toys are like so many batteries you charge with love, or hate, and they can carry all the weight of feeling in their crafted form, as though the power comes from deep inside instead of all your fairy darkness.

How your coming to this world has doomed them, doomed them all.

You think, again, of all the bones.

You climb inside the pile, pull them up around you, feel their heavy weight.

You close your eyes—

"You didn't know," Medoro says. "How could you?"

"We didn't think to know," the general says, "And we have suffered for it."

He puts his hand out, and Medoro takes them softly in his own. Another flash, and then his eyes glow blue.

"It really is the Flare," he says, his voice so full of longing, full of home. "I still do not quite understand . . ."

"Nor I," you say, "but I am starting to believe that these sweet makers and our fairy lines are more connected than we understood. There is a bond there—something that's outlasted memory. Something like the Flare—though I do not know how such a bond could be."

"And what now?" asks the general. "What can we do?"

"We fight," Paige says, "and take the portal down."

Her mother wished her strong, you think, and something in you breaks. For she is not just theirs, but yours, your child, gifted with your strength, so that they took you easy and returned you to that room to wait for her to grow and change and circle back for your release. But she was worth it, worth the years, for now she's done what you could not have thought. You want to save her—but you need her—and these truths wave back and crash and wave again away. Your mind is like a violent sea. Your stomach heaves and clenches tight.

"Are you okay?" Medoro asks, and you do not know what to say.

Okay?

You've killed a world.

You've been a prisoner.

You've made a child.

And now you're going to have to watch her die.

"I'm not," you say, a whisper only he can hear, because you cannot lie to him. "I do not have a plan. I fear we won't return. I know we still must go, and stop them, if we can, but . . ."

"Oh, Alexio." He puts his head to yours. He smells so different, like the fires, and the wet deep stones of caves. "You take things on yourself, and they are like the bricks that make a wall that keeps you in. Believe, and let them fall."

So pure.

So true.

But you are not a toy—

—and you cannot believe.

You smile weakly, and he smiles back. He might believe you, but again, he might be drifting worry down a river like a paper boat, to catch, again, at night, when you're alone. You'll scare the girl, and cricket, too, *Alexio, pull yourself together, please.*

"Excuse me?" says a voice outside the door. "I do not wish to interrupt, but I must say that there is something in the cave."

"What thing?" the general asks.

"Or, what I mean is many things, an army . . . toys I think." The unseen toy is speaking brightly, but she cannot help it. This is how she's made. "The Deathsprites seem to have sent them when they sensed—"

"I see." The general squares his shoulders. You think of how he told you to be ready, and you weren't, and he is not, for no one can prepare for everything. *We didn't know. We do not know. We'll never know.* "Then we shall meet them at the door."

The cricket leaps to Paige, and you're surprised—but then again, the two are friends of sorts, you think, now that the girl has proved herself. Paige puts a finger out, and cricket presses head to tip, a little bit of courage for them both. The girl then takes the axe again, and you take breaths you hope will calm this madness in your head.

"We fight," Doriel says, "and win, or die a glorious end."

***

THE WORKROOM IS A CLOUD OF chaos: toys with arms ripped from their stitches, dents in metal chests, the sad small cries of innocents who've served as shields instead. Some use their weapons—tools like hammers, carving knives, and wrenches—while the others leap on larger toys with fire in their eyes. There are no Fae here, not when they could send their army in their stead—and they are probably at the portal now, you realize, waiting to descend.

"The left," the cricket cries, and you veer that way while Paige takes the right. The general splits the center, waving swords in both directions, taking down as many as he can.

A box leaps toward you, and out spits its springs, with tank guns firing wildly in their unaimed melody. You leap, and take a gun, then feel the sting of a bullet to your upper chest near the shoulder, a high clean wound that luckily has missed the organs there.

"Alexio!" Medoro calls.

"I'm fine."

You leap, again, and swing. A tank gun falls, and then another, then the box, impaled by sword and axe as Paige meets from the other side. You face, together, your next foe: a red piano with a duck mouth stuck inside the lid that quacks and bares the knife-y teeth that nature would not give him. Paige throws the axe, which finds its home inside the palette mouth, and takes the demon down. Then, quickly, before you act, the cricket squeaks a warning and Paige throws her fist clean through a stuffed giraffe with truck wheel legs that sought to run you over from behind.

"Any ideas?" she says, and takes another toy.

"Is there another way to leave?"

"Let's see."

She's gone, somewhere beyond the crowd, and you, again, are swinging at the toys that force their way past others at the door. Or, she is gone at first, until the sound of violent swings ring out so loudly everyone must turn. The entryway begins to shake, and with a crash, large boulders tumble down onto the heads of foes still finding light amidst the tunnels that have led them here. The air smells strong of rock and dust and death, and stuffy, too, as though the air has already escaped.

You take a breath, *Just try to breathe*, but find your chest as tightly closed as that new wall of stone.

Mountain of stone.

There are two kinds of lies.

Mountains of bones.

You won't be surprised.

"This is the lie!" you shout. "This is the lie! This is the lie! This is the lie!"

CHAPTER THIRTY-TWO

LILY

WHAT FEELS LIKE AN ETERNITY PASSES, and then the hands are back at her shoulders, shaking her.

"Lily," Petta voice calls from very far away. "Lily, we need to go now. Come on, Honey. Open your eyes."

Lily forces her eyelids open. Petta is there, brighter now, like she has brought the very sun with her upon her return. Her hair is frizzy where it has come loose from its holder, and her shirt has a few rips in the arms. The collar is looser, having lost two of the buttons, and Lily can see the end of a scar there, where a breast used to be.

"There's no time like borrowed time." Petta adjusts her shirt so that the scar isn't visible. "I probably should have told Paige that part, too, shouldn't I?"

Shouldn't.

Should.

Borrowed time.

Time when she should have told her parents the truth—that she did not want to go back to school, or move to a big city, or buy a fancy apartment, or marry a man they'd call the son they never had.

Lily's mind spins, and she clutches at her head to quiet the shifting vision in front of her. "I'm sure you had your reasons."

"Yeah." Petta laughs again, that hollow laugh of hers, and it's the sad sound of a dented bell. "I was afraid—and I really, really, *really* didn't want to."

"You're not the only one." Lily lets her hands drop, and the room is still. "So now what?"

"We run." Petta puts out her arm, and Lily threads her hand through it. The skin there is moist and hot. "Just stick close to me, okay? Hallway, fire escape, car."

"Hallway, fire escape, car," Lily repeats. Her mouth feels disconnected from her brain, as though she's repeating the words without actually remembering them. Then, she is being wrenched from the wall, so that the room disappears in a flesh of shadows. Her arm aches at the socket. Everything spins.

When her vision settles, the hallway is a littered alley of bodies. Many of them moaning, and there are some bleeding puddles of red that splash at the interruption of Lily's shoes. The smell is of iron and sweat, and something else, too—a kind of wooden earthiness. Lily tries not to look down, but then she does, at Mike's black t-shirt, and then Len's web tattoo with that spider sitting motionless on his forearm.

"Mike?" Lily whispers.

She nudges the guard with the toe of her shoe. There is a whisper of breath from Len's mouth, an up and down of Mike's chest. They are alive.

"I didn't kill any of them," Petta says. "Just put them down long enough to escape. They'll be taken to the hospital and stitched up, and then they'll live on to fight another day as my sister's henchmen."

"Thank you—"

Then, Petta's arm is pulling, and Lily is flying again, each leap a frog's wild hop over the log of a fallen body.

The window is a stamp in the distance—

—a portrait of sky in the distance—

—a wall of blue that startles her in its cloudless loveliness.

Petta shoulders the frame, and then there is fresh air, the subtle rush of cars in the nearby intersections, a bird calling from the top of one of the nearby stores.

"Which car?" Lily asks, for there is a line of them in the alley. They are all strange vintage cars in weird colors, like a red Buick from the 50's and a pink VW Beetle, with peeling paint and dents in the hoods.

"That one." Petta points to the car at the front of the line, the only van. "If the others behind are captured . . ."

Again, Lily is pulled through the air, this time down the fire escape and past the line of windows. She catches only a flash of each driver, but she sees enough to understand that these people in aprons and flannel shirts with leather work belts or toolboxes abandoned on their passenger's seats are toymakers like Paige. Where have they come from? And how did they know that the women running past them needed rescuing?

Finally, with a shove, Paige throws Lily into the still-opening door of the van with a swift push. The interior is empty of people, but there are several musical instruments tethered to the sides with bungee cords. Something seems familiar about it, as though Lily has seen it on the street—or maybe she is imagining things again.

"Let's get out of here," Paige says, pounding on the wall that separates them from the driver.

With a sudden acceleration, the van peels out of the alley. Lily sinks to the floor, and instead of getting up, she just lies there, breathing.

Will she ever see her parents again?

Will they ever *want* to see her again, once Camilla tells them what she's done?

She closes her eyes. Toy Palace appears, bright red and gold, gaudy now like the terrible curtain of some cheap traveling show. Then Rashi, her smile, the bracelet that matches the one around Lily's neck shimmering in the pool hall bar candles. Finally, the girl with the light blond hair, innocent as a child in Toy Palace, strong as a warrior on the boat where she was pulled to another land Lily will never see—can barely even believe exists.

I should have asked for her number, Lily thinks, drifting down into her exhaustion.

But what difference would that have made?

CHAPTER THIRTY-THREE

THE DOCTOR

She returns an hour later. Fintan has just finished putting out the tools for the following morning, which his workers will use to sedate and then take apart the carousel for his initial restructuring. They will need to ask the Deathsprites to hunt down the sharks, of course, but that should not be too hard—and, really, any aquatic form will do.

He's returned, she says as a greeting.

So I've heard.

Aren't you curious to know how he's faring against your children?

He shakes his head no. *They are on their own now.* He tries to keep his eyes on the drawing, but his eyes drift away, then back again. *Did you come just to tell me what I already know?*

Of course not, she whispers. *I have a new project for you.*

A new project? He can't help himself—his pulse is already quickening. *What kind of project?*

She takes him by the hand and leads him to the supply closet—not the one they use, but the extra one, where only at night Fintan visits the work that no Deathsprite may ever see. He flicks the switch, and here are the loveliest of the tools, all gleaming with the voice's radiance. The table in the center houses a project he has forgotten since the previous night—strange, how that can be possible, and his mind wants to linger on the thought but is wrenched back, again, to the beautiful gleam of sterling steel—and he inhales its sweet, sterile scent.

But I have already completed my task. Fintan runs his fingers over the heart on the table, which pulses once at his touch. *A heart. A new kind of power.*

Not new, she corrects gently. *Old as time itself.*

She always has the right words.

You are slipping, she says, still gently, but slightly less so. Fintan runs his hand through his stringy black hair and is surprised to find it greasy and matted.

They ask a lot of me.

Oh, Fintan. You cannot fool the one who loves you.

And she is right. He loves his work. He loves the terrible Patched creations. He loves their teeth, and their mismatched bodies, and their deadly red glows—

—Or does he?

For now that he recalls their faces, he is repulsed by the images, and his stomach clenches at the stale bread lying there. Has he contributed such horrors to this world? What have they done to deserve this fate, besides welcome his kind and give them a home?

As I said, the fairy whispers, *you're slipping away.*

He shakes his head. *I don't want to. I want to stay here—with you.*

And you shall try very hard, I'm sure. The sparkling hand caresses his cheek. *But you can only be two halves, Fintan. Never whole. You must find the balance between them, or you will never see me again.*

I will not let that happen. Or will he? He is starting to feel confused, like his brain is an ocean with two storms crashing against each other. He moves away from the table to the wall of tools. He wants to busy his hands. *So, what is this project, then?*

I'll show you.

The fairy presses her palm to his forehead, and Fintan nudges her like a cat for a loving stroke. Then there is a flash of white light, and a vision appears: a body, much like a fairy's gangly form, but part toy, too, in its steely strength.

From scratch? His voice is doubtful, but excited. *The heart was hard enough . . .*

Oh, please. She places her lips against his cheek, not in a kiss, but some other kind of sweet caress. Whatever it is, it thrills him. *The heart was just a warm-up for a doctor of such caliber. Your talent has much more to show, I'm sure.*

You're right. He lifts his chin and nods. *I know just how to build it.*

Good.

The fairy slips to the door and pauses there, her gossamer dress shimmering, her face moving in and out of existence. He can see her, when she reappears, with long white hair and dark black eyes that haunt his dreams—when he remembers them.

You have until tomorrow.

Impossible! He drops his hammer on the table. *The heart took weeks—*

Back then, we had them. Now, we have mere hours—just the time to prepare the form for what is yet to come.

Fintan opens his mouth to argue, but he finds he is alone. He sweeps the room with his eyes and finds a pile of metal he has never seen before—or maybe he retrieved it when he was someone else.

A body. Fine. I'm ready for the challenge. Did you hear that, Fairy? Cricket? Hello?

No sounds.

No curves of a gossamer skirt.

Fintan ties his apron on and gets to work.

CHAPTER THIRTY-FOUR

THE FAIRY

"BREATHE."

His voice is in your ear, low, soft, the hidden layer of down beneath the prickly threads of his playful fur. Medoro. You follow the voice, blink your lids, focus on the breath that meets your cheek. The heat revives you, and you let him pull you up to standing so that you can see the damage Paige has caused. The enemy is dead, laid in a grave of stone, and toys on your side huddle like the mourners of their very funerals. The room is dark, and growing darker still as one by one the candles flicker out. It smells of stale dust, wounded Fae, and water that is very far from reach.

"I had to," the girl says. She sits upon a boulder, wooden legs crossed sharply, so that thin knees press against the distressed jeans and show their joints. "They never would have let us leave."

"And now?" Doriel asks.

"We need to think."

The toys are frantic. Little mutters, tapping hands, breaths like baby birds that cannot even squeak for worms but merely open mouths to wait. Doriel paces back and forth, marking his memories, the castle watches, training days—they run him through like blood inside his veins that pumps him more dependable than you. He's like a toy that plays its part, *go right, go left, walk front and raise your sword*—or maybe this is just how you would think of him, so that you could ignore that all these years you've let them saddle you and make you tame. He would have fought. He would have gotten out. And you just sat there, singing, while the Land of Toys was scorched. The fiery bones, they weigh your chest, so that you put a hand there so you'll feel you're still alive.

Believe.

I try . . .

Medoro mutters to the cricket, who has sought his shoulder, safer ground, and mumbles something you cannot discern.

"We can't go up," Medoro says to Cricket and to all who listen, "or else they'll catch us well before we reach the portal. If we go down, what would we meet?"

"The lake," the cricket says.

"I thought it, too." Doggish smile, here, for he has not realized what you know, and why the pressure in your chest is greater still than when the stone built up the tomb. To go inside the lake is to leap from a grave into a fire, where the Land of Toys houses its darkest of designs. "We'll get as close as possible, then swim across without the Deathsprites' notice."

The girl might not be strong enough; in fact, she cannot be. At least a mile, maybe more, to pass the forest edge and meet the water's beach. They tell her this, their hands upon her shoulders, saying: *It's okay if you should fail, but please, you must believe that you might not.* You wish you could. You wish she could. You've made her strong—but nothing is as strong as that, not any living thing at least. She has her arms, her wooden fists, but she would need—

"I know!" You rise, and they all turn to you. "Add on the shovels there. She is a toy, you see, and as a toy can alter to your liking. You're makers, yes?"

"But we would be no better than—" the toys all shout.

"The Deathsprites?" You laugh a hollow echo of a sound. "What makes them is not altering, but owning, so that they might tell a toy to move and it would roll without a thought. I do not want to change her head—it's lovely as it is—but merely make her hands two more effective tools."

They think on this. It hurts them, changing things, for they have plans for toys they follow like an architect would follow structures of a building so it would not ever fall. To alter is to make a risk that need not ever enter. To alter is to lose control. But they must understand that you have lost it all already, that you are desperate mice inside a trap, that you must eat your leg or say it's time to die.

"All right," they say. Then gently, to the toy: "Come here, my dear, if you accept, and we will make this quick."

The marionette agrees and sits upon the makers' stool.

Quick work they drill two holes that make her wince. "We'll bring our tools," they say, "so when we reach the end, we'll pull them out, and plug the hole with filler."

Paige lifts her hands and waves the shovels, dancing birds with wings stretched flat upon the wind she makes. You feel the breeze a little, on your face, or maybe this is hope that flies so close.

"Let's go," she says, and clanks her hands together. "We have Deathsprites we must overtake."

The shovels work as you had hoped, so that the stones fall at her feet like nuts cracked open at a pecking beak. A passage soon emerges, and you and the toys and Doriel inch farther, farther, farther down the corridor. Paige does not falter, cannot sweat, machines her way along in steady beat, so that you are reminded of that song, again, and hum it in your head. You need not share your madness. It is the lie. It is the lie. Legs and noses. None supposes—

A hand takes your and squeezes tightly at the palm. "I missed you."

Oh, Medoro.

"More than you can know," you say, and squeeze him back. "I thought I'd never see your eyes again, that impish grin. I thought I was alone."

"You feel it still?"

"I do."

"So many years . . ." He is imagining your days, your haunting hums, your mountain bones, reading you like the manual the toys would use to build you, if they could. "But we're together now—"

"Until the end."

He nods. He does not drop your hand, not even when the tunnel shakes so violently that you're sure you're doomed.

"Uh, whoops," Paige says, and strikes again, *clank-clank, clank-clank*, but this time with a bit more tempered strength.

"What awaits us on the other side . . ." You wish you could request he turn and flee, hide anywhere he might, for if you lose him now, again—

"We'll meet the threats together."

The cricket, who has left to take Doriel's shoulder at Paige's request, cries out that she can sense a change in airflow here.

"I smell the algae," Cricket says. "I smell—"

The wall ahead breaks like a mirror to the ground, and all the shatters leave behind the puzzle pieces of the sky. There is the lake, a glowing reddish-blue about a mile long, with dead toy fish and plastic frogs who once could leap themselves over the others in a one-upped joy along the edge, their bones crushed flat beneath the feet of Deathsprites on patrol. And there are many other bodies, too, of toys long dead and stripped for parts, and you must look away before they drag you down again.

"A lying lake," you say. "The water has been poisoned."

"I can smell it," Cricket says. "It's like the Flare, but something else, a coal-like thing that burns the water red. It lies below, a smoldering, rocky thing, that they have laid—"

"To fuel what lies above." You point, and they all crane their necks to see what you have spotted. At the far end, there's a reddish magic column from the water to the sky, swirls of red and black and gray that lead to glowing stone where fairies fly to meet their Earthly forms. There, they'll add the excavated piece, once lifted from the earth. "They did this on our world, only the lake was our whole Flare, and turned it to a bloody red, to mix with their small power and create a jump. They pull not just from this small water, but the core itself, the planet's heart, that's what they drag up to their hungry whirlpool mouth. They'll turn the stone into an altered portal, and when they know that they can flee for good, they'll leave this land a cold hard rock where nothing can remain—and enter an entirely new universe ripe for their destruction."

The toys all gulp. The cricket gives a disapproving chirp, though whether for the Deathsprites or your too-untempered telling of their acts, you do not know. You'd tell the truth, despite their fear, for lying is an Earthly trait that you will never wear—but maybe time it better, next time, if you can.

"So, we go on?" Paige asks. Her hands are raised, and toys are prying shovels from between her fingers. The putty will not ever feel the same as wood—but then again, the body that she wears is always wrong, so what's a little filling in a hole that she should never have?

"We must." You face the lake, and what you've sensed there. Should you tell them? You have lost perspective, and, besides, what difference does it make? "Into the water, and deep down, to avoid capture and to meet the place where hungry vortex draws its strength."

"All right." The marionette squares up her shoulders, and, again, the cricket leaps to them. "We swim so we can save this world, and ours."

You take your shirt off, and your pants, so that you're left with just your underthings to pull you down from water's heavy weight. Medoro does the same, and silly, he's still wearing what you gave him that last night, your own white shirt, which he had promised to return when night fell back against the bed to sleep. How long ago it feels to you, when he knows nothing but the blink of one long dream—

You put your toes up to the water, feel its heat. Do not touch it, yet, for when you do . . .

"You hesitate?" Medoro asks. He rips a piece of shirt and ties it tightly 'round your upper chest and shoulder so the bleeding might be stopped. "What are you keeping to yourself?"

You take a breath and step inside the lake. Instantly, the surface glows a deeper red around you, like a hunter calling sharks with bloody meat. Your bluish glow shines bright, a single bulb inside a shadow room, and then the red becomes the great black body of the beast. The toys all stare, their mouths agape, too late to even scream.

"Atilla of the Sea," you greet her, as her red eyes glow their new possession. Long ago, you watched this very plastic beast do wide loops in the lake, which now are devil darts shoved forward by the great propellers they have thrust into her sides. They should have known—the Deathsprites would not waste so great a monster as Atilla, not when she could be of murderous use. "Take us across, you demon of the Deathsprites."

She thrusts up, blocking out the sun, and bites her mouth over the party so the tent of teeth and ground for one small second feels much like the cave you've left, then drags the dirt and toys and Fae and marionette all up in single bite, which, swallowed down her gullet, leaves you in the dark, damp waters of her chamber stomach. You hear them now, delayed, the screams of terror and impending death. The marionette calls out for Cricket, who is here, a voice chirped in the night, and there, a hand, still in your palm, a calm inside a storm.

Your chest goes tight.

This is the lie.

But you have hope, too, for the floor drops down to slide you where the beast will go, amongst the glowing coals of fairy power, and you have the girl, an axe, and several swords besides. If you cannot escape, what difference will it make, then, to be swallowed, for this whole world will end so soon, with you atop it, anyway.

Breathe, Alexio.

Just breathe.

PART FOUR

CHAPTER THIRTY-FIVE
PAIGE

PAIGE IS INSIDE A GIANT DEMON SHARK.

A giant demon shark swimming inside of a deadly lake.

A giant demon shark swimming inside of a deadly lake sitting at the center of the Deathsprites' conquered kingdom.

She takes this in as the low waters of Atilla's stomach slosh first this way, then that way, in response to the jerks of her middle and the swishing of her back end. A plastic duck floats by, flapping its wings frantically at the motion. What a day. The air here is as stale as the cave, but it smells different, like decomposed flesh and algae and bacteria probably eating its way through her damp wooden body as she stands there, swilling in it. The toys are frantic; barrel monkeys beat their little fists at the walls and stab their tools at the plastic there, while a carousel horse rams the sides with her painted hooves. They act as though the thick lining could be breached by such silly weapons—Paige might breach it, though, when she finds out what Alexio has planned.

There is his glow, finally, and Doriel's, two fireflies in an otherwise lightless forest. Paige steps through the stomach sludge, losing her shoes in the process, and only realizes halfway to the Fae that Cricket is still holding onto her shoulder.

"You all right?" Paige asks.

"I'm being eaten alive," Cricket says flatly. "So, no. I'm not all right—not even close."

They meet the Prince and Doriel, who are whispering to Medoro about something relating to the other side of the lake. When she joins them, they tell her that this shark will get them to the source of the vortex's power—but that they don't have a plan for how to actually destroy it once they arrive.

"So, you just got us swallowed *without a plan*?" Cricket hisses. "Oh, the illogical nature of Fae. Just flitting around, whining about the Flare and, overall, just making a mess of everything. If it wasn't for this marionette—"

"So, you *have* grown fondness for her," Prince Alexio says, smiling weakly. Paige wonders how long he will last, even with the power of the Flare now inside of him.

"My choices here are limited. At least she's learned her lesson about *withholding the truth,* Alexio—"

"You would not have come, if you had known."

The cricket crosses her legs, but she does not argue.

So, they are aimed like a missile, but with no weapons to fire at their arrival. Paige thinks of her mother, and how she's probably being held in Toy Palace, maybe even in those same chains that Alexio escaped. She wishes she could have told her that she understood, now, why they spent the years so far away, and ask her why she chose to finally return—

Withholding the truth.

Something falls back on itself, and Paige turns the repeating phrase over in her mind, wondering at it. Her mother hid so much, but there were also many things she told—at night, when in the caravan they lay together, heads upon a pillow that they'd share until they slept, her mother's breath so sweet and lined in red, exchanging silly stories. Paige's were about the real world, little girls who went on big adventures and came home to roost, or girls who found their missing parents, or the ones who struggled with some truth. The tales were signs that Petta seemed intentionally to miss—but maybe she could see them plain as leaks above their heads, instead was powerless to change the fate her family had passed down to her, and she to Paige again.

Petta's tales were often of a land away from theirs, a land of toys, where her creations came to life and did such things as fall in love and run a kingdom where they all lived happily ever after.

The Land of Toys.

In the stories, Paige worked with the toys on all their silly problems. She fixed the car's engine. She helped the penguin waddle straight. Petta was always sure to include her, making her a little toymaker who the toys all accepted as one of their own without question or even second thought. She lived here, in this very world, for all those years.

How could she have forgotten?

Of course she knows why. The truth is that she barely listened to those stories, too busy resenting Petta for all she imagined she had lost due to her mother's selfishness. She wanted walls. A bedroom door. A TV, where she'd watch whatever other girls watched. And meanwhile, Petta spoke to her of things she now wishes she understood—the clues of saving all these toys.

Think, Paige.

She runs the index of the stories through her mind. The little toy car. The penguin man. The plane that could not fly. There, suddenly, her finger lands upon the title she is searching for: the marionette who could not tell a lie.

Pinocchio.

But he is not who she demands, none of them are, for what she seeks is just the truth that she now knows: the world, the toy and human realms, were already connected way before the Deathsprites came. Even the Flarewhispers did not form the bond that clearly brought the stories of these real toys to the family who then passed them down as lore. So how did the Vitaleys know? What linked them? And how can she use it when the answer comes?

The shark dips down, and Paige loses her balance and must clutch Alexio's arm to stay upright.

This is the lie of the toymaker, his voice echoes in her mind. God, that terrible phrase, how she hates it—

No.

Something is different.

The lie is the truth.

She grasps at something that slips through her mind like the minnows in the waters at her feet. If the Vitaly family knew of this realm, then they had to have been there, right? But there were no Flarewhispers to slip them through the realms back then, nor a vortex to place them into the bodies of the toys.

Or, wait, that isn't necessarily correct. The Deathsprites didn't make the stone, just used it, and Toy Palace was the tether at the other end. Maybe the Vitalys had been visiting The Land of Toys through the vortex for years, entering the consciousness of the toys here the way the Deathsprites had been entering the bodies of toys on Earth.

Or maybe they weren't visiting at all.

Maybe they *were* toys, returning home to visit when they could.

And how happy I am, now that I have become a real boy!

"Alexio," she says, gripping his shoulder so tightly that he winces from the pressure. In her excitement, she had forgotten his wound. "You could have made me any toy in the world. There are things much stronger than wood, after all—metal, and iron, and lead. How did you decide to make me a marionette?"

The prince moves her hand into his. "Ah, my little wooden girl. You've solved it now, haven't you?"

"Solved what?" the cricket asks. Then, she gasps. "You're kidding, Alexio. It's impossible."

"Just believe," he says, smiling that pale, weak smile of his. "A fae who passes through the stone becomes a toy, but when a toy steps through . . . But thank goodness the Deathsprites haven't figured that out yet, nor Camilla, whose imagination for the Patched would have no limit—"

The shark halts her terrible motion, and they are all thrown forward, marionette on top of prince on top of toys. A dog's snout presses into her back and then leans away. Cricket hops frantically on Paige's cheek.

"We're here," Alexio says in Paige's ear.

Paige rises from the pile and reaches for her axe. "The story's finally coming to an end," she says, and she feels Petta somewhere just out of reach, waiting for her. The axe rises, glowing in Alexio's blue Flarelight. "It's finally time to go home."

CHAPTER THIRTY-SIX
THE DOCTOR

THE BODY IS A THING OF BEAUTY.

The head is a smooth, chrome canvas, onto which Fintan has painted the soft white eyes out of pure inset silver. They can dart in astute motions, as well as sweep gracefully. There is a nose, long and thin, that sits firmly above the mouth like a ledge above a delicately carved cave. The lips are thin, long, handsome, a mouth that one would like to kiss, except for the way they close tightly in a secretive pursed position.

And the neck. Oh, it is slender, beautifully meeting the long, flat plane of the bare chest like the top of a vase meets its base. The arms, too, as Fintan rolls them playfully in their sockets.

Perfect movement.

A graceful warrior's form.

Below the chest are the legs, more muscular than the top, built for running and kicking down doors. There must be a balance in the robot's function, so that he lies there quietly as both a deadly warrior and sleeping beauty, ready to embrace or murder depending on his programing.

Now that is the *pièce de résistance.*

Fintan licks his lips, thinking of it. The web of wires. The tangle of life, which carries messages from the computer in Fintan's hands to the delicately carved limbs. It is covered now, but Fintan is tempted to remove the back plate, run his hand through the hair of his own creation.

He is not yours, the voice reminds him.

Yes, yes. He is just the creator, and the time has come for him to set down the controls and leave the supply closet, to find his bed and collapse there until morning comes for him just a few hours later. To forget this entire thing—and, already, the world is starting to turn, so that he feels nothing but the desperate need to *leave.*

You've done well, she whispers, and the sound of her voice grates on his nerves, repulsing him. How did he ever find her beautiful? Why did he do what she asked?

I must . . . He throws himself at the door, a caged creature who desperately craves release.

Goodbye, Fintan. And thank you.

CHAPTER THIRTY-SEVEN
PAIGE

THE SHARK'S SIDE IS TOUGH TO the touch, and when she throws her axe into its hide, the blade slips from its target and falls back again to her shoulder. No, this will not work—not without an extra boost of power.

"Will you do the honors?" Paige asks Doriel.

"You test me," he says, though he smiles. She will give the weapon back when this is all over—if it's ever over.

The general places his hand on the blunt edge of the blade and closes his eyes. Blue light emits from his palm and enters the axe, where the metal glows a dull blue in response. Not full power, not even close—but maybe enough.

This time, Paige throws her full weight into the axe's blow, and the sharp edge slices into the shark's side like a knife into a soft cheese. Once she has breached the outer later, water drips around the axe, threatening entry, and she knows she must move quickly now.

"Prepare to swim!" she cries, and then she jerks the axe down hard.

Water gushes, and she feels herself buoyed by the rising tide and thrown against the opposite wall. The shark jerks in pain, and Paige is sent back across again, toward the opening.

She cannot get her feet on steady ground, but she manages to impale the axe near her previous injury and makes a second line, horizontal, to create a kind of flap. Now the water is all around them, above her head, making a pool, and the shark is sinking from the weight of it. Alexio and Doriel are sent first, and then the toys swim by, exiting the stomach in an orderly line. Paige leaves last, her wooden body urging her with every push to rise, rise, rise.

And she would, would allow herself to be risen and floated like a stick on a lazy river, except that the shark has found some bit of strength at the end and gotten her by the foot. She cannot feel much of the fangs, but Atilla jerks her back and forth the way a dog would jerk a stuffed toy, so that Paige's vision blurs and she can barely find the blue glows far above her at the surface. She can see the whirl of the red vortex, though, even in these final moments.

Just believe.

She kicks at the shark and gets her squarely in the nose. Atilla loosens her grip, and Paige kicks again, this time managing to release the hunting trap of the teeth long enough to secure her leg from its grasp. The shark glares furiously at her, and then the red lights dim and fade away to empty black.

Swim, Paige orders, and her legs obey.

The others are floating at the top of the lake. Alexio and Doriel tread water, while the heavier toys float on the lighter ones, with several of the barrel monkeys secured on the back of the plastic duck, who seems pleased with its new purpose. The duck fusses at the toys on its back, and they, in turn, hug its neck and pat its yellow rubber side. *Toys are strange creatures,* Paige thinks, and then she remembers that she's one of them.

"Now what?" she asks.

The Fae do not seem surprised to see her, and in fact they don't seem to have realized she was ever caught at all. The proximity to the vortex seems to be affecting them, so that they all seem slow and strange. Prince Alexio seems most attracted to the light, so that now he watches the glow in thoughtful communion while General Doriel opens his mouth and then closes it again. He does not seem to want to speak before his leader, and his leader does not seem like he will ever speak. His eyes pass slowly to Alexio, to the stone, and then back to Alexio again. Then he moves past Alexio, to the bank, where Paige finally realizes what has rendered them speechless.

Everywhere, excavation has mounded the earth like an endless trench, so that they seem to be held captive in its frightening slant. Unseen diggers tear at the ground, sending sprays of dirt and red sparks above the top. The sound is metal on metal, and she wonders what could be there, what unseen bones, that Fae might use to send them to her world for good.

"Speak your mind, General Doriel," Medoro says. His dog legs kick at the water playfully. "Alexio is lost in thoughts."

"Oh. Yes." Prince Alexio finally looks at them with the startled blink of someone just awakened from a vivid dream. He is so pale, and Paige imagines that if she could touch him, he'd be as cold as a frosted window. "Do you have a plan?"

"The start of one," General Doriel admits. "Without wings, we're useless . . . But what if we could get some?"

Prince Alexio raises his eyebrows. "You mean—"

"Yes." General Doriel looks to the lake bank. "Take the wings from the Patched toys there and attach them to our toys instead. We'll ask the toys, and if they say they will—"

"It's dangerous," Alexio says. "There could be Red Fire in the veins of those parts, and if it mixes into their blood . . ."

"We'll be careful," General Doriel says. "We'll make sure there is none of that terrible liquid in the pieces we use—and besides, a little Red Fire cannot conquer the strength of a toy, can it?"

Alexio shakes his head. "I do not know."

"It's our only option," Paige says. She is worried, too—more worried than her voice betrays—but there is no arguing with the fact that the vortex is hundreds of feet in the air, and they are down on a bank, trapped behind a mountain of detritus, stuck on the other side of a great divide inside of which some unknown threat is being excavated. They can rise in the air and try to turn the vortex off—or they can watch the Deathsprites do their work.

Alexio nods. He is too weak to argue much, or offer any other plans, and Paige fears yet again that he will not even make it to the portal's opening.

"My prince . . . ?" Paige asks softly.

"My marionette."

"You need to rest—"

"I'll rest when we have won."

He does not say anything else, but finds a rock at the bank and sits there quietly, lost in thought. The mound is close enough that they could touch it, and she does, feeling loose dirt slip through her fingers or catch in the grainy grooves, leaving streaks of brownish-red across the wooden plains of her palms. Paige wishes she could open up the prince's head and listen to the whispers there, the mountainous bones that sing their tunes upon his skull, so she might ease his guilt and take a bit of burden—but then again, she needs to keep her focus on the plan.

"Can you address the toys?" General Doriel asks from next to her.

"What, me?" she asks, though she already knows what he means.

"You're one of them," he says, and shrugs. "They'd hear you better than a Fae."

Paige gulps. She hates big crowds, and stares, and expectations—*This is why I run the register, remember?*—and it's also why she hid at all the conferences, so that Petta could not march her through the rooms, her trophy daughter, bragging all about her budding maker skills. Paige knew she had no talent, not the true kind, not like Petta, with her graceful brushstrokes and her agile carves along the wood. Paige merely watched her and learned what was expected, nothing more. And now, the toys are staring from their little huddled crowd, expecting something great to leave her mouth. The carousel horse whinnies softly in anticipation. The muscle man flexes his muscles, as if a child is squeezing his chest to the beat of Paige's heart. The monkeys are tossing their weight from fist to fist, their feet swinging in time to the seconds that pass in silence.

"Uh . . ."

Just believe.

She gulps. ". . . We think that we can take the wings from Deathsprite toys—"

The toys cry out in indignation, audible over even the pounding of the excavation on the other side. They have done what she has asked, attached the shovels, but they hate the way the deviation feels, would like to go back to the manuals, for protocols are made for their good reasons—

"—and put them on you—"

Now the talk is louder. No one wants the demon wings, and what if Deathsprite power comes along with them? What if their eyes turn red too, after all, no one can know the true work of the fairies' power?—

"—so that we fly to the vortex—"

They cry in fear. The vortex?

"—and steal the stone before the excavation is complete—"

They would not approach that swirling madness for the world, no, they have done what has been asked, and got the Fae to where they might take up their swords and fight their battle, but sweet toys are not created for such war, and plus—

"—STOP!" Paige finally yells.

The toys go silent, though they blink their bubble eyes in panicked disapproval.

"At any moment, Deathsprites will rise up with their discovery and then descend on Earth—my planet." Paige's palms are tingling, but she clenches them and takes a breath. *You can do this.* Then she continues, "All the hope there, all the bonds between the toys and children, will be totally destroyed. A hope that I lost, or maybe never had, until I came to this realm and met all the toys here who have shown their bravery and strength. Cricket. Medoro. And all of you, who fought the Fae and left your cave and took down great Atilla. You're stronger than you know. You think the Fae can take that all away with just a nail or two? A pair of wings? I doubt it. They'd need to take your spirit, too, and let me tell you, no one here is going to let that happen. Okay?"

Blink.

Blink.

Cheers.

"Shh," Doriel hushes. "We cannot alert the enemy we're here. We need the element of surprise, if we have any hope of overtaking them."

The toys all nod. Doriel leads the pack, and quietly, they move along the bank, so that the underbrush, more like a forest now that she is small, can hide them from the guards who watch the land there. Wet sand mixed with soil squelches under her weight, while, against her arms, cattails brush their soft brown heads. Blue spikes of flowers send up clouds of dragonflies around her face, and clumps of rushes hold the soil firm against her stomping feet. How strange, to traipse through such a pretty underbrush, when right beside a wall of soil hides a planet's grave.

Along their path, the makers gather bits of fallen toys that they might use themselves—propellers, wings of airplanes, even parachutes from soldiers who have lost their lower limbs. But there are not enough—so Doriel points them up, into the trees, where Paige understands that they will need more wings from demon toys who flit across the sky on their patrol.

"I really hate heights," Paige says.

She never was the kind of kid who climbed trees—and what trees would she climb, anyway, without a yard, or neighbors, or even a park where she might wander from the picnic blanket over to a group of kids and follow them between the outstretched branches? They were always moving, always on the road, or parked in cement lots where nothing green could grow, and climbing trees was just about the last thing Paige would think to do when she was busy making toys with Petta, or filling out the paperwork for their next stop, or wandering the streets of yet another unfamiliar city where, for just a week or two, she'd call the strange streets home. But she was never the kind of kid who did any of this—traveled through portals, or fought in battles, or tried to save a whole universe from destruction—and yet here she is, doing all of it. *Wanting* to do it. "Do you not hate the death of your entire species more?" Cricket asks from her shoulder.

Point taken, Paige thinks. *So, I guess I can officially add terrifying climb to my growing list of firsts.*

The tree Paige picks is half-dead. Bark strips at her grip, and she can barely find a place to fit her fingers without falling back again. Her feet find landing posts on branches, but with a double snap, they fall away and crash into the underbrush.

"Shh!" General Doriel says, and Paige just shrugs—what can she do now? Then his branch falls away, and he is hanging twenty feet above the ground, then ten, then landing in the underbrush and rolling off the impact.

"The trees are—" Paige begins.

General Doriel's eyes are wide and somewhere past her head. "Paige, look out!"

She whips her head around to find a toy behind her. Patched thing, a creepy doll, with frizzy hair and broken cheek that turns her like a teacup shattered on a kitchen floor. And it has wings, a plane's, fused at her sides instead of at her back, so that the messy metal seams look like the doll's been dipped in tar and left abandoned.

"Take her down!" the General cries, and Paige leaps from her branch and grabs the Patched doll around the middle. The toy bee buzzes back and forth across the sky, then upside-down, then spinning like a jet on ambush, while Paige holds on as tightly as she can. Another body hits their deathly dance, and Paige finds Doriel beside her, with his sword impaled in the doll's neck. The head cracks into pieces, and the doll descends, so that they have to leap away or be destroyed on impact.

"Catch her!" Doriel yells, and the toys below manage to grab the dead doll before she breaks her wings upon the ground.

"Quickly, drain out the Red Fire and start attaching wings to toys so that they might battle any aerial attacks. The rest of you will join, when we have found more to attach to you."

The toys take the plane wings off the Patched with the little saws hooked to their leather belts and then look amongst them, wondering.

"I'll do it first," Paige says. She bends her knees so that the toys can reach her back. "Just do it quick—"

"No, me." A soldier toy steps forward. "If it doesn't work . . ."

"You're sure?" she asks.

"We need you, Paige."

You do?

Paige stands and lets him take her place. The toys all get to work, and soon the wings are hinged onto the soldier's back, so that he snaps them up and slips them down whenever he commands. They check his eyes, but there's no sign of red, no Deathsprite magic, and Paige breathes again.

"Go try them out," the General says. "Report back on your sightings."

The soldier snaps his wings and flies. He dips at first, but then he finds the wind and pushes with it, so that soon he's disappeared somewhere beyond their sight.

"Who's next?" the cricket asks.

The toys all raise their hands.

CHAPTER THIRTY-EIGHT

THE DOCTOR

FINTAN WAKES TO THE FRUSTRATED CHATTER of the guards somewhere far down the hall. No, it is not just the guards, but the Fae, too, all complaining that the toys with Prince Alexio are ruining their work.

"Pegasus wings on a marionette," one of his workers is saying. "It's appalling."

"And airplane wings on a soldier. Who would think of such a thing?"

Fintan blinks and tries to pull himself from sleep. He is so tired, as though he only just fell asleep a few hours ago. His muscles argue with the strain of merely rising from his pillow. Is he sick?

"Doctor," one of his employees says from the door. "You'll never believe what's happening."

And so, he hears it—all of it—and the thought of his beautiful children being disassembled and pieced onto the wrong toys makes him clench his fists in rage. *But I thought you didn't care what happened to them?* The sarcastic voice mocks, and this time, Fintan does throw his fist, taking down the poor Fae who delivered the news.

"I'm sorry," the Fae says from the floor. He's just a crumpled, ugly body, innocent of everything except his sloppy existence. *Not exactly a deserving target.*

I know. Fintan fights the urge to punch the Fae again. *I'm just very, very frustrated.*

You and I both. I wanted to escape this place eighteen years ago, remember? But nooooo, you had to stay and be the evil hero, or whatever it is you call yourself.

I'm a doctor, Fintan says, then realizes, too late, that the voice knows his title perfectly well. *Oh, go away and leave me be.*

Gladly, the voice says. *But I'm going to enjoy what happens next.*

Fintan helps the Fae up and apologizes vaguely, claiming that he was interrupted from a bad dream that had left him quite on edge.

"No apology needed," the Fae says, bowing gratefully. And he does owe Fintan, after all, for the doctor is the only reason they are still alive today. "I should not have startled you."

The Fae tells Fintan what has happened: Prince Alexio has indeed returned, and worse, he has found General Doriel, too. And toys, who've long hidden in the woods, now right outside the prison doors and bent on taking down the vortex.

"And your beautiful unearthing, too," the Fae adds, cringing with the news in anticipation of another blow.

"What unearthing?" Fintan asks.

"You know." The Fae pauses and then adds, in confusion, "The one that will let the Deathsprites travel through? The one we've been digging up and building back for all these years . . . ?"

Fintan shakes his head. There is that feeling again, like the haze of an early morning fog, threatening to drag his brain back to sleep. "Oh. Right. Of course."

He thinks, *Was that you?*

Oh, please, says the sarcastic commentator, *you must be joking. You know I just sit and watch the show.*

Not the toymaker either, then, for he allows Fintan to remember what he's made, but someone else—someone darker. He feels a strange breath on his cheek, warm and ash-smoked. Fintan shakes his head a few times, trying to remember, but gains only a headache.

"So, what are we doing about all of this?" Fintan asks.

The worker shrugs. "The Deathsprites are trying to get the machine working, even though your plans are not complete. Our guards are leaving now to join them."

"Oh." Fintan blinks. "So, are we free, then?"

"I suppose?"

"Well."

Neither of them says anything more, and then the worker leaves the cell, probably to flee with the other Fae who have suddenly found themselves the kings and queens of the Land of Toys. There will be the silly amalgamations to deal with, once the dust settles—but they are nothing Fintan's own toys can't take care of, with a little guidance and dedication.

Fintan leaves his cell, and indeed, the hallway is empty of guards.

There are no footsteps anywhere.

The prison is empty.

"Not quite, Doctor. Turn around slowly, and if you value your life, don't make any sudden movements."

CHAPTER THIRTY-NINE

LILY

THEY DRIVE FOR HOURS. LILY FADES in and out of consciousness, until the taste of cool water at her parched lips revives her enough to see a concerned Petta hovering above her head. There is another woman there too, a strange woman, with red-blond hair and a corset top that would make Lily's parents whisper behind their hands—*and at her age*. Her stockings are white with tiny yellow daisies; her boots are red cowboy boots with black roses stitched on the sides.

"You look familiar," Lily croaks.

"I was on the boat," the woman says. "With Paige."

Lily nods. Her muscles feel stiff—and of course they would, since she's been sleeping on the hard van floor. She works her elbows under her body and sits up, and then Petta feeds her a little more water, which runs over the side of her mouth and dribbles down Lily's neck.

"Where are we?" Lily sits up all the way. Through the doorway, she spots a dense forest and a small clearing packed with some of the same cars as the alley. "And who are they?"

"We call ourselves the Organization of Traditional Toymakers," Petta says. "But we're really just old friends who have an . . . interest . . . in preserving the traditional ways of our ancestors."

"Like Arnaldo Vitaly?"

Petta smiles at the familiar name. "Oh, much older than that."

Petta lifts Lily from the van and sets her on the grass, with her back against one of the van tires. From there, she can watch the others moving about the clearing, exchanging tools and tying their aprons back on. They appear to be preparing for something, although Lily cannot hear any of the words they mutter to each other as they bustle from one side of the clearing to the other.

"I'll be back," Petta says. Her eyes are on the others. "I must speak with them—alone."

Lily nods—what choice does she have?—and watches as Petta joins the crowd. They flock to her and form a tight circle, from which no words escape, only low mutters. Sasha has stayed with Lily, and she wonders why this woman is not permitted to hear whatever Petta must say.

"I'm not a toymaker," Sasha says. She sits on the ledge of the open van door, close to Lily. "Just a singer who happens to have gotten involved with the escape of the daughter of one."

"Paige." Lily nods. "I saw you when the portal opened."

"And you are . . . ?" Sasha lifts her eyebrows.

"Lily Jones." Lily manages to raise her hand to shake Sasha's. "Manager—well, former manager—of Toy Palace."

"Ah." Sasha puts her other hand over the one Lily is shaking. There are little blue veins there, webbed like the flowers on a porcelain plate, and lots of silver rings with big purple and blue gemstones, accompanied by an all-metal skull on her ring finger. "My condolences."

"Thanks." Lily tries her legs again and finds that this time, she can stand on her own. Now, she can really take in the setting—a wall of thick brown trunks, the dense foliage of their tops, the tangled underbrush accompanied by the telltale leaves of poison ivy and some sharp thorns. There is one break in the trees, a long dirt road carved from the forest that seems to stretch on forever, down which they must have driven before they parked. "Where are we?"

Sasha shrugs. "Somewhere in Indiana. I just followed the directions Petta gave me—I don't know much more than that."

Petta is still talking, but now the toymakers hug, embracing each other with tight squeezes and heavy pats on their shoulders.

"What's going on?" Lily asks, though she knows Sasha doesn't have any idea. "Are we leaving?"

One of the toymakers, a man with a long beard and an old-fashioned tweed hat, leaves the group to walk to the red Buick. He retrieves a brown leather suitcase, closes his trunk, and returns to the group, where the other toymakers gather to look at what he has brought. Lily cranes her neck, but she cannot see through the tight huddle of the onlookers.

"Oh," Sasha says, her voice full of wonder.

Lily shifts her weight so that she can look from Sasha's angle, and there, in Petta's hand, is some kind of broken glass. But rather than being able to see through it, Lily is almost immediately blinded by a strange blue glow—the kind of glow that emanated from the man in chains right before he disappeared.

"What is it?" Lily asks, her voice coming out in a whisper.

Sasha does not answer—perhaps she cannot speak. The shard seems to have that effect, for Lily, too, descends into muted wonder. The toymakers take a step back, so that they are standing in a circle with their shoulders touching, and then Petta raises the shard into the middle of the circle so that they can all place one hand on the long, sharp edge. Lily expects them to hesitate—after all, the edge looks like it could cut clean through their skin—but they all take up the shard without hesitation.

"It must be together," Petta says.

Her eyes drift over the shoulders of the toymakers across from her, and then she finds Lily's gaze and holds it. She nods, as though to say *Thank you*, and Lily nods back. Then, shifting her gaze to the shard, she cries out a phrase that will echo in Lily's head over and over again in the days to come:

"One with the Flare!"

"One with the Flare!" the toymakers repeat.

"One with the great white light!"

"One with the great white light!" the toymakers yell, stepping together again to raise the shard as high as they can above their heads.

Lily waits.

And waits.

And waits, until her gaze has drifted up to the passing clouds in the sky from boredom.

Nothing happens.

CHAPTER FORTY

PAIGE

THEY ARE TOYS OF FLIGHT.

Paige's wings are bird bones stripped off of a Patched flying horse, a hawk-like Pegasus that took a chunk of wood out of her shoulder in the fight—and yet, she'd do it all again to fly just once like this, with all the trees below her, and the castle in the distance with its mound of bones, and all the Deathsprites at their fires, cooking up their hand-crafted demons. They are terrible, even at this distance, their great metal wings flexing open to glisten their blades in the glow of the fires and then folding back behind their stubby forms like hawks' wings as they prepare to dive for a kill. Their chest plates announce the ones they have melted down and hammered and chopped and nailed—a cemetery of toys. One close to them presses a button on the pack around its waist, creating a cloud of dust as it lifts the Deathsprite unsteadily into the air, and then there are the wings again, balancing their armory in the unhelpful wind. Paige wonders what the point is in all this metal, all of this weight, when with just their own bones and skin stretched taut might carry them more gracefully.

"They do not wish to fly," Alexio says by her ear. He rides Medoro, who has added kite-wings to his back, and they whip wildly back and forth and seem, for just a moment, to forget they're riding to their death; beside him, General Doriel is on the back of a plane monkey, with its drum around its neck and tail a perky "S" of joy.

"They wish to kill. Think of a scorpion, with wings for a stabbing tail. Think of a predator, who spends its days sitting in wait until its insect prey makes the mistake of passing by its pincer claws. Think of the way they must digest their food externally, then suck it up, the flowing red of Fae and other beings we can only guess."

Paige swallows hard and looks away. There is the strange circle from which Fae excavate something from the ground, which her crew knew only as a sound a few minutes before but now looks like it means to hang the lake, or the whole land—though how, she still cannot determine. In the groove of the dug-up dirt there are metal bones, and with them, the Fae workers who pour new metal into the spaces between the bones and nail and solder them. The smell is stifling, like inhaling the smoke and heat of air beside a bonfire.

Her body tells her she should turn away, but there is no choice but the one ahead.

"Let's go," she says, and as she thrusts her body forward with her wings, the toys fly at her side, like one great flock of birds.

"We need to find a way to take it down," Doriel calls out on the wind. "Once we determine—"

"There." Paige points to the strange tubes of red liquid feeding into the top of the stone, which she could not see when they were on the ground. "Do you know how it works?"

He shakes his head no.

The air is wild beneath their wings. It's growing faster, colder, as they meet the vortex air around the spinning light. None of this makes sense—

They do not see them coming. Suddenly, they're everywhere, an army of the Deathsprites, like a hive drawn out to sting an unsuspecting hand. Paige braces for the impact, and the metal wings thrust her away, so that she barrels backwards in the air. Her vision swims; wind whips at her cheeks and over her hair. She tries to find Alexio, and there he is, amidst the Flarewhispers and toys, appearing and then disappearing as she spins. Finally, she activates her wings, spreading them wide to catch her in a sudden hammock of resistance. Then she thrusts her wings backward, sending her body like a slingshot through the air toward Alexio, who's being wrenched from poor Medoro's back. Medoro howls and bites at them, but they don't care about his rage, not when they are so close to their prize. A Deathsprite slices poor Medoro's cheek, then hits him squarely in the jaw with a blunt fist, so that the dog's thrust back enough to loosen Prince Alexio's grip.

His balled fists hold fur, but no Medoro.

The Deathsprites swarm him.

He is being taken up.

Of course.

This is why they kept him for all of those years, Paige thinks as she flaps her wings wildly upward, *while they gathered the power they would need to open the portal for good.*

This is the lie.

They carry their cargo up on their tide, while Paige and the other toys beat at the back line of Deathsprites with their wings and fists and feet. Paige manages to loosen some of the metal from a wing so that she then can stab the bone into the neck of its original owner, and Red Fire spurts from the wound onto her chest. It glows there, almost pulsing, for a moment, sending smells of sulfur up her nose, and then the blood dries instantly into a dusty red. The injured Fae careens away, revealing the next Deathsprite in the flock, who barely turns her head as Paige rips off her wing. The Deathsprite tumbles, but almost immediately, another warrior takes her place. Paige's body strains against the double effort of the blows and flapping wings. No matter how many hits she lands, the Deathsprites will not be distracted, not even when she hooks their metal bones and pulls or hits her axe into their chest, not even as they die. It's like they think as one, one swarm, one foe, their only goal to get Alexio *up* to activate the portal.

She pushes in again, but despite her efforts and one more fallen Fae, they crest their wave at the stone. Paige is pushed backward again, and the Deathsprites form a strong perimeter. Inside the circle, two Fae strap Alexio to the stone with rope, so that his body is like a glove over a hand.

"Alexio!" Paige screams, flying at the closest Deathsprite, but with his attention squarely on her now, he lands a stabbing blow of his talon into her upper arm and sends her reeling back in pain. The other toys attack in her place, and then they fall—a paratrooper with his rubber pterodactyl wings ripped off, a patchwork doll with eyes removed so that she aims her helicopter blades in wild directions, one of the monkeys clutching at the empty air without its hand. Paige can't decide if she should pull the others back or forge ahead, and her eyes dart wildly, trying to find the answer in the crowd.

"Save the prince!" Cricket cries, as though that is not what they are all trying to do, as if there is any hope at all.

Paige thrusts into the battle again, axe meeting Deathsprites, but there are far too many. One beats at her with the metal bones of his wings, and when she finally lands an axe blow to his chest, the next Fae impales the tip of her talon into Paige's upper thigh. Again, she rings the axe against the metal chest; again, the next Fae swipes their glowing sword, shaving off a bit of shirt and splintered wood. There are so few toys around her now, and those that still fly breathe in ragged breaths and wave the stumps where other limbs should be. How can she send those who remain to certain death?

"Quickly, quickly!" Cricket cries. "They've almost done it!"

Paige opens her mouth to stop the toys, to say that they are through, but they won't hear her over the sudden commotion of the vortex, which now emits a strange and squealing sound, as though it is trying to halt. Then it begins again, only this time, it kaleidoscopes the other way. The swirling air glows blue—not pale, but brilliant, like a star about to burn itself into oblivion.

"Watch out!" Paige cries.

The vortex sparks, and all the Deathsprites scatter. The swirling air in the center churns faster, becomes a hungry mouth into which toys and Fae are sucked with screams and cries for help. Paige grabs for them, but they slip through her fingers and are consumed. The vortex shakes, and light beams stretch their wild winds. The other toys are hit, and they plummet to the lake like rocks thrown by a reckless hand.

"What's happening?" Paige cries.

Then, below her, on the ground, she sees the vortex lift a newer object—one that until now has laid in settled rest inside the mound. Two nostrils, deep gray pits inside the metal nose, which brings behind it a snout and glowing eyes, red fires tinged with blue, like evil stars. Behind them, a horn, a sword-top that could skewer a whale in one sharp thrust; and then the serpent neck, the spikes; the chest as large as a castle face; two great leg towers; catlike claws that find their purchase in the earth and take the body from its grave to shake the thighs and spiky tail. And then the wings—like tents, or planet shrouds, so that they block the lake completely as they stretch and fold—which after testing find their angle and begin to beat.

"A dragon . . ." Paige cannot believe—and yet, how else to call the metal beast they've dug up from the earth? She's seen a small toy of the same design once, on a table in front of a candy store—3D printed, a sign announced. When she held it in her hands, the articulated pieces curved and swayed in a way that was both appealing and unsettling, like holding a live snake. How can the design be so new, and yet this toy so old? And how can they possibly think to tame it, when, with one determined stomp, it might destroy a world, or many?

The dragon, now uncurled, sets upon the realm, lifts its wings again, and rises to the sky. The shadow on the earth is like the shadow of a meteor, or like a dying sun, the kind of shadow that announces all will end—and there is nothing left to do but close your eyes and wait for it. The dragon flies one time around the lake and then above, to where the vortex swirls its wild blue, and spins a circle there until the teeth barred in the snout can meet the dragon's tail and find a hold.

It's like a ring, Paige thinks, as quickly now the dragon-circle spins. The stone beneath Alexio glows brighter, and the dragon too, all blue and flame, and then it takes the vortex light inside its body, in that circle, like a bubble wand that holds a filmy surface, thin and malleable. The dragon drops, and hinges so it rests upon the earth, a spinning vortex disconnected from its source, and yet containing it. How does it work? How can it hold that glow?

It might yet fail—but then the center holds, and holds, and holds. The glow becomes opaque, and then it turns so black, an absence, like an empty hallway between worlds.

Paige looks again high up, where Prince Alexio is watching from his slumped position on the stone. His hand is out, as though to take hers. What is he doing? Then she sees her own hand, also stretched, and glowing blue. He's guarding her—but not for long. And now the air is stilling, so that the Deathsprites flock to the new vortex with barely a glance in her direction. They know that soon the magic will fade, and the marionette will be unable to stop them. Better to pass through while they can. Better to leave.

But what can I do? I'm just one girl—

—one piece of wood.

Below her, the toys float on the water, passed out or maybe gone for good. The demonic dogs wait at the shoreline, waiting for the toys in the water to make the mistake of coming to land. Their teeth snap. They want blood. Even if the Deathsprites leave, there is little hope that these toys will ever stop hunting the rest.

I can't do this, Alexio.

"Oh, come on." The voice is Cricket's, and only now does Paige remember that the insect still sits on her shoulder. "None of this was ever possible, Paige. But did it stop you?"

"No." Paige squares her shoulders and grips her axe. "Okay. Let's take one last stand, for those who still survive below—"

"—and for all who have been lost," Cricket finishes.

Paige darts around the crowd of Deathsprites and hovers in front of the dragon's ring-shaped vortex. She lifts her axe and takes a battle stance, knees bent and one shoulder back. How many will she take before they overwhelm her?

"Let's finally burn this marionette," one of the Deathsprites says. Paige has never heard them speak—did not know they even could—but their voices are low and rough, like sandpaper on wood. She shivers. The world is going strange around her, darkening, or perhaps that is just the shadow of the wings as the mass of them moves closer, closer, closer. Soon, she will be eclipsed.

Together, they fly at her. They move quickly and wildly, like snakes darting for a hand, but the light around her glows a protective cocoon which they cannot enter. They beat their wings, bang their metal claws, while Paige manages to land the axe on one, two, three of them. More take their place, and now they are closing in, forming a husk around her shell that, when the glow does fade, will crush her into splinters. She can see the horrible red glow of their bloodshot eyes. She hears ringing in her ears, or maybe that is the shadow of a heartbeat she no longer contains. Wildly, she swings the axe, landing a sharp slash across the chests of the three Deathsprites in front of her. She is so tired. The glow around her is starting to fade.

Come on, Paige. Keep moving!

"Move, Paige!"

The voice is not the crickets, nor Alexio's, but it is familiar. Paige whips around. She knows that voice—but how can it be here?

"Mom?"

CHAPTER FORTY-ONE

LILY

How tired their arms must be. How much their throats must ache. It's been hours, but again, Petta takes up her cry, and again, the toymakers repeat her call. *They're probably all completely insane,* Lily realizes, looking back to the circle. *And I might be, too.*

"How long will they stay here?" Lily whispers to Sasha in a brief break between toymaker yells.

"Until it works, I'd bet," Sasha says. She has removed a little bag of beads and is stringing them on a stretchy strand of plastic. Her fingers move quickly, and in just a few minutes she hands Lily the jade necklace with an insistent, "Keep it."

"Thanks." Lily slips the necklace over her head and draws it far enough away from her body that she can look at it. "It's really pretty."

"Keeps my hands busy." Out comes another plastic bag. "I sell them, too, when we do the bigger festivals. Not much more than gas money, but hey, it helps."

Lily wishes she had something to do with her hands—counting coins in the register, or running a pencil's eraser across a line of boxes as she counts the inventory at the end of the month. *Not exactly rocket science,* her dad would say, or on his harsher days, *A trained monkey could do it.* But she loves the pride that surges through her as she adjusts the numbers based on what her team has sold.

Loved, she corrects. *That life is gone now, and you can never get it back.*

But where will she go? She has a bit of money saved, but it's still less than a year of her salary—not enough to live on. And she doesn't have a place to stay—not without asking her parents for help cosigning on a lease.

Has this all been a mistake?

Have I actually ruined my life for good this time?

Maybe she should have gotten an internship one of those summers instead of coming home. Maybe she should have moved to a big city at the end of her senior year. Maybe she should have folded up her Toy Palace t-shirt and placed it in a box on a shelf in her closet and left it there, like everyone else. Maybe she should have seen the job for what it was—a desperate attempt to cling to her childhood, back when she was just a perfect girl who adored her parents and did everything right and never ever *ever* thought of girls in dirty hoodies the way she had been thinking of Paige since the day that she met her. Maybe she still could do all of those things, if she turned around now and went home, if she packed her thoughts into a box and slid it up onto the top shelf of her mind, if she—

"You can feel it too, can't you?" Sasha whispers.

"What?"

"That pull—his special brand of revelation and regret."

How had she missed it before? That feeling, the weight of the air, blowing this time over the grass like an ominous wind?

"It's actually going to work" Lily says in awe, and she and Sasha rise at the same time to look at the group of toymakers still standing in the center of the clearing. The beads that were on the van floor next to Sasha roll away, but neither of them moves to catch any of them.

There is the familiar cut through reality.

There is a break in the forest.

There is the wind, whipping faster and faster, as though it aims to wrench them all from their world and drag them like a tide into some other realm on the other side.

Then there is an even stranger sight: a wooden marionette with bird wings and the man who was once chained in Toy Palace fighting off what look like demons. Their terrible blade wings flash in the blue glow; their faces are the scrunched and scarred fury of death itself.

None of this is possible, Lily tells herself—and yet she finds that she does believe it. Petta's words echo through her mind, too: *Set the bar for reality there, okay?*

As though she has heard Lily's thoughts, the marionette turns, and the surprised face is that of Paige. She looks different now—not just because she is made of wood, or because of the wings, but in the expression she gives, like the flat and determined hull of a boat insisting its way through the violent seas of an unrelenting ocean—but it is her, nonetheless.

Beautiful, Lily thinks as the marionette meets her eyes.

The marionette smiles a little, as though she is reading Lily's mind—and maybe she can, for, after all, anything seems possible now. Or maybe it's the creature on her shoulder, some kind of insect, which seems to lean over to whisper in her ear.

Lily raises her hand in hello.

Paige does the same back.

Then the toymakers are rushing through the gap—or, at least, they used to be toymakers, though as they meet the space the shard has made, they turn into something else entirely. Marionettes, of course, but also dolls, tin soldiers, and other toys Lily cannot even identify in the flash of their rush. Into the battle they thrust, their tools raised up to meet the bodies of the fairies who Paige appears to be trying to conquer.

Then, in another flash, the portal and all the toys inside of it are gone.

CHAPTER FORTY-TWO
PAIGE

THROUGH THE VORTEX, THERE PETTA IS, standing in a forest. The wind that swirls between them whips her hair into her eyes, but Petta does not blink. Behind her, many people stand—people Paige knows, somehow, though she cannot quite place them.

"Move!"

Paige thrusts her body back, straight through the crowd of surprised Fae, so that she stands behind them like a shadow. From the vortex, the whole crowd on the other side comes through the passageway—but they look different, as they move from realm to realm. First, Petta turns to wood, a marionette much like the maker but with grains that pattern her so beautifully. Then, others turn to iron, porcelain, and plastic, unicorns that catch them as they fall, and army men with parachutes, and flying fairy princesses that whip their wings like seed pods on a breeze.

Of course.

The conferences, where all the makers came together, talked of toys and magic they could make with them.

They're not makers, but the ones who came across the vortex long before.

They're toys.

"Go," her mother says from her seat on the top of a wooden airplane, and then she nods her head up toward Alexio. "Quick, before they—"

Paige shoots up above the fray before she can hear the rest of Petta's warning. She finds the prince as she has seen him, slumped and almost drained.

"Let's get you off of here—"

"No. Wait." He shakes his head. "If I leave, and the portal closes, no one will get home."

"There will not be a home, Alexio." Paige's voice is stern and strong. "Get off, and let it close."

The prince nods, and she gets to work untying all his bonds. They're Fae-charmed, but the axe still glows its Flarewhisper blue. The ties fall off and plummet to the water, while Paige takes up Alexio in her arms.

"You're going to be okay," she says.

"Oh, Paige." He smiles weakly. "You know I'm not."

She flies him down, around the clashing swords and metal wings, until they meet the ground where the good toys battle the bad. Paige takes down a dog with a sharp kick to its side, and then a doll by throwing her shoulder into the Patched toy's chest. Then there is Medoro, finally, who takes the prince in his own arms so that Paige can protect them. His fur is matted with blood, and it sticks up in all the wrong directions. One eye has a growing bruise, and one arm is slashed in a thin X of sword marks.

"My love," Medoro says. He buries his face in the prince's shoulder. "You cannot leave me."

"Oh, Medoro." Prince Alexio puts his hand through Medoro's fur. "We always knew how this would end. *Until we meet again, in this world or the one that we have made.*"

"No!" Medoro cries, but a sweet blue glow emits, then flickers out.

Alexio's head falls to the side.

Medoro howls, the worst sound Paige has ever heard, and ever will again.

She cannot breathe.

No, she thinks, *please don't, Alexio. We all need you. I need you. Please, please, please—*

"He's gone." Medoro sits hard on the ground. "He's really gone, Paige." His perky ears lie flat on wetted cheeks. "Oh, my sweet Alexio."

No, no, no, no, "No!"

***

THE BATTLE ENDS, THOUGH PAIGE DOES not look up to see it. The dragon flies away, and no one can explain where it has gone.

Somewhere close, her mother calls her name.

At her side, the general weeps deeply.

This is the lie.

This is the lie.

This is the lie.

CHAPTER FORTY-THREE

THE DOCTOR

When Fintan turns around, it is Gwynn who holds a gun up to his chest.

"What are you doing?" the doctor asks.

The Fae uses their spare hand to pat the doctor down, but he has no weapons, not even a screwdriver. Satisfied, his assistant takes a step back without lowering the gun.

"I can hear her too, you know." They tap their temple. "The fairy with the glistening hand."

"What?" Fintan blinks in confusion. Something plays on the edge of his mind, but it's slapped off the edges of his memory before he can recall it. "What hand? What are you talking about, Gwynn?"

"I know it's different for you." Gwynn sighs. "Just one voice among many, am I right, Doctor?"

This is going to be good!, the sarcastic voice squeals suddenly, so that Fintan clutches at his temples at the sudden harshness of her voice. *Get me some popcorn!*

"I don't know what you're talking about—"

"You don't remember it, do you?" Gwynn shakes their head, so that the glistening sweat on their hair falls like a dog after a wash. They must have been running before they came for Fintan—but running where? "The body in the basement?"

"We have lots of toys there—"

"Well, what about the stone shifting the vortex?" Gwynn is taunting him, and Fintan's hands ball in fury. "Do you remember that?"

Oh, they are onto you! They've got you good, Fintan!

"No, but I'm sure I've just been distracted by—"

Gwynn is giving Fintan a pitiful smile, and how the doctor wants to slap it off his smug assistant's face. What does Gwynn know about voices, or bodies, or the vortex? They could no sooner build a toy than sprout wings and fly.

"By your madness." Gwynn's smile falls away. "We weren't meant to build, Fintan. Your arrogance has gotten the best of you."

Fintan flies at Gwynn, slapping the gun from his assistant's hands and getting them by the neck, so that the pulse is right there, under his palms, ready to beat its final thrum.

Oh, Fintan. The voice is sweet, and pure, and glistening, and he finds his hands loosening under its possession. *The time for your games has finally come to an end. Embrace your bloodline, my child, and be remade.*

"We are ready for the transfer, Doctor."

The glistening hand holds Fintan's shoulder, anchoring him in the present moment. He will not slip away now. He will not even blink.

PART FIVE

CHAPTER FORTY-FOUR

PAIGE

"Paige? Wake up, honey."

Paige opens her eyes. Above her, a fresco, gold, like funeral flowers above the headposts waiting like four deathly ghosts. She turns her neck to find a window, far too blue, a mockery of what should be power from a Starsprite prince's hands. Blue pillows by her side are just three bodies piled lifeless on the graveyard bed.

This is the lie.

"Paige?" Her mother presses her hand against her daughter's head. "Paige, honey, can you hear me?"

"You should have told me." Paige sits up and fights the spinning room. "Why didn't you tell me?"

Petta looks like she would say something to argue, but instead, she gives a heavy sigh and looks out through the window. "I'm sorry."

So, they are trapped here now. The Land of Toys. Paige wishes she cared more, but she feels numb, like even at her core she's turned to hardened wood.

Petta stands and goes to the window. Paige imagines Alexio there, staring out at the death that he had brought, and her heart aches to see him there again. She should have saved him. She should have found a way—

"My grandmother entrusted me to save our family name." Petta sighs again. "She told me where we came from—really came from—and said not to tell my father or my sister. Even then, Camilla seemed so different than the rest of us—she saw the world as something to be conquered, not created. My grandmother didn't trust her."

"I know the feeling." Paige wants to be numb, but a prick of anger stabs through the coldness of her chest.

Petta hangs her head. "Things went awry, and . . . well . . . you know the rest. I thought that finding all the other toys would help, that together at our conferences we might find a way to save this place . . ."

Paige thinks of all the days spent waiting in the caravan, while Petta claimed she learned to etch new patterns, or to stitch a bear more pleasantly. The nights spent driving, searching for some clue she could not comprehend. "But you couldn't figure out how to get back."

"I thought Alexio was gone. If I had known Camilla had him . . ."

"Then you'd have used him, too?" Paige crosses her arms. "He wasn't just some power source, you know. He was my friend."

"I know." Petta comes back to the bed. "And I know what it's like to blame yourself—"

"I don't," Paige says, but of course she does. She looks down at her hands, which, finally, appear familiar even in their textured timber. "So, why'd you come back to town, then, anyway?"

"Oh, Paige." Petta seems like she would cry, except she can't. "I wish I could say I came to save the toys, or even that I thought of them at all. The truth is that I'd given up, a year before, and that I actually came to reconcile—"

"*What?*"

"—because I found out I was sick."

"Sick?" The room goes sharp, and suddenly Paige is herself again. "What do you mean, sick?"

"Let's not speak about it here—it doesn't matter now."

"What do you mean, it doesn't matter?" Paige's voice is angrier than she has ever been out loud. "Can't you even tell me—"

"Fine. I was dying, okay? And I knew that she was all you'd have—"

This is the lie. Paige lies again against the bed and closes her eyes. Her own mother couldn't even tell her truth, not even at the very end—and this is her inheritance. A bunch of lying, thieving, manipulative toymakers who care only about their own self-preservation. No different than the Deathsprites—just less powerful. *And you're a liar too, remember?*

"I want to be alone," Paige says, her voice as hard as she can make it. But she doesn't really want to be alone—she just wants to be with someone else.

"Okay. I'll give you time."

Petta walks across the room and shuts the door. Her wooden footsteps echo down the hall, even when Paige brings up the covers. There's the smell: rosewater, lavender, and burning wood. *Alexio.* Oh, she cannot even bear it, cannot bear to lie here when he lies in death. She throws the covers off, and sees, again, the flowers painted up above her head. *Medoro. Yes. I need to find Medoro.*

CHAPTER FORTY-FIVE

LILY

THE SILENCE OF THE FOREST SEEMS deafening after the whirl of the wind in her ears. Lily sits in the grass, felled by her shock, while Sasha is like a statue stuck in place beside her. Lily opens her mouth as though to say something, but she cannot mutter even a quick *Did you see that?* or *Are you okay?* Several minutes pass of that quiet, and then a curious squirrel hops across the clearing where once the circle of toymakers stood and takes up an acorn in its greedy paws, waking Lily from her daze.

"What do we do now?" she asks Sasha.

"Now I guess I'm supposed to drive you home," Sasha says.

So, Lily was never going to go with them through the portal—and, really, she has known that all along, though Petta never said it directly. *I really, really, really didn't want to,* Lily imagines Petta saying later about why she didn't break the news beforehand—assuming she lives long enough to tell Paige why the shopkeeper from Toy Palace was standing in a forest with her, that is.

This is the lie of the toymaker, Lily thinks, and then she laughs out loud, a kind of strange release of whatever fear and anxiety has been building up inside of her.

"I don't even know where I'll go." Lily's mind drifts to the red columns, the gold foil letters, the closing and opening of the registers, the empty chains that once held her and Petta prisoner. Then to her house on Mulberry Street, the empty driveway from which her father and mother would have driven to go search for her—or the pool hall where they might have found Rashi and been told the story of a girl who could not be their daughter.

There is no home.

There is no escape.

"Don't be silly." Sasha puts her arm around Lily's shoulder, bringing incense and smoke. "You'll come with me."

Sasha gets in the driver's seat of the van, and then Lily climbs into the passenger's seat next to her. Sasha starts the car, and the silence becomes the croon of some slow country music song. Lily realizes the sound is familiar, and she wonders if it's Sasha's voice on the track—and if the instruments playing along behind her are the same ones that are strapped inside the cabin behind them. They accelerate, and the cars they are leaving to rust and make homes for the squirrels and other creatures who live in these woods grow smaller and smaller in the rearview mirror.

"Any chance you play any instruments?" Sasha asks as they emerge from the tight woods. They pass a farmhouse with a garage door labeled Michael's Toy Shop in swirled blue lettering, and Lily wonders if one of the toymakers from the clearing owned it.

"Violin," Lily says, "but I hate it."

"That's too bad." Sasha thinks for a moment and then says, "Maybe you can be our band manager?"

"Maybe," Lily says. She leans back against the headrest and shuts her eyes. If she thinks hard, she can recall Paige's face—the way she looked so bravely out onto the battlefield where she might meet her death. "All I know is that everything I do from now on is for me, and no one else."

"Well said." Sasha puts the windows down, and the breeze whips through the front of the van with a familiar promise. Then Sasha leans over, not taking her eyes off the road but threatening to at any moment, and says with a teasing smile: "So about that look I saw between you and Paige . . ."

"There was no—" Lily starts to say, but then she catches herself. "Yeah. I know."

Sasha turns up the music, and Lily realizes it's a love song—or, rather, a song about lost love. She wonders who inspired Sasha to write it, but she doesn't ask—not because she thinks Sasha would lie to her, but because she knows she'll tell the truth. Better to let the woman tell Lily her story on her own time, if she ever wants to share it at all. Just like Lily will tell Sasha her own story, she thinks, as the song whittles down to its final notes—but not until she's ready.

"Be on the lookout for a gas station," Sasha says in the break between tracks. "One that looks like it might have some food, too."

Then the song changes into an upbeat piece with a wild banjo solo, and the road becomes an endless highway, and Lily turns her mind away from the girl on the other side of the universe—at least for now—and sets herself to the practical matters of what she'll do next.

CHAPTER FORTY-SIX

PAIGE

SHE FINDS MEDORO IN THE GREAT Hall, looking up at a portrait of Alexio hung high enough to last the murderous raid. Besides the pictures, the whole hall is empty but for some shattered beams and broken chairs tipped over on their sides. The stone floor's cracks remind her of a spider web, or of that doll, her face cracked like an egg—

"Don't." Medoro does not turn around.

"What?"

"Don't slip away."

"Okay."

She shakes her head and dusts the echoes from her mind. Then she goes to his side and looks up, to the sweet face of a prince so full of life she barely recognizes him. His cheeks glow blue with pleasure. He wears his crown, a dapper coat, and most shocking of all, a smile aimed somewhere beyond the painter's gaze.

"I stood right here," Medoro says. His ears are still flat against his head. "The piece took hours, but we never looked away. He said he wanted to preserve the way he felt—and that, though this portrait would hang in the Hall, it would really be for me."

"He loved you." Paige threads her hand through Medoro's arm. "Against all odds, he did."

"And I loved him." Medoro drops his gaze. "What now, my marionette?"

She shrugs. The world has ended; all she knows is halted time.

"He'd want us to move on," Medoro says, "though he would never do the same."

"I know." Paige squeezes tightly on his arm. "Is there another option?"

"Hah." He squeezes back. "If you can think of one . . ."

"Hey, wait." Paige drops his arm. "We could leave here, you know—if we could make the portal work again. Find the dragon. Make it send us to my home."

"But who would make the bond between the realms?"

"Why, you!" Paige puts her hand up to his chest, where deep inside the pointed Shard lies like a child sleeping in a womb. It might awaken—if they wish it to. "We could escape this place, and make a new life there—"

She does not think of Petta, does not let herself doubt, for she has spent her whole life playing someone else's game. *I'm not a pawn*, she thinks.

"Of course you're not," Medoro says, and puts his head to hers. "But make sure it's the time to make your move. In case we cannot return . . ."

Paige puts her cheek upon his shoulder and closes her eyes, smelling the same scents that still lie in Alexio's bed. Rosewater. Lavender. Wood. She hopes that when they leave, she'll still be able to remember it—remember *him*. Medoro takes a deep breath, too.

"You will."

CHAPTER FORTY-SEVEN

LILY

THE FOREST IS QUIET, AS THOUGH the soft feet and delicate wings of its inhabitants are aware of their new guest. Lily sits on the porch, sipping the scalding tea from what Sasha refers to as *Paige's mug*, lost in thought. Maybe it is the two blue birds perched on the painted porcelain side, their feet threaded through the petals of two brilliant sunflowers, that remind her of the way the blue light of the portal hit the side of Paige's face; maybe it is the way the rocking chair sounds, like the creak of the Toy Palace floorboards, that carries her back to the memories she has told herself she must forget.

Pull yourself together, Lil. It's almost time to go.

In just an hour, she has an interview for a manager position at the Italian restaurant chain down the road. Not glamorous, but it's a start—one where no one knows her father, or the ways she "should" be applying her skills. She has already dressed in a smart collared shirt from Sasha, and the most sensible black skirt she could dig out from the wall of lace peasant skirts and mini dresses and stockings hung from the waist that danced their legs in wild abandon when Sasha pushed them to the other end of the rack. *That's as boring as I can get,* Sasha had proclaimed, hiking the pencil skirt over Lily's waist and pinning the extra inch in the back. *But it'll do.*

Luckily, she'd held onto a pair of vintage penny loafers, and with a bit of toilet paper stuffed into each toe, they fit Lily perfectly. The purple blazer was the final touch, but when Lily slipped into the sleeves, she was surprised to find little bits of dust and wood ingrained in the fabric.

"How could this pass through the portal?" she asked, raising her collar.

"Well, people can," Sasha had said with a shrug, "so I guess why not anything else too?"

How little they know about the slice through space, or the blue glow of the Flare, or the Land of Toys, or anything, really, outside the backyard of their universe. Lily feels so small when she thinks of it, like one of the birds on her mug at the face of a flower so large and beautiful it must turn its face away and sing. Sasha has seemed different since they got back, too—quieter, and less ready to go back on the road the way she'd claimed she would. It all seems so unimportant—or maybe that is just Lily projecting herself onto the woman currently humming at the stove, cooking up what she calls an "English breakfast" of burnt toast, vegan sausage, an egg like a doll's rolling eye, and mushrooms Lily has not had the heart to tell her taste like dry dirt. She made the same meal the night before, and likely tonight they will warm a can of beans, or sear some tomatoes with a sprinkle of salt, and add it to the leftovers. Of course, Lily could offer to cook instead . . . but to do so would require staring at the oven long enough to allow thoughts of her mom to flood her brain, and she isn't ready to do that—not yet. She has called from a payphone and told them she is all right, and for now, that is enough.

"Thirty minutes," Sasha calls out through the screen door. She'd be letting the heat out, if only she'd allow the furnace to warm the house in the first place. "Better eat something, in case they want you to stay and fill out paperwork."

"Coming," Lily says, but she kicks her feet off the ground and rocks backward, just a little, to create a gentle lulling motion. The creak returns, and then a grinding sound, like gravel under a set of tires—or, wait, the sound actually is a set of tires, attached to a truck slowly ambling over the holes in the dirt road. "I think you have company—"

Wait. Lily knows that dusty red pickup, the little wooden duck on strings around the rearview mirror, the girl at the wheel with the dusty blond hair in two messy braids that disappear behind the dash. There is a man beside her, handsome in the pretty way a man can look, brown hair curled at the neck and tucked under a leather tricorn hat that reminds Lily of a duke or maybe a very wealthy pirate king. The truck comes to a stop a bit away from the house, and then the driver's door opens, revealing the rest of Paige—only now, instead of a hoodie, she wears a pair of green cargo pants and a tan cable-knit sweater. She looks the same, and yet entirely different, from the last time Lily saw her—perhaps it is her stance, with her shoulders raised and feet setting themselves firmly toward their goal, or just the weight of all she has taken on, carried around her neck like an invisible anchor she must resist with the straightness of her back. Or maybe Lily is projecting again, for this is the weight that has kept her in the rocking chair for almost two hours, hoping the gentle movement will ease the load.

"Lily Jones?"

How surprising, the low, melodic tone of Paige's voice—then again, Lily has not heard her speak since that one day in Toy Palace, when her own voice drowned out most of what Paige might have told her of the women in the portrait.

"Yes?"

Paige comes to the steps but does not ascend. "My name is Paige Vitaly, and we met a few days ago—you gave me a tour."

"Yes." Lily wants to say something else, but her mind is as slow as the runners knuckling their way back and forth across the porch.

"My mother asked me to find you."

Lily's rocking speeds up. *Is Petta Vitaly dead? Is she injured? Why didn't she come back herself? What happened when—*

"She's fine." Paige smiles a little, and the movement brings a dimple to her left cheek. "Better than she would have been here, if she'd stayed."

"Good." Lily's brain is telling her mouth to talk, but the words have not formed, and her mouth is numb, and nothing in her body seems to be working at all. She is like a doll of herself, only able to say *yes* and *good* and maybe soon an *okay*.

"We got the store back," Paige says. Finally, she is climbing the steps, and now she leans her back against the railing so that she is so close to Lily she could kick her leg out and brush against her shin. Not that she would, of course—and yet Lily's eyes go to the long green leg, the little space where her stomach shows between the waistband and her sweater, the arms crossed over her chest in a loose pretzel that seems to say, *No, I'm not nearly as nervous as you are. Why do you think I would be?* "They were pretty outmatched, to be fair. Medoro is a skilled fighter, and he can be quite vicious, when he wants to be."

Lily's eyes go to the truck, where the man who must be Medoro is waiting. Are they together?

"And there's the matter of my strength . . ." Paige shakes her head a little, as though she is puzzling something out. "Not quite as strong as it was, but still there."

"Yes." Lily's mouth is dry, and she has to try a second time to get out her next words: "Your mother was like that, too."

"Hmm." Paige's arms drop. "I guess we have time to figure it out. More pressingly, we've decided to reopen the store—and we'd like you to come back with us and run it, if you want to."

"What?" Lily finally finds herself about to speak, as though the shock of the request has given her a good shake. "But I can't possibly go back."

"Why not?"

"My parents . . . Well, they'll be furious. And I'm not sure what they've been told about me . . . about the store, I mean, though I guess I'm not sure about anything—"

"Lily." Paige kneels down so that she is looking up at Lily from very close. Her hand is on Lily's knee. Her eyes are locked onto Lily's, so that even when Lily tries to look away, she finds that she can't. Paige's irises are so green and pale, like moss in the sun. Her eyebrows are thick arches of blond peppered by light brown. Her forehead is higher than Lily noticed before, or perhaps it is just uninterrupted now that her hair has been parted like a golden curtain. But it's not just that she is beautiful—she is powerful, like being in the other realm has charged her with some kind of energy she lacked that day in Toy Palace. Lily half expects that if she reaches out a finger to touch her, a spark will shock her hand. "If there is one thing I've learned this week, it's that you have to go after what you want—regardless of what anyone else says or thinks."

"But that is what I am doing," Lily says. Her voice is harder than she means it to be. "I'm making my own path—here."

"No, you're not." Paige shakes her head, so that the braids dance on her shoulders. "You're hiding."

Now Lily's voice is so hard it's like a sheet of ice on a frozen pond. "You don't know me."

"No, I don't." Paige puts her hand out, as though Lily would want to take it. "And I'd bet that not many people do—but that is entirely up to you." Her empty fingers curl into a fist, but Paige's face isn't angry—it's just strong, like a shield. "You don't owe anyone anything, Lily Jones—not an explanation, or a five-year plan, or some kind of stepping *out* when people haven't earned their place *in* with you." The fist drops by her side, and Paige stands up so tall Lily has to crane her neck to see her. "But I do know a little something about what it's like to lie to yourself—and that's why I'm here, asking you to come back. For *you*, Lily. Because you want to."

There is the hand again, not lost but only waiting for another chance to reach out. Lily stares at the long, calloused fingers of the toymaker's daughter, still etched with paint under the nails, and thinks that Petta would be surprised that Paige is taking up her profession after everything she put her through. All of the goodbyes. All of the new towns. All of the lies, and the family secrets, and the almost-deaths. Why would she continue to put herself through those painful reverberations of the past, rolling through her present and threatening at any moment to topple what comes next?

But she wants to, Lily thinks, finally putting her own hand in Paige's, so that there is the spark of the girl's touch after all. *And that is enough.*

EPILOGUE

THE WORKROOM IS SILENT. BRUSHES STAND in their glass jars, drying. Tools lie in their places on the workbench, waiting for the calloused hands of their makers to reach, again, for their wooden handles. The smells of paint remover, shaved wood, soldering alloy, and a bit of coffee still evaporating at the bottom of a cup fill up the space where soon the bodies of the makers will return to sit upon their stools and bend down to their work. *Paige*, one sign hung on the right wall says, and on the left, *Medoro*. Between them, on the table, lies an open binder full of printed pages, each one labeled *Manager's Log* and signed Lily Jones.

Past the workroom is the long hall leading to the store, where shelves of dolls, bears, and wooden cars all wait for 9:00 A.M. to chime upon the clock. Nothing moves here without the child's hand to lift it; nothing sounds a single beep or note or invitation. These are the toys of lost years, brought into their times as antique keepsakes for the children of the ones who still remember them, remember sitting with a single doll to play, for hours, with a set of clothes, or a tea set, or a long book that, when it ends, feels like the waking from a sleep.

Maybe the memories will echo through these purchasers to those who will receive them—

—or maybe they'll be lost.

Above the first floor, there is an office. Where once the fine wooden panels of the walls announced the luxury of the family name, now axe marks and flame burns mark the scars of their removal. Where once a wooden desk proclaimed ownership of all who worked in the store and those outside of its walls, now the piece serves as a shelf on top of which the framed portraits of the Vitalys and the other pieces of their history lie stacked like tombs in a catacomb. Where once a safe held the secrets of the past, now the metal enclosure contains the personal items of the former owner, soon to be packed and shipped to her Italian estate.

We held the world in our hands, she'd said as Medoro tied her hands. *We could have ruled them all.* And she had looked so royal then, in her pearls and her glowing red stone and her button-down blouse, her hair without a single strand out of place—as though she still expected that at any moment the Deathsprites would set a crown of metal and matching stones upon her upraised head. After all, that is why she stayed for all of those years, wasn't it? And why that week she had waited in that banker chair, long after the guards who had seen their fallen comrades in the hallway fled Wintroster, until the wrong two people slipped through the shard's break in space and demanded that she finally step down from the throne she'd built for herself?

It was not until the end, as Camilla left Toy Palace for the last time, that she'd mentioned something that stopped Paige and Medoro as they passed through the door: *The Deathsprites were just the offspring of a greater power—even they feared what is to come.* She wore a smug smile on her face, which widened as her eyes took in the surprise of theirs. *Perhaps I'm glad I'm not going to be here to see it, when it does.*

They had untied her hands and put her into a car, and then they had watched the intersection where she'd turned long after the vehicle disappeared and the road had emptied of cars.

What do you think she meant by that? Medoro had asked. His shoulders were thrown back under his fitted brown coat and his wool trousers creased at the knees, as though he meant to battle whatever threat might appear. His right hand rose, as though to take up a weapon, but instead, he pulled at the bristly hairs of his goatee. His eyes, brown with flecks of auburn, darted from under his tricorn hat and down the road, then back, again, to the buildings beside them.

Lies, Paige said, *to scare us.*

But there had been a chill in the air, and later, as the first snow fell on the town, Paige had pressed herself into her friend's embrace and closed her eyes tightly and wondered, for the first time, about the vast and empty space from which they all had come. Toys. Fae. Humans. And something else, perhaps—something greater—that sat on the other side of time and space, waiting.

***

On the second floor of Toy Palace, past the office, there is also another room—a dark room, kept bright by what appears to be a shard, kept in a locked glass case that requires passwords and a special key. Flare blue flutters at the shadows on the walls. All the passing days are made short by recollections of its final use. Now, it sits thoughtfully in wait, the way the hammers sit, and nails, and brushes, too. A tool made powerful by only those who wield it.

Now it sits—but then, unlike the silent nights that have come before, a swirling wind begins. At first, it pulls the paper from the walls, then, growing stronger, takes the ceiling, floorboards, and the door. A portrait too, of two toys: wooden dolls, a mother and a daughter, posed in their last hug before the younger girl's departure from the unfamiliar land. All near is pulled into its churning power, with the exception of the glass case, still unmoved by all the wind the vortex makes.

A light appears in the center of the whirl.

A hand emerges.

White.

Glowing.

"*There are two kinds of lies, you won't be surprised.*"

On closer inspection, the hand is not the soft touch of familiar flesh. No, it's hammered joints, and pieces added up to make a whole, a robot hand of metal and wood and even bone.

"*—short legs and long noses—*"

The arm comes next, run with wires that carry the messages of movement to the hand before it. The elbow bends and opens. Swings right and then left.

"*—but no one supposes that there is another much worse than the others—*"

Now the chest, a plate of steel, with a glowing white hole at the very center from which the initial light seems to have appeared. And the face, too—at once familiar and completely strange. High cheekbones. Sharp nose. Haunted white pupils that look through everything before them in dull disinterest.

"*—and this is the lie—*"

Finally, the crown passes into this world and declares its conquest.

"*—of the toymaker.*"

The robot settles his gaze on the glass in front of him. He takes two heavy steps and punches his fist so that the case door shatters, setting off alarms throughout the building that he barely notices. Feet pound from above, where the apartment shared by the co-owners of Toy Palace keeps them close to any danger that might threaten their home. The door opens, right as the robot takes up the Shard.

"Alexio?" Medoro asks, rubbing sleep from his eyes.

"It can't be," Paige says from behind him.

"*Until we meet again,*" the fairy says, and thrusts the Shard deep into his own chest. The room explodes in light. The humans who were once toys clutch at their heads.

"*This is the lie . . .*

This is the lie . . .

This is the lie . . .

. . . of the Toymakers."

THE END

ACKNOWLEDGMENTS

My heartfelt gratitude goes to Kat Georges and Peter Carlaftes, co-founders of Three Rooms Press, for believing in my retellings before anyone else did. Arden Gray, thank you for being an incredible editor, and for diving deep into the lore of this world with me (several times!). Thank you to my agent, Anne Tibbets, for rolling with me on this wild journey, and to my fellow author and friend McCormick Templeman, who has mentored me throughout this process.

To my family, thank you for being here every step of the way, from my first book about moving in kindergarten to this third retelling. Thank you to Jason for supporting my work in so many ways, including watching our kids so that I could travel to speak in the city that ended up inspiring the opening scene of this book. Zoe and Lyla, thank you for always believing in me so purely, and for making me think so hard about what it means to parent honestly.

Finally, thank you to everyone who has read my books and said that they wish they'd had these versions of the stories when they were kids—in my opinion, until everyone is represented by our reimaginings, there are not enough of them.

ABOUT THE AUTHOR

Kelly Ann Jacobson is the author of several acclaimed reimagined fairytales including the queer young adult novel *Tink and Wendy*, which won the *Foreword Reviews* Indies Gold Medal for Young Adult Fiction, as well as the queer young adult novel *Robin and Her Misfits* (Three Rooms Press), an Indies finalist. She has published numerous other works for adults and young adults, including the chapbook *An Inventory of Abandoned Things*, winner of the Split/Lip Press's Chapbook Contest, and the literary speculative fiction novel *Weaver* (Livingston Press). Her short pieces have been published in *Boulevard, Southern Humanities Review, Daily Science Fiction*, and many other literary magazines.

Jacobson is the Assistant Professor of English at the University of Lynchburg, where she currently lives. She also teaches the course "Completing the Novel" for Johns Hopkins's MA in Writing. She received her PhD in Fiction from Florida State University in 2021.

For more information, visit www.kellyannjacobson.com.